Psychic Surveys Book Seven

Promises to Keep

Psychic Surveys: Book Seven

Promises to Keep

How far will you walk down a dark dark path?

SHANI STRUTHERS

STORY
LAND
PRESS

Dedication

For Louisa Taylor – with me (almost) from the start.

Acknowledgements

Yet another book is completed! It's been lovely to catch up with the Psychic Surveys team again. They truly do feel like old friends, and – call me psychic – but I'm sure there are many more adventures for them to endure yet (seriously, who'd work for the PS team? It's all drama, drama, drama!). Thanks also to my beta readers, who help me so much when it comes to shaping my stories. They are Robert Struthers, Louisa Taylor (to whom the book is dedicated), Amanda Nash, Amelia Haire, Sarah Savery, Lesley Hughes and Kate Jane Jones. I really appreciate everything you do. Thanks also to Rumer Haven for editing the book – it's wonderful and magical to be working with you. And for all the artwork, thank you to Gina Dickerson, who, as well as being such a wonderful friend, is the most creative spirit I know.

Prologue

Ness

"LYNDSEY, it's me, Vanessa. Are you there? Lyndsey, please, if you can hear me, let me know. That's what tortures me, the not knowing. I don't think you're in the light. I *know* you're not. Lyndsey, please! I'm sorry about what I said. I was young, I was…hurt. Lyndsey, that's your name. Such a pretty name. You were so desperate to know it, well, now you do. Your name is Lyndsey, you're my twin, and, damn it, I miss you. I miss you so much."

Ness could barely hold back the tears as she sat in the living room of her modest terraced Victorian redbrick in Lewes, the curtains closed, no lights on at all, peering into the darkness.

Lyndsey, where are you?

How many times had she said the same words? For how many years? Waiting, praying, *begging* to be answered. Just as Lyndsey used to beg her for answers too.

"But I didn't know the answer, not then! No one talked about you, and what happened. That, at least, wasn't my fault. How could I tell you what I didn't know? But I found out, Lyndsey, as soon as I was able to, and…well, I'm telling you now, aren't I?"

Lyndsey was stubborn and wilful too. She was mischievous, playful, spiteful, sweet, happy and sad...a person of complex, varied emotions, someone who'd never lived, not in this world, at least.

At birth, Ness had been the only one of them to draw breath, filling her lungs with air and kicking and screaming as all newborns do, her tiny face becoming redder and redder, furious at having been ejected from the comfort of the womb. A twin but embarking on life's journey alone.

What effect the loss of her twin had had on her parents, her mother in particular, Ness never knew. The woman hadn't been one to show the softer side of herself, if, in fact, one existed. Certainly, Ness had never witnessed it, although her siblings argued differently and displayed more loyalty. Oh, how grief-stricken they'd been at her funeral, whereas Ness had just stood there, dry-eyed. Perhaps that's why she was estranged from them too, because they'd noticed that – she'd been the same way at her father's funeral a few years after, and they despised her for it.

No matter. Being despised was something she was used to. Her mother had seen to that.

"What's wrong with you?" she'd say, she'd *sneer* at her. "You're not right, in here, I mean." She'd point at Ness's head, stabbing at the flesh there. "You're all...wrong. Yes, that's it, you're wired up wrong. Thank the Lord there's only one of you to contend with."

How Lyndsey would cry to hear such cruel words, standing there beside Ness as the tirade continued, listening to every word. Not that their mother had shown any signs that she was ever aware of her. The one who'd grown in spirit was invisible to everyone but Ness, who could see her as if she were flesh – not a wraith, something vague and mysterious, but as real as she herself was, as vital. And she always had been, ever since Ness could remember.

As a young child, she would chatter to her twin, point to her, laugh with her, play games with her, and the more she did it, the more incensed her mother would become.

"The devil's in that child, I swear it!" she'd scream, her father not agreeing with his wife but not denying it either. He'd always been such a weak man.

Don't get bitter, Ness.

No, she wouldn't, she mustn't. In doing so, she'd only pile fresh pain on top of old.

No one spoke about the child that had passed, or seemed to care. No one ever mentioned her by name. But a thing that was nameless remained just that: a thing.

"Find out what I'm called." All the time, her twin would ask that. "Find out!"

"How?"

"Mum will tell you."

"She won't."

"She will! You've got a name. I want one too. Please, Ness, please."

How could she ignore the plea in the other girl's voice? She couldn't; it haunted her.

But asking her mother had always been a mistake. She'd been beaten for it. Yet still, her twin had insisted she try, would sit on her bed, her body shaking so pitifully with sobs.

The clock on the mantlepiece – chiming midnight – interrupted Ness's reverie.

"Oh, Lyndsey," she said, tears breaking rank now. Good. Let them. If her twin was observing, let her see how sorry she was. "Why do you torment me like this!"

Shit! Now she sounded just like Lyndsey, like a kid again. *It's not fair! It's not fair,* she used to say. *I want a name, d'ya hear? Find it out. You have to, Ness!*

She'd got so sick of it, her constant demands and what they caused. But Lyndsey refused to stop. She got worse, breaking things if Ness tried to ignore her, making the TV go fuzzy or interrupting the radio at a crucial point when her parents were listening to a play, and always, *always,* Ness would get the blame. She was dubbed a problem child. A troubled child. Unnatural. She was all that and more, the beatings continuing, filth and accusations pouring from her mother's mouth as if it were she who was possessed. As if…as if… Ness had no proof of this, none whatsoever, but it was as if her mother had *known* her daughter wasn't lying, and that's why she'd reacted in such an extreme way, because she'd *hated* knowing.

Ness rose to her feet and started to pace the confines of her living room. This suspicion plagued her too. After all, psychic ability could indeed be something inherited, handed down from person to person through the generations. Was she, Vanessa Patterson, the exception to that rule or no such thing? Had her mother had similar abilities? Lyndsey'd thought so. *Sometimes, Ness, she'll turn her head and look straight at me, straight into my eyes. Try again. Ask her about me. It might be different this time. She might tell you.*

And so Ness would, bracing herself for the onslaught.

"*She* doesn't have a name." Spittle would fly from her mother's mouth. "*She* is dead!"

But it was lies, all lies, the former as well as the latter – yes, she was dead in a physical sense but not spiritually, and she had a name, one that had first blossomed in her parents' minds, then become a mere technicality, something to write on a piece of paper for the purpose of law, the purpose of cremation. Not just a secret, it was worse than that – like her twin had never been, her memory not something to hold close, to cherish, but something to erase. People dealt with grief in various ways; the adult Ness realised that. Did that mean she should cut her mother some slack? She couldn't.

And then her mother had suffered another loss, a miscarriage. Home alone with her, Ness tried to help, but the way her mother had looked at her – as if even that had been her fault.

Coming to a standstill, Ness screwed her eyes shut, her hands clenched into fists.

That terrible, terrible night.

If only she could take it back, what she'd said, not to her mother but to Lyndsey. If only her gift extended to include the impossible: rewinding time, rewriting history.

When her mother had heaped yet more blame on her, it had not only hurt her, it had caused the anger inside to become white hot.

Lyndsey loved her. Ness knew that. She'd tell her over and over. *I love you, Ness. I always have. I want you to live, for both of us.*

But Ness hadn't wanted to live, not anymore.

Aged just thirteen, she'd taken a knife from the kitchen and drawn its sharp, serrated edge across her wrists, watching as blood flowed from her, so much of it, like a stream.

She'd attempted suicide, but not before she'd spoken to her twin, who was watching her in horror, begging her not to hurt herself, pleading with her to change her mind. *I'll tell*

5

Mum what you're about to do, she kept saying, she kept threatening, and so Ness had replied:

"Tell her, and tell her this too if she's listening: she's a monster, and I will never forgive her for denying what I am, especially if it's her I've inherited it from. And there's something else – I blame you just as much. Both of you have driven me to this."

Terrible words, but there was worse to come.

"I never want to see you again, not even when I'm dead too. If you break that rule, if you try and contact me, if you plead, if you cry, even if you beg, I will ignore you. I will never, *ever* acknowledge you again. I promise."

And now, ironically, it was Ness who was crying, who was pleading and begging. *I didn't mean it.*

In the darkness of her living room, Ness was on her knees now, her hands clasped together, held up and resting against her mouth, tears drenching them.

"You're stubborn, you know that, just like Mum was stubborn. And I was stubborn too, a stupid, stubborn kid. I found out the very thing you wanted me to but still there's no sign of you. You're Lyndsey Dawn Patterson. That's your identity, the thing that sets you apart. Don't stay in the darkness; you don't belong there with other nameless things. You're Lyndsey, *my* Lyndsey, and I've always loved you too."

This cursed silence!

"What are you trying to do? Drive me to the edge again?"

No! She mustn't say such things. Nothing was her twin's fault, nothing!

"I just want to know you're okay."

Her twin who'd saved her, because she *had* alerted her mother to what Ness had done that night, somehow, her mother having no choice but to call an ambulance, to try to save her too.

"Oh, Lyndsey."

No hint of her presence at all.

Her twin hated the darkness, had told her that so many times.

And yet Ness had banished her into the depths of it.

And because of that, she was stuck in the darkness too.

PART ONE

Corinna

Chapter One

IN the Rights of Man pub, Corinna sat waiting in one of the booths for Presley, his brother Cash, and Ruby to arrive. Nursing a bottle of San Miguel, she was busy contemplating an article she'd just read on her mobile, concerning some woodlands close by. They were haunted woodlands, or so it was claimed, a variety of strange events having taken place there. It wasn't somewhere she'd been before or, indeed, even known about until recently when she'd talked to a friend who'd visited there on a ghost hunt. The friend, Anya, had been bursting with enthusiasm about it.

"It was incredible, Crin. We were there in the dead of night, trying to see, ya know, the dead of night!" She'd laughed uproariously at this joke before continuing. "Three people have been found dead there, *three*! And all of them in mysterious circumstances. Like, there were no marks on them at all, no indication of how they'd died. They'd just wandered into the woods…and died."

The article also informed her that dogs had gone missing in these woods on a regular basis and, once upon a time, a horse! The owner of that particular horse had apparently sworn to the police he'd tethered it securely before walking a few feet further into the woods to relieve himself. When he'd retraced his footsteps, the horse was gone, no sign of it anywhere.

Corinna was shaking her head at this, unable to believe such a large animal could just disappear like that. The deaths, though, were for real, the first having taken place in the 1970s, then 1982, and, finally, in 2001. There'd been investigations, of course, including those of a paranormal nature, the latter hopefully a bit less sensational than the ghost hunt Anya had paid good money to attend. One man in particular, Tom Witcher, was very vocal about the woods, this article quoting him as well as other articles that Corinna was now browsing through. His theory? A black-magic cult practiced there, the Cult of Badb – a word that meant 'crow', apparently, in Irish mythology, popularly regarded as some kind of harbinger of doom, foreshadowing death.

Corinna shivered, feeling really quite cold despite the warmth of the day – it was the month of August and very hot; in fact, Sussex was experiencing something of a heatwave. Did she want to read any more about these woods? After having dealt with Blakemort, both recently and in her past – a house she'd had the misfortune to spend five years of her life in, aged five to ten – the last thing she wanted was any more dealings with anything tainted by the so-called black arts. Her job, aside from a part-time bar job, was all about the light, sending grounded spirits who'd remained tethered to the material world home towards it to rest awhile. Spirit rescue was an interesting job, one she loved and was good at, and there was simply no need to get involved with anything deeper or darker, although sometimes, admittedly, you could tread a fine line between what was dark and what was light. It was, she supposed, a hazard of the job.

But these woods, now that she'd found out about them, were intriguing. And three deaths in thirty years intrigued her too: the first a woman, the same age as Corinna herself, twenty-three; the second a policeman who'd been investigating the girl's death; and the third another woman, this time older than the first, in her early thirties. Gaynor Sanderson, Jim Fowler and Samantha Lawrence had been their names, respectively, a quote from Tom Witcher reiterating there'd been no wounds, no bruises at all on their torsos when found. They'd all been lying on their backs with eyes and mouths wide open…

"Hey, babe, what you Googling this time?"

Presley's voice made her jump. "Oh, hi," she said, placing her phone on the table and jumping up to give him a welcome kiss. "You scared me."

"Did I?" Presley grinned. "Go me, eh? Frightening the world's bravest lady."

Their lips met, sending, as it always did, a shiver down her spine, the good kind this time.

"Oh, how you flatter me," she replied as she drew away, grinning as much as him.

They'd been a couple for over a year now…not an easy time, not considering there'd been Blakemort to deal with during that period as well as the death of his best friend, Danny, the drummer in his band, Thousand Island Park. But they *had* dealt with those issues and become all the stronger for it, the pair of them now on the hunt for a flat to move into. Older than his brother by a couple of years, he was thirty-two to Corinna's twenty-three, and he worried sometimes she was too young to make the decision to live together. She'd assured him, though, she was plenty old enough. Dealing with something like Blakemort made you grow up fast.

Presley Wilkins hadn't come to the table empty-handed; he was carrying a pint of Olympia for himself, a local summer ale, and another bottle of San Miguel for Corinna. As he settled himself beside her, he repeated his question. "So, what are you Googling?"

She glanced at her phone and shrugged. "Nothing."

"Really? You looked proper intense when I came in."

"Don't worry, it wasn't Tinder."

"Worried? Me? How could you possibly replace such a fine specimen as me?"

Again, he was joking, being as far from arrogant as it was possible to get. Incredible, really, because, like Cash, he was lovely to look at, his slightly darker skin – courtesy of his Jamaican-born mother – was something she envied, hers was so pale in comparison, his dark brown eyes easy to get lost in. So often, people remarked on what a good-looking couple they made, she with her Titian curls tumbling halfway down her back and eyes that flashed green. As modest as she was by nature also, she was happy to agree, albeit privately. There was no doubt in her mind he was 'the one', as there was no doubt in Ruby's mind that she'd met her match in Cash.

Which was just as well, considering Ruby was married to Cash and carrying his child.

Ah, there they were, having entered the Rights of Man too, Ruby's stomach burgeoning.

Immediately Corinna began waving. "Hey, Ruby, Cash,

11

over here," she called, both of them adopting smiles on spotting her.

"Hey, Corinna!" Ruby closed the gap between them, her arms outstretched to embrace Corinna, the pair of them hugging as hard as her bump allowed. This was the first time they'd met since the pair had got married a few months before – their reception held right here, in the Rights of Man. On that day Ruby had been glowing, full of eager happiness. She'd suffered from sickness before that date, but with all the excitement of the wedding, perhaps, the sickness had abated. Unfortunately, in the latter stages, it was back with a vengeance, along with swollen legs and tiredness Ruby described as 'debilitating'.

"How you feeling?" Corinna asked.

"Still tired, but, hey, I'm getting there. Not long to go now."

"Can't come quick enough, eh?"

"Too right," she replied, lowering herself gently into the chair opposite Corinna.

Presley did the honours regarding drinks, another Olympia for his brother and a Coke for Ruby.

"You miss the rum in it?" Corinna quizzed as Ruby lifted the glass to her mouth.

"Ugh, no. The mere thought of alcohol, or any food that isn't white…"

Corinna crinkled her nose. "Huh? What do you mean? What's with the white food?"

Cash was the one to elaborate. "What she means is that she – and, subsequently, our baby – exists on nothing but baked potatoes, pasta and cheese, eschewing any of my more colourful creations, the ones I've built my reputation on: spag bol, lasagne, jerk chicken. It's a nightmare!"

"Oh, poor you," Ruby said, giving him a dig in the ribs.

Cash raised an eyebrow. "Or…is it just an excuse and you never liked my food anyway?"

Ruby shook her head. "I did! I do! Especially your spag bol. It's hormones, it's all down to that. Honestly, Crin, you wouldn't believe what they can do! Literally, right now, place any food with any colour in front of me and it'll trigger the sickness." She pointed to her glass. "The only exception seems to be Coke, which, you guessed it, I crave."

Corinna relaxed into the conversation. It was so good to see Ruby and Cash again, to be able to talk like they used to, socialise together. She'd missed it so much. And she'd been worried too, she might as well admit it. Very worried. Yes, her friend was pregnant, and on and off she'd been suffering ill health because of that pregnancy, but that wasn't the only reason she seemed to be shunning everybody.

Ruby was strong, determined. Her business – Psychic Surveys – hadn't just been a source of income for her but a way of life, her vocation. Women worked through pregnancies; Ruby could have worked through hers. But she refused to because of Blakemort, Corinna was certain of it, that damned house. Something had been said to Ruby by the boy there, the boy whose beauty belied his evil. Corinna didn't know what, exactly, but she knew well enough the way evil worked, suspected he'd planted an idea into Ruby's head, then retreated into the shadows to watch it grow as the baby itself was growing. And, in a way, Ruby had also retreated into the shadows, removing herself as the head of her business, giving up her lease on the attic office she'd once occupied, leaving her colleagues to continue her work without her. Psychic Surveys comprised Corinna, Theo and Ness now, three when there should be four. Ruby was trying to keep her baby safe, but from what, she wouldn't say.

The fact she was out, though, had begun mixing again, could it be a good sign? Did it mean she was stronger? Less fearful? Surreptitiously studying her from her position across the table, Corinna couldn't get behind that idea, try as she might. Ruby looked as tired as she claimed to be; there were dark circles below her eyes, her complexion was pale and her shoulder-length brown hair lank.

There was no way Corinna was going to broach the subject of work – what cases the team had been working on recently, for example, and how Corinna's abilities were developing since having faced up to Blakemort, plus the enquiries that promised to develop into future cases. It'd be like rubbing salt into an open wound, because although Ruby had made the decision to quit, not being involved hurt her. It was so bloody obvious, but Cash…well, Cash was often a law unto himself.

"Come on, then," he said, producing a somewhat startling clap with his hands, "tell us all. What spirits have you sent packing lately?"

The silence that ensued was cringeworthy.

"Cash…" Ruby began.

"Cash," Presley said too, a split second later.

"Cash," Corinna added, perhaps a little more beseechingly, but he remained oblivious.

"Presley was telling me one spirit gave you the right old runaround, pretending it'd gone to the light, then returning. Happened about three times, didn't it? Having a laugh at your expense."

He was right; that had happened. Not all grounded spirits were full of fear and anguish. Some chose to linger, knowing full well where the light was but taking their own sweet time heading towards it, deciding to have a little spooky fun in the meantime, knocking on doors, thumping around on stairwells, sending a vase or two crashing to the floor, no real harmful intent behind any of it other than enjoying their newfound skills. During the years the four had worked together, they'd come across plenty of cases like that, would laugh about them, laugh *with* the spirits too, gradually persuading them on, though having to be creative about achieving this with the most mischievous. But this time, there was no laughter to be had. Although Ruby was still a friend, as a colleague she'd left a massive hole, which, Cash aside, no one wanted to be reminded of.

"Cash—" Corinna tried again, but he was on a roll, asking yet more about what Psychic Surveys – thankfully, Ruby had encouraged them to keep the business name – had been up to.

"I miss it, you know," he said, taking a swig of his ale, "the *craic*, as our Irish friends would say. Remember Highdown Hall? The first case I joined you on. Christ, Cynthia Hart was a piece of work, wasn't she? A right diva. The good old days, eh? Times change, I suppose. Talking of which, Presley was also saying something about a house in Lindfield you've been contacted about. No one can get a clock to work in the kitchen, is that right? Time stands still in there."

Corinna briefly closed her eyes. Brothers talked to each other, of course they did, but if only Presley had mentioned something about discretion too.

"Ruby," Corinna said when she was finally able to get a

word in edgeways, "it's you I want to hear about. Have you got everything you need for the baby? What about clothes, what have you bought him? Did you bring the scan picture? You got a 3D one, didn't you? They're so cool."

Ruby grew even paler. "Erm…no, sorry, Corinna, I forgot it."

"You forgot?" Corinna was incredulous. She'd have thought she'd be dying to show it off.

"It's great that it's a boy, though, isn't it?" Cash said, the widest grin ever on his face. "A mini me. What are the chances?" He cocked his head to the side. "Well, about fifty-fifty, I suppose."

"It's brilliant, mate," Presley replied, holding up his glass for a celebratory clink.

"Yeah, yeah, fantastic," Corinna added, also holding her bottle aloft but suddenly feeling like crying rather than celebrating. Ruby was struggling – why was Cash so oblivious? Or could it be that he was simply trying to gloss things over, for his own sake as well as Ruby's? Inwardly, she sighed. The pair of them were in a strong, loving relationship; having a baby was a good thing. They were the perfect age to be parents, or so Corinna thought, Ruby twenty-seven now and Cash thirty. It was progress, taking them to a whole new level. But Blakemort had ruined it for her.

Cash started talking again. "We've got a few names we like—"

"I'm really sorry," Ruby interrupted. "This Coke…"

"What about it?" said Cash.

"I don't know, it's…" She swallowed hard, lifting one hand up to her mouth. "Normally, I can't get enough of the stuff, but right now, it's not agreeing with me. Shit, sorry."

Immediately Corinna reached out to grasp Ruby's free hand, which felt cold. "Hey, don't be silly, there's nothing to be sorry about! Do you think…are you going to be sick?"

"I honestly don't know."

Still with Ruby's hand in hers, she stood up. "Come on, let's go to the toilet."

She was surprised when Ruby duly obeyed, surprised because for some reason she thought she'd resist, not wanting to be alone with her. The fact that she didn't heartened her.

It was the beginning of the week, so the pub wasn't full. Thankfully, there was no barging their way through other drinkers to climb the flight of stairs that led to the ladies' and gents'. En route, Gracie Lawless, who ran the pub, waved to them from behind the bar, a smile on her face but her eyes growing sombre as they fixed on Ruby, probably wondering why she hadn't seen her for such a long while too. Once in the toilets, Ruby went straight into a cubicle and did indeed start to retch, Corinna dutifully holding her friend's hair as her body convulsed. It was dry retching, though, and eventually it came to a stop, although Ruby continued to shake.

"Oh shit," Ruby was murmuring. "Oh God."

"Come on, over here, there's a chair. Sit down."

As though she were a small child, Ruby allowed herself to be led to the wooden chair, Corinna pushing her gently down upon it. She then knelt by her side.

"You really are suffering, aren't you?" she said.

"The nausea passed. It went away. I don't know why it's come back, and this tiredness. Honestly, Corinna, it's relentless." Forlornly, she shrugged her shoulders. "I guess some women bloom in pregnancy and some don't. Trust me to be one who doesn't."

"Was your mother the same? Did she suffer from morning sickness?"

Here, Ruby emitted a laugh, a bitter edge to it. "Morning sickness? That's such a misnomer. Lately, it's morning, noon and night sickness! As for Mum, nope, not a day's sickness throughout it," she rolled her eyes before adding, "sickeningly. You know, I count the hours, the minutes, the seconds 'til this is all over."

"Like you said, not long to go now."

"Yeah, another five weeks. That's if he arrives on time. It's not uncommon for firstborns to be late. I just...I can't wait to feel normal again. Right now, it's hard to imagine I ever will. Ow!"

"Ruby, what is it?"

"The baby." Briefly Ruby screwed her eyes shut. "He knows how to deliver a hefty kick."

She attempted another laugh, not a bitter sound this time, just weak, how pitiful it was piercing Corinna to the core. Corinna couldn't help herself – she reached out and drew Ruby to her.

"I miss you," she said, her voice a muffled whisper against Ruby's hair.

"I miss you too."

"It's like...nothing's the same without you."

"I'm sorry."

Releasing her, Corinna shook her head. "Stop apologising! You can't help feeling so wretched."

"I know, but...I worry about you all. We were such a strong team, weren't we?"

"We were," agreed Corinna, "and hopefully we can be

again. We've already told you, we'll keep Psychic Surveys afloat until you're ready to come back."

"And I've told you, I can't come back."

"Ruby—"

"Corinna, I can't. The baby's my priority now."

"There are plenty of working mothers, Ruby!"

"I'm not saying I won't work, just...not that type of work."

"Try as I might, though, I can't see you doing anything else."

"I have to. Take my word for it, okay? Believe me."

"Ruby, what happened at Blakemort? Because that's when you made the decision not to—"

Corinna stopped talking, not just because Ruby was holding her hand up but because she'd gone from sad to thunderous in a split second.

"What is wrong with you? Why can't you respect my decision? What's so hard about it? I am *not* returning to Psychic Surveys."

Before Corinna could respond, Ruby stood up, shock delaying Corinna by a few seconds from doing the same. Once on her feet, she was the one apologising, but Ruby was having none of it.

"We'd better get going. The boys will be wondering where we are."

"Okay," Corinna said, still contrite, cursing herself for having pushed Ruby where she clearly didn't want to go.

As Ruby moved towards the door, Corinna followed her, another woman entering but barely glancing at them. Just before Ruby descended the staircase, she turned.

"This case you're working on, the one in Lindfield, it's an

ordinary case, isn't it?"

Ordinary? Only a psychic could say such a thing and get away with it.

"Yeah, I think so. I'm doing a follow-up visit tomorrow."

"Good. Keep things ordinary, Corinna."

"Uh-huh—"

"Don't court the dark stuff, not anymore."

"I wouldn't willingly—"

"Because it's not worth it." Ruby was holding her stomach now, cradling it. "Stick to spirit rescue. It's what we were good at, what Psychic Surveys was set up to do in the first place, domestic spiritual clearance, experts in it."

"Believe me, I never want to encounter another Blakemort," Corinna said.

"God no," Ruby replied, but she averted her eyes as she said it and stared at the ground.

"Hey, there you are!" Cash, having entered the stairwell, was standing on the bottom step. "Me and Presley were wondering if you'd climbed out the back window or something."

"Poor Ruby, that Coke—"

"I'm fine," Ruby said. "I wasn't sick after all. We just got chatting. You know how it is."

"Yeah, yeah," he said, his eyes travelling from Ruby's face down towards her stomach, a hand extending to pat it as she reached him. "And little Hendrix is fine too?"

"We're not calling him Hendrix, Cash."

"Hendrix?" queried Corinna.

Cash smirked. "It's a family tradition, isn't it? Naming the kids after the musical greats."

"Hendrix," Corinna repeated, testing the name on her

tongue. "It's quite cool, actually."

Ruby was having a boy. *A beautiful boy.* Corinna was glad she'd only thought those last words, not said them out loud, words synonymous with Blakemort and the boy there. *Oh, Ruby…*

Ruby was staring at her as if she had, in fact, uttered those words, so many emotions on her face, a whole smorgasbord, including horror?

Ruby… Again, she only thought it, but if Ruby caught that too, Corinna had no idea, as her friend had turned, following Cash back into the bar, where she then made her excuses and left, citing tiredness, leaving Corinna to stare after her, so many questions on her lips. *Why are you so scared? You're glad you're having a boy, aren't you?* And: *At this rate, will I ever see you again?*

Chapter Two

THE case of the house where no one could get a clock to work in the kitchen was, as Ruby might describe it, a pretty ordinary one. Corinna, along with Theo, had already made a preliminary visit, getting the feel of a happy family home, one in which the Bow family resided – parents Karen and Luke and their children, Ben and Lola. The village of Lindfield, where they lived, was beautiful, with a church dating from 1098, a hunting lodge thought to have been used by King Henry VII, and an ornamental lake complete with fountains. The Bows' house was set back from the high street and itself dated from the mid- 1800s.

Corinna recalled her and Theo's first visit, how it had been clear the Bows weren't frightened by the prospect of anything supernatural. Quite the opposite – they were intrigued.

"You see," Karen had said, homely and blond and somewhere in her late thirties, "we knew this was a problem here, that whole clock-and-kitchen scenario, when we bought the house. The previous owners told us about it. They said they'd been told by the people they'd bought the house from too. We didn't take much notice at first, if I'm honest. I didn't even have a clock in the kitchen, but then we redecorated, got one of those lovely big Thomas Kent clocks from Tufnells just down the road. Spent quite a bit of money on it, hung it up, and, sure enough, it stopped working. Took it back to the shop, ordered another, same thing happened. Tried other clocks, and, yep, you guessed it – same old, same old. Take the clock out, though, place it elsewhere in the house, and voila! The hands start moving."

"And the clock on the microwave or the central heating boiler?" Theo asked.

Karen laughed. "Maybe they don't understand digital clocks, 'cause they're fine."

Theo had then gone on to ask whether the more traditional clocks stopped at a certain time.

Karen's husband, Luke, answered. "Doesn't seem to be an issue. Whatever time the clock's set at, it stops the moment it's brought in here."

Theo nodded at this, Corinna eyeing her surreptitiously, part amused, part enthralled, as she always was by the eldest of the now depleted Psychic Surveys team. In her early seventies, short and rotund in stature with pink hair, her physical appearance often caused people to raise an eyebrow. If they knew about her psychic abilities too, however, they'd be blown away. Corinna still was, after years of knowing her. *What are you thinking, Theo? Is this house haunted?*

Karen and Luke had continued to talk, plus there was the sound of the children from elsewhere in the house, scampering feet and high-pitched squeals – but Corinna tried to set those noises aside, to focus on her colleague as Theo had trained her to do, to 'catch' her thoughts.

There's something here. Not sure if it's intelligent or residual, not yet. Can you feel it?

Corinna almost squealed too. Theo's answer – despite the fact she hadn't opened her mouth to speak – was loud and clear. She was amazed her abilities had extended to include this particular talent. Since the night that Blakemort had burnt to the ground, there'd been a shift within her, as if something had been released, requiring her to no longer hold back. Dubbed a sensitive before, someone who could sense spirits but not see them, she was blossoming, as Theo described it. The theory – again according to Theo – was that her childhood experiences in Blakemort had caused her to shut down her abilities as a means of protecting herself against its terrible onslaught, but now that the house no longer had a hold on her, she was able to be who she truly was.

"Do you think your house is haunted?" Corinna now asked of Karen and Luke, causing them to look at each other and shrug.

"We're happy here," Karen explained. "The kids are and Petra too – that's our dog, by the way, a rescued greyhound and supremely lazy. She's asleep in the front room, probably."

"A rescued greyhound?" Theo repeated. "Likely she's earnt the right to be lazy, then."

"Oh, she has," Karen enthusiastically agreed. "She was really ill-treated, and yet she's such a sweetie. She's the second greyhound we've rescued; we had a boy before, Georgie. Wouldn't be without a dog, would we, Luke? And they're sensitive, aren't they, like cats. Soon let you know if there's anything to be worried about."

"So you're not worried?" Corinna checked.

Luke shook his head. "We're just curious, you know, as

to the reason why a clock won't work in here. We've exhausted any logical reasons, so…you know…"

"You're looking for an *il*logical reason," Theo said, but tongue-in-cheek.

"Well…yeah," replied Luke, his cheeks flushing a little. "Look, your rates seem pretty reasonable, and from your website you've had a lot of successes, so we thought you could maybe conduct a little investigation, solve the mystery for us."

A little investigation… Corinna had smiled to hear it. Just an ordinary case. The paranormal – which, technically speaking, encompassed anything outside of normal – really was becoming more acceptable in modern society, with people even guilty of undermining it, making it into something twee. Most people called spirits 'ghosts', a word that neither she nor her colleagues tended to use, and with some there was the thrill of the chase, those that wanted to hunt them down, to experience something, *anything*, so they could wheel the experience out again and again at a dinner party, perhaps, making themselves the centre of attention. *Yeah, we had a ghost in our house – these people, psychics they were, confirmed it. We were so scared. The damned thing terrorised us, you know, stomping around in the middle of the night, that kind of thing. But these psychics, they came in, made contact, and sent it packing. It was evil, really evil. It had to be.* And everyone would laugh, everyone would sigh, declare they were jealous, even, that they wanted their own house ghost. Psychic Surveys were well versed in dealing with these kinds of people, could sniff them out a mile away, but Karen and Luke Bow were genuine, not exactly thrilled they had an in-house spirit, but their imaginations weren't running riot because of it.

A second meeting had been set, Corinna, Theo and Ness turning up to the house in Lindfield on yet another sweltering August day with not a cloud in the sky.

Karen and Luke's greeting was as warm and friendly as it had been before, Corinna introducing them to Ness as they were ushered indoors.

"Aren't there four of you usually?" Karen asked. "I'm sure I read there were. Ruby…Ruby Davis, that's it. Is she ill or something?"

"Ill?" Theo raised an eyebrow, a frown on her face that she quickly erased. "She's pregnant. That's why it's the three of us, for now."

"Oh, I see," Karen replied before offering them tea, which they accepted. As Luke set about making it, she enquired what she and her husband should do, "you know, whilst you're busy."

"If you leave us in the kitchen, we can do our best to tune in, see what we can detect," Ness answered, her voice, her whole demeanour strained, the lines around her eyes a little more pronounced than usual. If she had other things on her mind or hadn't been sleeping properly, she hadn't mentioned anything to her companions on the journey over, and, given she was such a private person, they hadn't probed either. "You can wait in another room," Ness continued, tucking dark hair behind her ears, "or perhaps go for a walk. It's up to you."

"We'll go for a walk," Luke decided, setting full mugs down in front of them. "We need some groceries from the Co-op anyway."

"We've done some research on the house, as we said we

would," Corinna informed them before taking a sip of tea. Normally, she took hers black, a nod towards veganism, which sometimes she was super good at and sometimes failed at. This was one of those fail times, as the milk was in the mug before the water had even been poured. No matter, she wasn't a pedant, not with a boyfriend like Presley, who, like his younger brother, ate anything and everything.

Karen and Luke were looking at her expectantly, and she hated to disappoint them but continued speaking anyway. "The house appears to have a clean history; we could find nothing that gave us any cause for concern. We've a list of owners here, dating all the way back to when the house was built in 1864." Producing the list, Corinna pointed to it. "As you can see, the first owner was a woman, Jessica Biggs. It looks like she lived here for forty-five years before—"

Fifty!

"What?" Open-mouthed, Corinna stared all around her, trying to work out who'd said that, noticed nothing except four faces – those of Karen, Luke, Ness and Theo – staring at her.

"What is it?" Theo said. "Have you...detected something?"

"I...erm"—Corinna glanced at Karen and Luke before answering—"think so, yeah."

"A ghost?" Karen breathed.

"A spirit," Ness corrected, always a stickler for the rules.

"Whoa!" Luke added, his eyes – a much darker shade of blue than his wife's – on stalks.

Theo struggled to a standing position, huffing and puffing as she usually did. "It might be best if you go and get that shopping you mentioned, leave us to it."

Corinna also stood, her chair scraping loudly against the flagstone floor.

"Shit!" The word was out before she could stop it. Mortified, she clasped her hands over her mouth, trying to get herself under control, listening to more from the spirit who'd contacted her.

Fifty years...lived here. My house...mine!

Who are you? Corinna shot back, using thought only, all the living continuing to stare at her. *Are you Jessica Biggs?*

Jess! The name's Jess!

Sorry—

Doesn't matter who I am—

Look, if I've upset you—

Not about me. About time. So much time...

Is that...is that why the clocks don't work in here? You're making a statement of some kind?

Understand!

Listen, I—

Theo had begun herding Karen and Luke out of the kitchen. "It really is best if we're left to deal with what's going on in here," she was busy explaining.

"But what *is* going on?" Luke asked.

"My God, our home really is haunted!" Karen declared.

"We don't know that, not yet," Theo insisted.

"But you'll tell us, you won't...soft-soap us?"

"No, Luke," said Theo. "We're not in the business of soft-soaping."

Corinna heard barking, Petra the dog having roused herself from her usual state of slumber if not actually moving from her favourite spot in the living room and putting in an appearance.

"The dog," Karen fretted. "I'll go and see to her. Thank goodness the children are on a playdate!"

"There's nothing to worry about," Theo reassured her prior to closing the kitchen door. "Most spirits are not malevolent, far from it. They're distressed or confused or they simply like it where they are; they have trouble letting go of the material world. Often, all it takes is a few words of persuasion or understanding, and they move on. You have a lovely home, and it may be that a previous resident thinks so too and…well, that's what we're going to find out."

"He or she likes it here?" Karen held the door open just a fraction. "In the kitchen? Is that…is that why time stands still in there?"

"Possibly," Theo answered, closing the door fully. "Possibly."

Shuffling around to face Corinna and Ness, who'd also climbed to her feet – such a sombre expression on her face as she too tried to understand the situation – Theo asked Corinna what she was experiencing. About to answer her, to tell her that she could hear a woman's voice in her head if not actually see her, she sensed a loud whoosh, as if someone had swept through the atmosphere to stand in front of her, who then started to poke at her.

Although stunned by what was unfolding, Corinna managed to answer her colleagues. "It's Jess Biggs, and she's jabbing me, right here, in the chest. Can you see her?"

"No," Theo said whilst Ness shook her head.

"Ow!"

Ness darted forward. "What is it? What's happening?"

"She's pulling my hair now! Ow! That hurts. Stop it!"

Theo closed her eyes. Corinna knew what she was doing

29

– surrounding them all in white light, using it as protection, contacting the spirit by thought too, also telling her to stop what she was doing. Meanwhile, Ness had come to stand beside her in a show of strength and solidarity.

"We're not at your mercy, and we don't entertain any tricks or stunts you might want to pull," Ness told the spirit. "We don't want to cause you any distress; we only want to help." She was repeating their ethos, the message they always worked so hard to convey. *We're here to help.*

Not that it impressed Jess.

"Shit!" Corinna swore again as this time she was shoved hard, the small of her back colliding with the cooker, and knobs and handles digging into her as the breath left her body. Not just shoved, she was pinned to the cooker, Jess Biggs as determined as they were.

But for what purpose?

"Wait!" Corinna uttered breathlessly, an instruction not meant for the spirit but her colleagues. "Let her speak. She…she *needs* to speak."

Time means nothing. Not where you are. Not where I am. Nothing changes. Understand! This house…good now. Another house…not good. Never. There are people. Things happened. Dreadful! Hard to speak. Things…happen again. Nothing changes. Understand! Change it. It's about time!

Gone. Jess Biggs – a woman who'd lived here for fifty years, not forty-five – had retreated, if only temporarily. Before Corinna could relate all that had happened to a clearly curious Ness and Theo, she checked her watch; it had stopped, just like it had the first time she'd set foot in here. Not a trick, not a ploy, but a message, one Jess Biggs professed was hard to convey – why was that? And one that had also gone unheard for so long. A message that didn't make sense, that was cryptic, that would take time to unravel. A lot of time, perhaps, and a lot of effort. The other house the spirit had talked of, the one that wasn't good, if so, what was it? More to the point, *where* was it? Also in the village of Lindfield? Certainly, Psychic Surveys hadn't had any calls from anyone else here complaining of paranormal behaviour. And if it was a bad house, how bad? Blakemort bad? No. No way. That was a one-off. It had to be. *Please no.*

"Fuck!" she said again, a variance on the swear words that seemed to spew from her since she'd stepped into the Bow household for the second time. "Fuck! Fuck! Fuck!"

An ordinary case?

It was looking like anything but.

Chapter Three

TIME means nothing, the spirit in the Bow house had said. But it *was* time to explore the village of Lindfield further, primarily to find any evidence of the bad house that Jess Biggs was talking about. Whilst it might not even be in the village of Lindfield, it was also the case that when Jess Biggs had lived, people tended to not move around as freely or as extensively as they did in more modern times, and so, if nothing else, it provided a starting point.

From the ornamental lake, they worked their way up the high street, taking their time, admiring the many ancient houses on either side of them that dated back centuries. Of varying styles and sizes – some were as big as manor houses, others far more modest – they were beautiful and picturesque, as were the lime trees that lined the high street, almost in full bloom and filling the air with their fresh scent. No bad vibes could be detected; it was all quite benign, although certainly there was a sense of the hustle and bustle of days gone by.

History – there was plenty of it in a village like this, prompting Corinna to Google what was on the net about it, reading aloud to the other two her findings whilst they walked.

"They started to hold annual fairs here in 1343, which carried on for centuries after. The Lindfield sheep fair was one of the most active in the country, later usurped by smuggling."

"Ah, good old smuggling," said Theo. "Always plenty of that in these here parts, me hearties!"

Corinna smiled before continuing. "All Saints Church," she said, pointing to a church that lay just up ahead, "is a thirteenth-century Gothic landmark, and the high street is lined with historic buildings, a mix of later Jacobean, Georgian and Victorian styles."

"Lovely," Ness remarked. "Just lovely."

"One of the more interesting buildings is Old Place, thought to have been built as a country cottage for none other than Elizabeth I. And next to Old Place is another intriguing house, this one possibly a hunting lodge for her grandfather, Henry VII."

"Oh!" Theo was impressed. "Where are they?"

"Erm…hang on, I can pull up a tourist map of Lindfield." Doing so, again online, Corinna stopped to study it. "They're just past the church, right at the top of the high street."

Theo started to stride ahead. "Maybe it's his house Jess was talking about."

Corinna nodded in agreement, keeping pace. She'd also previously relayed exactly what Jess had said to her. They'd mulled it over then, and she mulled it over now.

"I wonder what she meant when she said it was hard to speak," she voiced.

Ness shrugged. "It could mean a variety of things, that it's painful for her to recall, perhaps?"

"And yet she's waited a heck of a long time to do just that."

"As I said, it could mean a variety of things."

"She also said time means nothing."

"Hence the clock issue," said Ness.

"Something I agree with, wholeheartedly." Theo was puffing a bit now from her earlier exertion. "Time is a man-made construct, nothing more."

"Do you think, now that she's made contact, she'll ramp up the haunting?" Corinna asked, worried.

"The Bows know to inform us if that's the case," Theo assured her.

And it was true – they did. Honesty was of paramount importance to Psychic Surveys, although on occasion they limited what they told their clients whilst working on a case so as to keep any fear or worries from escalating, not wanting to feed any delicate situations further. Of course, they'd had to explain to the Bows something of what had occurred in their house less than an hour ago, and, as they did, Corinna also apologised for swearing.

"It's fine," Luke had said, a carrier bag of groceries still in his hand. "I'm sure it's par for the course, isn't it? You know, when odd things happen and take you by surprise."

"Sometimes," Corinna said, feeling her face flame in colour, most likely the exact same shade as her hair. "As you know, we made a connection. Unfortunately, it was fleeting."

"So there's definitely a ghost?" Karen was clearly torn between excitement and unease.

"An old woman," Ness elaborated, "one that means no harm but has a message to convey."

"A message?" repeated Luke. "About what?"

"Time," answered Theo, "and how meaningless it is. It could be, now she's imparted this message, she may not bother you anymore. Then again..." She glanced at her watch.

"So, she hasn't gone?" Karen said, checking her own static watch.

"Maybe not," Theo told her before waving her hand in the air in a somewhat frustrated manner. "Look, terribly sorry about this, for being vague, but sometimes that's exactly what the spirits are: vague. We need some time to process what she's told us. As though it were a riddle, we need to work it out. One thing we do know, she's not a troublesome spirit, just...a very patient one."

"I suppose we'll be all right, then," Karen said.

"We always have been all right," Luke reassured her. "And we like it here."

"We do," she said with more conviction. "We love it. But you won't forget about us, will you?"

"Of course not." Ness's ever so serious tone settled them further. "We'll be in touch regularly, and you can contact us should anything concern you, anything at all."

At that point Petra had finally put in an appearance, sniffing at the air but otherwise content, settling herself in front of the AGA. That she was content to be in the kitchen was a relief to all, and the Bows had agreed they were happy enough with the results for now. The team had taken their leave, intent on exploring further, now coming to a standstill outside Old Place and the hunting lodge.

"Wow!" Corinna declared. "They're awesome."

They were. Old Place, with its thatched roof and black and white timbers, was a country residence fit for any queen.

As for the neighbouring hunting lodge, it was resplendent with its timber frame, peaked gables, oak mullions and soft red bricks in a herringbone style.

"Wonderful," breathed Ness, doing as the other two were and staring at it.

"No proof that the pair of them ever did visit, though?" Theo checked.

"Doesn't seem to be," Corinna said. "Not according to the articles I've read, anyway."

"And now they're private residences?" Theo asked, turning to look at Corinna.

"Looks like it. Do you get a sense of any…royal visits?"

Theo's expression was slightly torn. "I get a sense some impressive gatherings were held here once upon a time, certainly, in the lodge, highborn types coming and going…"

"As highborn as the king?" Ness queried.

Theo shook her head. "No. Not him but people that society considered important, a steady flow of them through the years. I'm talking generations, decades, centuries." She stopped for a second and then shut her eyes as if trying to see further. "Some gatherings were…dubious, yes, that's it. Secret. Private. I'm sensing a clique. A circle of people. A little magic. The dark kind." Before her colleagues could comment, Theo's eyes snapped open. Instead of looking tense or even horrified, she smiled. "Par for the course, isn't it? The upper echelons love a secret society."

Ness frowned. "So, no sacrifices went on here as such?" She was clearly only part joking.

"Nope," Theo replied, "no sacrifices and no summoning of demons. Most of these secret societies only tended to go so far. There's darkness here, as I say, but only a tinge."

Ness turned to Corinna. "Remind us what Jess Biggs said, her exact message."

Luckily, when Ness and Theo had been wrapping things up at the Bows', Corinna had excused herself, citing a need to pop to the bathroom. Once there, she'd typed Jess's words into Notes on her phone whilst still fresh in her memory. Her mobile still in her hand, she swiped at the screen and recited it to her friends for the second time: *Time means nothing. Not where you are. Not where I am. Nothing changes. Understand! This house...good now. Another house...not good. Never. There are people. Things happened. Dreadful! Hard to speak. Things...happen again. Nothing changes. Understand! Change it. It's about time!*

"That's quite an impassioned plea," Theo remarked.

"It is," agreed Corinna. "It's so strange that of us all, I was the one who sensed Jess, who she, like...picked on, for want of a better phrase. For so long I've lagged behind you all."

"Things *do* change," Theo said, winking, "contrary to what Jess says. Circumstances too."

Ness resumed gazing at the hunting lodge. "Do you think one of these houses is the one she's referring to? That she was aware of what used to take place here?"

A few moments of silence ensued as each contemplated her answer, Corinna sighing before being the first one to reply. "Like you said, Theo, it was an impassioned plea from Jess, so, if what you're sensing here is only a tinge of darkness, it doesn't equate."

"True that," Theo replied. "You'd think we'd be hit by a tidal wave of the black stuff."

"Exactly."

"But"—again Ness was sombre—"there is *something* here,

at these houses, and, if nothing else, we can bear it in mind."

"We can," Theo conceded.

"Shall we continue walking around the village?" suggested Corinna. "See if anything else, you know, jumps out at us." She grinned, adding, "Figuratively speaking, of course."

"Let's," agreed Theo, "but not before a spot of lunch. I noticed a rather nice tea shop further down the street, and do you know what? I could murder a quiche and salad."

* * *

Theo's quiche and salad were followed by a huge slice of coffee-and-walnut cake, which she attacked just as enthusiastically as her first course. All the while, Corinna and Ness sat nursing their individual drinks, black coffee for Ness and a green tea with jasmine for Corinna.

Ness had been quiet during lunch, had hardly eaten a thing, picking at a cheese-and-pickle sandwich she'd ordered and making Corinna wonder, yet again, what was on her mind, not that there was any use in utilising her newfound talent of catching thoughts to find out. Theo might be training Corinna to pick up on thoughts, but equally, she was training her how to cloak them – something Ness was particularly expert at, and who could blame her? A useful skill between them when they needed it, conversely, it was also a massive invasion of privacy.

Even so, she was getting something about a girl...a young girl...

Ness looked sideways at her, and immediately Corinna flushed.

"I saw Ruby yesterday," she blurted out, seeking to divert attention.

"Did you?" Theo's mouth was full of cake as she said it. "How is she?"

"She's very pale, and she's feeling sick again. In fact, she *was* almost sick. We were in the Rights of Man, and she had to rush to the loo. I went with her. She was, like…fine at first but…a bit agitated towards the end. Just not the Ruby we know and love. And miss."

Theo swallowed the last bite of her cake. "Oh, that's the stuff," she commented. "The very stuff." Picking up a napkin, she wiped at her mouth. "Corinna, sweetie, we *all* miss Ruby. I keep in touch with her regularly via text, but apart from that, she really is determined to keep her head low."

"But why? Aside from how wretched she's feeling, I mean. Because…because I think there's more to it, and…I'm worried."

Theo patted at Corinna's hand. "She knows where we are, that we're here for her."

"But it's not the same, is it? The four of us, and Cash and Jed, were so strong together."

"And we still are, even as three instead of four. We keep this ship sailing. We agreed on that, when Ruby told us she was retiring. Isn't that right, Ness? Ness? Are you listening?"

Ness lifted her head. "What? Oh yes, yes, absolutely, we keep this ship sailing, we keep it afloat. I hope Ruby's all right, though. I worry about her as well."

"I know." Theo's expression darkened temporarily. "But she's in safe hands with Cash."

Corinna leant across the table. "Does Blakemort have

something to do with the way she is? Theo, do you know more than you're letting on?"

At once Theo shook her head, almost as if expecting to be asked this. "Blakemort is over."

Believe it, she was saying, what she'd probably said to Ruby. *It's over.*

"It's just…" Corinna persisted, "she told me to keep things ordinary, she was emphatic about it. Stick to spirit rescue, she said, what we're good at, don't court the dark stuff."

Ness's attention was wholly captured now.

"Go on," she urged. "What else did she say?"

"That's it, really, in a nutshell. Keep it all as light as we can."

"If only," Ness replied, her voice barely above a whisper.

Corinna pressed her lips together before sighing. "We can't let her retreat from us, though, because that's what she's doing, as if she's trying to protect us too. We're a team. Always."

"Look"—Theo looked first at Ness and then Corinna— "let's get the bill, shall we? Get on with this infernal walk around the village. It's not a case of out of sight, out of mind, Corinna, believe that also. No one's forgetting about Ruby."

With Corinna deciding she had to be satisfied with that for now, they did as Theo suggested and continued exploring Lindfield, calling it a day after an hour or so because Theo claimed her legs were swelling so much, they resembled an elephant's.

Back in Corinna's car, they drove out of the village, Corinna frustrated there'd been no obvious 'bad house'. Still, she was looking forward to a relaxing evening, staying over at

Presley's flat, him doing the cooking, and a thriller on TV they wanted to catch up on…

"Stop!" Ness yelled, causing Corinna to quickly check the rearview mirror and nudge the left indicator before pulling into a thankfully empty space.

"Ness?" she said. "What is it?"

"Yes, what is it?" Theo shifted around as far as she was able. "Calling out like that, you could have caused the dear girl to crash—"

"Over there," Ness said, ignoring Theo's reprimand and pointing to a house on the opposite side of the road, partially concealed by tall hedges. "That house…there's something about it. Something…bad." She then turned to Corinna. "Sorry, love, so sorry. Theo's right, I shouldn't have called out like that, but that house, call it instinct, but we need to take a look."

After all three had bundled out of the car and crossed the road to stand on the pavement outside the house, Ness asked Theo and Corinna if they were sensing anything about it.

"It's certainly beautiful to look at," Corinna began, and it was, despite not being as grand as Old Place and the hunting lodge, although like Old Place, it too had a white stucco facade with exposed black beams – not original, Corinna suspected, as Old Place was, but certainly a nod towards what was a popular architectural style. The roof was tiled as opposed to thatched, patches of lichen evident. It was also rather substantial in size, somewhat higgledy-piggledy, that term jumping somewhat randomly into Corinna's head, and she sincerely wished it hadn't. It was the term she'd used as a child to describe rambling Blakemort. *Blakemort is over!* She had to repeat Theo's words, and her insistence, before

41

prompting Theo for her opinion on it too.

"Oh yes," replied Theo, "this has more than a tinge of darkness about it. Far more."

"Another place for gatherings?" Ness suggested.

Theo agreed. "And it's another private residence. Can't exactly barge our way in there to find out more, can we?"

"Look, there!" Corinna had edged closer to a black-coated wrought iron gate and was peering in. "It's got a name to the right of the door, on a plaque. Low Cottage. I'll Google it."

"Go ahead, oh techno queen," Theo quipped, causing Corinna to smile as she retrieved her phone to yet again check the internet.

Ness, meanwhile, had also moved closer to the gate. "Bad mojo indeed," she murmured. "But…mojo that knows how to cloak itself."

"From the likes of us?" Theo said, all traces of humour in her voice gone.

Ness nodded. "Yes, exactly. Theo, what can you sense?"

"Not as much as you, dear, not this time. That barrier is most effective."

"If we could get in there," Ness continued. "If we could find a way—"

"All I can find out about the house for now," Corinna said, "is its sales history on Zoopla. Wow! It's an interesting sales history, that's for sure. This house has changed hands so many times, like…nine times in the last fifteen years. I kid you not. There's a couple of images of its interior too – look, low beams, a big old fireplace, farmhouse kitchen, beams in the walls as well as the ceiling. Award Estates was the last to sell it. We could get in touch, ask them—"

"What are you doing here?"

A male voice startled them all, Ness turning in the direction it had come from and Corinna promptly lowering her phone. She hadn't realized she'd actually pushed the gate open, had started to venture down the path a few steps, drawn forwards unwittingly, it seemed.

"Sorry..." began Corinna, returning back to the pavement, where the stranger also stood, observing him all the while. He was tall and lean, in his forties – the latter end of them, she guessed – his nose somewhat large and pointed, and blue eyes bulging slightly. A hawk, that's what he reminded Corinna of, observing the three of them just as pointedly. "We were just saying, what an...erm...stunning house this is. So...charming."

The man raised an eyebrow. "Charming? You'd call it that?"

"How would you describe it?" Ness's voice held the merest hint of a challenge.

"Oh, I could think of other words," was his somewhat enigmatic reply, "ones more apt."

Theo came straight to the point. "Do you live here? Are we in your way?"

"Live here? No."

"Do you know who does?" she continued.

"It's available for rent, I believe."

"Is it indeed? How interesting."

"Is that what you're doing here?" the man probed further. "Because you want to rent it?"

Theo smiled. "Maybe."

Rather than returning her smile, he frowned. "The rent will be expensive."

"Undoubtedly."

"Do you have family?"

"Do you?" she batted back.

The man's nostrils flared as he shook his head. "Look, this house, it's got a history."

"Oh?" queried Ness, an eyebrow raising.

"We know it's changed hands a lot," Corinna told him, "over the past fifteen years, anyway."

"For a reason." The man was chewing at his lip now.

"Look, who are you?" Theo said. "What's your name?"

"My name? That's no business of yours."

"Correct, but I was being polite."

"Who are you, then?"

Theo offered her hand, which the man took but only lightly and very briefly too. "I'm Theo Lawson. This is Ness Patterson and Corinna Greer."

"Oh," was all he said, his hand back by his side.

"This dark history—"

"Who said it was dark?" the man replied quickly enough.

"But it is, isn't it? Very dark."

Corinna looked at Theo as she continued speaking, surprised at how far she was taking this. What was she trying to do, put the fear of God into the man?

He knows more than he's letting on!

Theo fired the thought like a bullet.

"Young man"—only Theo could get away with calling someone in his late forties that—"as potential tenants, is there anything you'd like to tell us about Low Cottage."

The man stared defiantly at her for several seconds, his nostrils flaring again. "Yes," he said at last, "keep away from it. If you value your lives, keep away."

Chapter Four

CORINNA'S evening wasn't as relaxing as she'd wanted it to be, not with that man's words still in her head. Why on earth had he threatened them like that? Before they could quiz him further, challenge him further too, the man had promptly turned on his heel and hurried to his car, climbing in it and driving off. At no point had he imparted his name, remaining a stranger, a dubious one.

As they had also driven away, Ness did some digging on Google regarding local letting agents and who might be responsible for Low Cottage. The agency was the one Corinna had already mentioned, Award Estates. A local firm, they'd handled past sales as well as current lettings. Ness gave them a call, planning to make an appointment to view the house, a man called Greg Warrington answering the phone. Ness informed him there were two other people in the car and that she was putting him on loudspeaker, after which he wasted no time in informing his captive audience there'd been a lot of interest in 'such a charming cottage', Corinna only partly amused that he'd used the same term as her.

"I really wouldn't delay," he continued. "It'll be snapped up. It's in such a beautiful village too, isn't it? A prime location. Is it a young family who'd be moving in?"

When Ness hesitated, Corinna stepped into the breach. "It's us, actually, myself and my two aunts," she said, noting Theo's amusement and Ness's *be*musement at her answer.

"Oh," Mr Warrington said, quickly concealing his surprise. "I see. Shall we pencil in a date?"

They'd decided on Thursday, in two days' time, Theo having a hospital appointment on Wednesday, although – as she'd taken pains to point out – it wasn't for anything serious. "They're monitoring my weight, my heart, the usual. A royal pain, really."

Two days to gear up for it, to enter a house the stranger had deemed life-threatening...

"Dinner's ready."

Snapped out of the agitated reverie she'd fallen into, Corinna looked up to see Presley handing her a bowl of food – spaghetti with cherry tomatoes, garlic, capers, and olives running through it and topped with pangrattato, one of their favourites. They'd decided to eat in front of the TV, catching up on the thriller they were following, although something else seemed to have caught Presley's attention, a show on Netflix.

"Can we watch this first?" he asked, and Corinna nodded, also intrigued.

Not a fictional programme, it was a documentary, one concerning a young girl whose body had been discovered along a side alley in the city of St Louis, USA. Aged twenty-three, she'd come from the 'right side of the tracks', apparently, was popular and beautiful too, holding down a good job and singing in a local gospel choir. She'd left home fairly early one morning to go and meet a friend for coffee.

En route, she'd run into evil. The strange thing was, when she'd eventually been found, there wasn't a mark on her. But, as everyone knew, a person didn't just drop dead in a dark alley, managing to stuff their own body behind a dumpster whilst they were at it. It was murder all right, but involving what method and by whom?

These kinds of documentaries, although somewhat dramatic for the benefit of the viewer and packed with loaded statements from attorneys and detectives, lending them that all-important edge-of-the-seat tension, fascinated both Corinna and Presley. Sometimes they discussed them at length afterwards, as usually the programme would end with no real conclusions drawn; what had happened remained steeped in mystery, similar to the deaths of the three victims in the UK's Rayners Wood – becoming cult mysteries. Regarding the latter and what she'd learnt whilst Googling it, it was quite possibly a cult mystery in both senses of the word!

The bowl of pasta was, as always, delicious, the pair of them chomping their way through it whilst engrossed in what was unravelling on the TV. Throughout the documentary, a black-and-white close-up of the girl's face kept appearing on-screen, with Corinna trying to read that face, staring into eyes that stared back at her, so large and soulful. They were eyes that had seen something in her final moments, seen *someone*, realising too late, perhaps, their intention and the horror of it... *What happened? Who was it? You know. You and the murderer...*

"Crin? You got the feels yet?"

Corinna turned her head towards Presley and forced a smile. The 'feels' was what he tended to call her psychic ability to sense things. "Nope. Just a big dose of…emptiness."

He took her empty bowl from her and placed it on the coffee table in front of them, stacking his on top. "No feels, eh? That's bad, very bad. Perhaps I can succeed where others have failed."

Taking her in his arms, she closed her eyes, breathing in the slight muskiness of his skin, her smile more genuine this time. God, she was happy to be with him, the brother of her best friend's husband. He was down-to-earth, supportive, kind, caring and hardworking, all that she valued in a partner, particularly the supportive bit, not getting as involved with her line of work as much as Cash sometimes did – his day job as a motorcycle courier and gigging with his band a few evenings a week kept him busy enough – but sticking by her through thick and thin, even during Blakemortgate, as he laughingly called it. *Particularly* during Blakemortgate. In the run-up to her return there, she'd almost had a breakdown.

As he began to kiss her neck, she dug her fingers slightly into his shoulders. This other house – Low Cottage – surely it couldn't be as bad, despite the warning that had been issued. And who was that man anyway? She'd never met him before, he was a complete stranger, and yet there was something about him that nagged at her, something…familiar.

"Corinna?"

"Uh-huh?"

"No more analysing."

"Just feel, huh?"

His lips grazed her mouth. "That's right."

Later that evening, with Presley asleep beside her – feels on the sofa having led them through to the bedroom – Corinna continued to lay there, content but wide-awake. So much was going through her head, yet more analysing, notably what Ruby had said about keeping their work as run-of-the-mill as possible, plus the stranger's bizarre warning.

At last she accepted the inevitable, that sleep – for her, at least – was a long way off. Moving gently so as not to wake Presley, she reached for her mobile, dimming its screen before Googling more about Low Cottage. It had last sold for just under six hundred thousand, the subsequent rent there, as the stranger had said, sure to be astronomical. Still, it cost nothing to look around, to tune in, sense what they could about it. If there was any chance that it was the property that Jess Biggs had meant, then they had no option but to explore it. Psychic Surveys, under the ownership of Ruby Davis, enjoyed an excellent reputation, with plenty of cases coming in via word-of-mouth as well as their website, which had an entire page devoted to testimonials. She, Theo and Ness felt strongly that they not only maintained this reputation but built upon it, and to that end Jess Biggs needed to feel confident that her message had got across, that the living were doing something about it, whatever *it* was. That way she'd move on, timepieces would start working in the kitchen of the Bow family home, and all would be happy.

Simples.

If only.

The following day, she had an evening shift at the pub to work, which left the day free. She resolved to go to The Keep in Brighton, where all local records were kept, and see if she could find out anything more about Low Cottage, exactly when it was built, the architect, any significant happenings that had taken place there that might have been recorded, and records of past owners as well. But that was still a good few hours away; right now, sleep still eluded her.

Almost as if they had a will of their own, her fingers typed *Rayners Wood* once again into the search bar. There was so much stuff on it, including YouTube videos, personal blogs, paranormal group investigation results and even an entry on good old Wikipedia. Although she'd already read it in the Rights of Man whilst waiting for everyone to turn up, she couldn't resist refreshing her memory: *Rayners Wood is a woodland area in West Sussex, England, close to the village of Rayner, which paranormal enthusiasts believe to be the focus of satanic cult activity, deaths and lost or sick pets.*

Wiki then went on to explain that, according to an article in a magazine that Corinna had never heard of but which specialised in supernatural matters, people claimed to have experienced nausea there, sudden patches of grey mist, and sensations of being pushed or followed – all since the 1960s. What people had experienced before that date, Corinna mused, was clearly not as enthusiastically recorded. It mentioned the three deaths that had occurred there and also that others, not including Tom Witcher this time, had made a study of the woods, finding no evidence of satanic ritual – as Witcher insisted there was – beyond odd campfires and a few suspicious carvings on trees.

That was the sum total of what Wiki had to say on the matter, whereas other sites, devoted to the paranormal, delved deeper. One YouTube video was fun to watch, a kind of amateur *Most Haunted* with a group of individuals on a ghost hunt, rather like Anya had been, spooking themselves stupid, insisting they could see strange lights flickering within the trees, hear garbled voices in the distance and twigs snapping several feet from them, as if something was stalking them. Corinna didn't believe a word of it, not least because, in between screaming, members of the group kept dissolving into laughter, pushing and shoving each other and generally having a blast. There was another YouTube video uploaded by the *Spectacled Explorer* that took the avid viewer on a walk through the woods, explaining the myths and legends places such as these were steeped in but refuting any supernatural connotations as 'nonsense' without actually explaining *why* he thought they were.

Tom Witcher hadn't uploaded any videos, or any direct information as far as she could see, but he was certainly quoted often enough from a book he'd written on the subject and which Corinna resolved to buy as soon as possible to do some delving of her own. Would she visit Rayners Wood? Maybe, when she had a free day. For now it was enough to be aware of it.

Another article caught her eye, something about *The Devil's Triangle* in the short synopsis below the headline. She clicked on it, also aware of something else: that her eyes were becoming heavier now, all this reading tiring her out at last.

One more article and she'd call it a night. Glancing at the digital clock beside her bed, she corrected herself – it was four in the morning; the night had all but disappeared.

The Devil's Triangle, what's that all about? Certainly, she'd heard of the Devil's Dyke before, an area of green hills that dipped and rose just outside of Brighton; she'd walked there plenty of times. The place was so named because, according to legend, the devil was furious at the people of the Weald for converting to Christianity and so decided to dig a dyke through the South Downs, allowing the sea to flow in and drown their villages. *Charming,* she thought wryly, picturing the devil as an angry horned beast complete with pitchfork in hand, stamping his feet in fury. The *Spectacled Explorer* was right: Sussex was rich with myth. "It's a hotbed," Theo had once said on the subject. "Who knows what's real and what isn't. Think about it, darling," she'd continued, "the past encompasses such delights as invasion, plague, witch trials, and religious persecution, so of course folklore will run alongside it, equally as deep."

The Devil's Triangle, though, was something different from the Devil's Dyke, although still within Sussex. It incorporated Chanctonbury Ring, Cissbury Ring and, oh look, surprise, surprise, Rayners Wood – three areas of landscape set at three different points.

Again surprise, surprise, Britain's most famous devil worshipper, known as the Beast 666, none other than Aleister Crowley himself, had also used Chanctonbury Ring to practise his particular form of paganism. He believed that ancient ley lines crossed and weaved their way through these sites, no doubt hoping to draw on the earth's natural telluric current for reasons best kept to himself. Whilst walking at any of these sites, not just Rayners Wood, people reported sudden, sweeping sickness, dizziness, problems with breathing and, most disturbingly, feelings of being pulled along or pushed by an unseen force – affecting both animals and humans alike.

Keep things ordinary, Corinna. Don't court the dark stuff, not anymore.

Ruby's words caused her own breath to halt. Something

deep within Corinna was saying the very same thing. She shook her head as if to disperse the warning but quickly stilled as Presley stirred beside her and mumbled something incoherent before settling back into slumber. The thing about the ordinary, she reasoned, was that sometimes it led towards the *extra*ordinary. You got a call from a potential client, just as she'd done from the Bows; you sensed a grounded spirit, as the team had done on countless occasions; then you made contact, got a message and, hey, presto, ordinary was done away with.

But what's all this got to do with the Devil's Triangle?

It was a good question, and one to which she had no answer, except... They'd visited three houses in Lindfield, if you counted Old Place and the hunting lodge as one, which she did because they occupied the same area of land. Houses that were a fair distance from each other, that could possibly equate to a triangle too? The thought was a potent one.

Ah, there he was, Tom Witcher, quoted in yet another article, a definite authority on these matters – on Rayners Wood, at any rate, which he focused on over and above Chanctonbury and Cissbury Rings.

"I will continue to monitor these woods," he stated, "as I believe that someone must, someone who is not afraid. There is danger here; that's a cold hard fact. People have died in strange circumstances. Animals have gone missing and still tend to, to this day. I believe there have been more deaths than those counted and that death may well occur again. Something has been unleashed in these grounds, and it must be stopped."

They were strong words, dramatic words, words that made her sit upright rather than slouch.

Like her – like Ruby, Theo and Ness – Tom Witcher pitted himself against what was insidious, what was unseen, but what was real all the same.

"Whoa!" Corinna said under her breath, settling down to read yet more, not worried about sleep anymore, not feeling tired at all. What did she feel? Alive. That was it. A strange choice of word considering her reading material, that it was death making her feel this way, other people's deaths and the likelihood of more. Yet tapping at the screen and scrolling, her fingers tingled. What with? Purpose? Yes, that again, because she agreed with Witcher, wholeheartedly. If evil was present in Rayners Wood, it had to be contained, not exploited.

God, the world around her was so full of mystery. Her *local area* was full of mystery.

What had gone on in Rayners Wood had nothing to do with her, absolutely nothing. And yet now that it had been brought to her attention, courtesy of Anya, she could think about little else.

Chapter Five

THURSDAY arrived, another glorious day, with temperatures set to soar higher still. It was only Corinna and Ness going to Low Cottage this time, as Theo was feeling unwell. When asked about the hospital appointment she'd had, she'd snorted down the phone to Corinna.

"All this gumpf about my diet. It's like listening to a stuck record!"

Corinna had suppressed a sigh, knowing full well Theo had been described by the medical profession as morbidly obese on not just this occasion but many.

"The thing is," Theo had continued to protest, "I don't eat a lot. I've the appetite of a sparrow nowadays. The weight, though, refuses to budge. Upshot is, I'm getting them to test my thyroid again. Has to be underactive, and that's the reason why any diet's going to have its work cut out!"

Yeah, yeah, yeah, thought Corinna, but not with anything akin to malice, only affection. And if Theo had caught that thought, she'd made no comment. Instead, she'd gone on to tell Corinna that she felt she was developing a summer cold so would stay at home so as not to infect them.

"But keep me updated if there's any news. Hopefully, I'll be back in the saddle soon."

Corinna hoped so too, just a little upset that four had now gone from three to two.

Ness was driving this time, very little traffic on the road between Lewes and Lindfield, and Corinna telling her she'd been to The Keep the previous day and what she'd found out about Low Cottage and the village it was in.

"It was the lime trees, or lindens as they were known, that gave the village its name, which literally means 'open land with lime trees'. It dates from 765 AD, when a Saxon king granted land there for the construction of a church, and then in the fourteenth century it was granted a market charter."

"Hence the sheep fairs you mentioned when we were walking around it on Tuesday."

Corinna nodded. "In short, it was an ordinary village that then became a pit stop on the London-to-Brighton coach route with pubs like the Bent Arms and the Red Lion Inn used as horse-change stops. For a while, pre-1700s, it flourished." Getting into her stride, Corinna continued with the history lesson. "From the 1700s onwards, though, as other coach routes were opened, it went downhill, only to rise again thanks to nearby Haywards Heath also becoming a stop on the Brighton-to-London route, this time via train. So that's when a lot of grand houses were built, during the Victorian era, Low Cottage being one of them. It dates from 1900, so not as old as it looks, and not as old as other houses in the village either."

"Okay," Ness replied. "And what of its architect?"

"No information on that, but checking various records, I found out its first resident was Phyllida Hylands, who lived there from 1901. She may even have been the one to have commissioned the build. She'd been widowed and moved in with a cook, a parlour maid, a housemaid and, later, a resident nurse to look after her. She died there in 1962 at the ripe old age of ninety-one!"

"And after that?"

"Well, after that, there's another gap in the records in that I couldn't find out who occupied it from 1962 and into the eighties. The records are patchy, but from thereon in, it's had owner after owner, as we know. The ones who stuck it out the longest were the Carver family, in the late nineties, who managed four years. Everyone wants to get rid of it pretty sharpish. The people that own it currently, Paul and Julie Winterton, have had it for just over a year."

"I wonder if they meant it to be a rental," Ness said, "or if they chose that option precisely because they couldn't stand living in it either."

"Damage limitation," murmured Corinna, "and avoiding stamp duty by reselling it."

"Maybe. Did you find out anything more about Jess Biggs?"

"Just her occupation. She was a weaver, married but widowed too and had no children."

"Right. Not a lot to go on, really, is there?"

"Sadly not. You know, I've also been researching something else."

Ness briefly glanced at her. "Oh, really? Go on."

Corinna found she had to take a deep breath before continuing. "I've been reading about these woods…"

"Woods?" Ness said, a brief look of confusion on her face.

"Yeah, Rayners Wood to be exact." Explaining as

succinctly as she could how she'd come to find out about it, she then – just as succinctly – related its somewhat murky history, including the bodies that had been found there in the '70s, '80s and as recently as 2001. "The thing is, Rayners Wood is part of what's known as the Devil's Triangle. Chanctonbury Ring and Cissbury Ring are at other points of that triangle, and all of them are allegedly paranormal hotspots."

"Yes, yes, they are."

Corinna was surprised. "So you know about them?"

"Yes," Ness repeated before adding more robustly, "what's this got to do with Low Cottage?"

"I had a suspicion about this triangle business, and it turns out I was right. This morning, before you picked me up, I looked at a map of Lindfield on-screen and roughly plotted out where the Bows' house is, Old Place and the hunting lodge, and Low Cottage too—"

"And they form a triangle?"

"That's right, Ness, they do. A triangle that sits within the larger Devil's Triangle."

There was a brief silence whilst both contemplated what had been said and its implication. Certainly, the positioning of the houses might be a coincidence – a concept Theo never held with – but by the same token, it could have been deliberate. Regarding triangles, both knew the significance of them. A symbol regarded as extremely powerful, it was adopted by many ancient civilisations and subsequently secret and satanic groups, the latter tending to prefer the inverted triangle as it pointed to hell rather than heaven – Low Cottage being at the bottom of its triangle, just like Rayners Wood was at the bottom and, therefore, something hellish. The mere thought caused Corinna to shudder. What would they encounter when walking through the doors of Low Cottage, a house that initially attracted people to it but then what? Repelled them?

Why did it repel them?

"I'm just wondering—" Corinna began, but once more Ness interrupted her.

"Preconceptions are dangerous," she said, her frown still evident. "They can influence what we tune in to. Let's keep an open mind for now, remain neutral like we're supposed to."

"Sure, fine," Corinna replied. "Like I said, the Devil's Triangle, it gave me the idea, that's all, to check out where those houses were in relation to each other. That wood, though, it's close by, not that I've been there, have you? You knew all about them, and yet I had no idea—"

"I haven't been there," Ness said, speaking over her for the third time, "and it might have nothing to do with the Bow case, okay? Low Cottage might not either. Don't get carried away, Corinna." Again, Ness turned her head to glance at her. "Just...don't get carried away."

* * *

Low Cottage was aptly named in one sense. It had beams everywhere, some hanging so low that both women, despite not being particularly tall, had to stoop on several occasions in order to pass beneath them. What wasn't very accurate was the cottage part of that description, not in Corinna's opinion, anyway. Cottages by their very name conveyed cosiness and warmth, a welcoming place to retire to at the end of a busy day, but there was nothing welcoming about this place. Despite the heat of summer, it was cool inside, verging on chilly, not a respite but as uncomfortable as the relentless sun. It was also vast, with various rooms almost warren-like, no real cohesion to them, a rickety staircase with uneven treads connecting the ground floor to the equally muddled floor above.

Greg Warrington, every bit the estate agent in his slim-fitting grey suit, white shirt and pink tie, had a habit of checking that his slicked-back hair was firmly in place before opening his mouth to speak. He was doing so even now as he led them from yet another living room – Corinna had counted three so far – into the kitchen to ask what they thought of the cottage.

Before answering, Corinna glanced at Ness, Ness holding her gaze. What a loaded question that was! How to answer it? Not truthfully, that was for sure.

This house was… Corinna struggled to find the right word. *Hideous* seemed too strong, rude almost, but as she could find no alternative, she rolled with it, albeit privately. It *was* hideous, though not in appearance. Many would be initially enchanted by its quirky layout – its numerous owners were testament to that – but not Corinna and not Ness either, judging by the looks they'd exchanged with each other throughout their tour, Ness really quite ashen, what little colour there was in her face draining entirely. The layout, Corinna couldn't help but think, was deliberate, as if it had been designed to confuse you, exit routes always out of sight, around another dark corner…

Although it had passed now, there were certain rooms in

which Corinna had felt nauseous, including the master bedroom and a tiny living room downstairs set up as a study – "Ideal for the homeworker," Greg had said, adding, "Aren't the views amazing?"

He'd then left his hair alone for one minute to point to a small window in the study that perfectly encapsulated the rolling hills that Sussex was famed for – the South Downs, in other words, patches of woodland interspersed amongst them. Innocent woods? Corinna wondered. Not Rayners Wood, at any rate; that was to the south of Low Cottage, not the north.

Another thing odd about the house was its smell, one of damp and all things rotting. If Greg noticed, however, he never said a word, but for Corinna it was pungent.

In the kitchen, seeming to note Corinna and Ness's hesitation in reply to his question, Greg continued onwards. "I do have plenty of other people interested, but if you want the house, ladies, I'll see what I can do, push you up the ladder a bit. You'll have to be quick, though, very, very quick."

Corinna could smell something else too: his desperation. Strange, really, as he wasn't the owner, but maybe the Wintertons had promised a bigger commission than usual, thus their desperation becoming his. Either that or he simply hated having to come here.

He was fiddling with his hair again. "I don't like to push for a decision, not my style, but this place, it'd suit you, I think." He focused on Corinna. "You and your aunt."

"Aunts," she corrected. "One couldn't join us today, which is a shame; she's suffering from a summer cold. Before we can make a decision, we need her to see it, really—"

Greg's mobile started to ring, a jarring bell-like sound that sliced through the atmosphere. "Oh," he said, his face lighting up as he checked the caller ID, "it's a client, one who's also registered interest in this house. Gotta take it, hope you don't mind." As he left the room, he winked, adopting a bit of a smug smile also. "Told you it was sought after."

Left alone, Corinna and Ness held each other's gaze for a moment before Corinna let out a great whoosh of breath. "Sought after? This place? You have *got* to be joking!"

Ness rubbed at her temple. "If I never set foot in this place again, it'd be too soon."

"If only."

Clearly, her comment took Ness by surprise. "Why do you say that?"

"Because…because…I don't know, it's just…this has to be the house Jess Biggs was talking about, Ness. The bad house. The evil house."

"She didn't say evil." Ness was quite emphatic.

Corinna stood her ground. "I'm not getting carried away, Ness. This place *is* evil. You can't tell me you don't think so too. In the master bedroom and downstairs in that nook, that study or whatever it is, you looked as if you were gonna hurl. That's how strong the feeling is."

Still, Ness tried to temper her. "We don't know if what we're tuning in to is residual. You know as well as I do that walls can be like sponges, they soak up energy, be that positive or negative, as does the ground below our feet. That energy can be strong, certainly, but still residual. I've picked up on nothing that suggests it's more intelligent than that. Have you?"

When Corinna didn't answer straightaway, Ness prompted her. "Corinna, have you picked up on anything more than residual?"

"No, I haven't, but...but..."

"Corinna?"

"Oh God, Ness!"

She could say no more – something was happening to her...something she hadn't bargained for. Images began flashing through her mind, so quick they were almost nonsensical, so dark she could hardly make them out. There was a figure in them but whether male or female, she had no idea, and they were running, was that it? Her chest constricted suddenly, causing her to lift a hand and rub at the flesh there. Flesh...she could see flesh, not her own but flesh that was...dead. It had to be, flesh that was...burnt? The stench of earlier became more intense, filling her nostrils, so ripe it caused her to gag, to double over.

"Shit!" she swore, pivoting on her feet and running towards the sink. "Shit! Shit! Shit!"

Once there, the breakfast she'd had earlier made a spectacular comeback, her body heaving just as Ruby's had a few days earlier. Throughout it all, Ness held her, soothing her, whispering her name over and over. "Oh, Corinna. Poor Corinna. What the hell's going on?"

Hell. She not only felt like it, it was as if she'd seen it too, embodied in the flesh of a burning corpse. But why had she seen it? What did it mean? And the figure she'd seen running, had it been running through the woods? Was there a connection after all, despite Ness denying it?

"As I said, that was someone about this property... Oh fuck, what the hell's gone on here?" Greg Warrington had returned, his mobile phone still in his hand and his eyes on stalks. "Have you been sick?" he continued, aghast. "In the sink?"

"Ten out of ten for observation." Ness's tone was acerbic. "Mr Warrington, instead of gawping, if you could pull out a chair for Corinna to sit down whilst I clean up, we'd appreciate it."

"A chair?"

"Yes, a chair. Now!"

Delaying no longer, he pulled out one of the chairs positioned around a long refectory table, gesturing for Corinna to sit down, even offering her a glass of water whilst he was at it. In reply she waved her hand in the air, refusing it. Right now, the prospect of imbibing anything in this house caused yet another wave of nausea, one that she did her utmost to quell. The visions were gone, that was the main thing, although the memory of them remained as vivid as ever.

Ness was running the tap, looking in a cupboard below the sink for some bleach or cleaning fluid. For a moment there was silence as she worked, but then she turned, her focus on the estate agent, addressing him and him only.

"This place," she said, "we'll take it."

"What?" Corinna all but mumbled, too weak to deliver her statement with any real punch.

"We'll take it," Ness reiterated, not even glancing at Corinna.

Greg, too, looked surprised, as if he hadn't expected them to want it after all, as if he'd somehow guessed the reason why she'd vomited – as if no one, but no one, could possibly want this house.

But someone did.

He waved his phone at them. "I'm sorry, it's too late. I was about to tell you that another interested party has just rung to say he wants Low Cottage. So much, in fact, he's prepared to pay over the odds to secure it. Not that I asked him to, nothing like that. He's moving in straightaway."

Ness was as shocked as Corinna. "Who? Who wants it?"

"Who?" said Greg.

"Yes. Tell me."

A slave once more to the command in Ness's voice, the estate agent readily betrayed any client confidentiality. "His name's Tom Witcher," he said. "He's the one who wants it."

Chapter Six

HOW was it possible to feel both relief and disappointment in equal measure? Corinna didn't know, only that it *was* possible. If Greg Warrington had said they could go ahead and rent Low Cottage, what would Ness have them do, actually move in there, Corinna and her 'aunts'? Ness would want to do that despite what had happened in there, the visions and the sickness?

"No, of course not," Ness said when Corinna asked her this very question on their return journey. "I wouldn't dream of moving in there, especially after what happened to you. Besides," she added wryly, "can you imagine me and Theo under the same roof for any length of time? We'd end up killing each other, or being carted off by the men in white."

"So…why'd you say it?"

"I said it because…as we know, there's something wrong with Low Cottage – very wrong, judging by how strong your reaction was. Those visions you told me about…"

"They weren't of that place, though, Ness. I don't think so, anyway. I think it may have been the woods." Corinna sighed. "Maybe I've been reading too much about the Devil's Triangle lately."

"There are so many devil's triangles," Ness said, although so low it was barely a murmur.

"Are there?" Corinna was genuinely surprised.

"Oh yes. The Bermuda Triangle, you've heard of that?"

"Uh-huh. Of course. Hasn't everybody?"

"I suppose."

"Didn't know it was also called the Devil's Triangle, though."

"It has been, at various stages throughout history. George Sand, I think, was the first to identify the triangular nature of the area where all the losses took place – ships going missing, planes going down, never to be heard of again, sucked into some mysterious vortex, another dimension entirely, according to some. Others have elaborated on this notion, I can't remember who now, but it's all there on the internet for the curious. And of course, there've been plenty who've disputed it. For those that do believe, the theory is these triangles are set along particular lines of latitude, or ley lines, places where telluric energy is strong and can be drawn on."

"Ley lines?" Corinna nodded her head voraciously. "Yes! Exactly! That's what I've been reading, that ley lines converge at our very own devil's triangle in Sussex, and do you know what else I found out? Crowley would visit Chanctonbury Ring and practise his rituals there."

Ness shrugged, such a nonchalant gesture. "Doesn't surprise me. Word gets out, people get excited, they buy into it, feed the myth."

"Do you think the Devil's Triangle in Sussex is caught up in myth?"

"I don't know," Ness admitted. "Partly, I should imagine.

67

So often it's a case of 'call it that, and they will come' – the devil worshippers, the thrill seekers, the bored and the opportunists. But in the course of our work, we've realised one thing, at least: if you feed something, it grows."

At that Corinna nodded again.

As they drove towards Brighton rather than Lewes – Ness dropping Corinna off at Presley's – their conversation continued, Corinna still trying to get her head round the offer Ness had made.

"So, if we'd been able to, we'd have rented the place but not actually moved in there?"

"Correct."

"You do know there'd have been a contract to sign? A lease? A deposit too."

Ness remained unfazed. "We'd have found a way round all that. Talking of which, the rent was actually quite reasonable, wasn't it? For a house of that size."

"So was the rent at Blakemort," Corinna pointed out, "and not for altruistic reasons."

"True," Ness conceded. Coming to a halt at traffic lights, she turned her head towards Corinna, brown eyes meeting green. "Apart from the adverse effect it's had on you, and its regular change of hands, we don't know anything about Low Cottage, and our job as Psychic Surveys is to find out, to banish negative energy if it's pooled there and to bring back the light. Also, if there's a spirit grounded, maybe even more than one, we need to send them on their way, especially if they're suffering, if they're traumatised, if they're…frightened. I didn't get the strength of feeling you got in there. It's strange, I did when we first drove past, but it seems to come and go. Although make no mistake, I certainly didn't like it, and I was nauseous too on several occasions, but seeing your reaction, I felt we *needed* to be there, in whatever way we could, hence my offer."

"Ness?"

"Yes?"

"The lights have changed."

"Oh! Okay."

Ness pulled away. They were just a few miles from Brighton, Corinna's head still swimming with all that had transpired.

"So this guy, Tom Witcher, beat us to it. I'm wondering if it's *the* Tom Witcher, you know, the guy that seems to spend his life studying the goings on at Rayners Wood."

"It's not a common name, is it? His surname, I mean."

"Yeah, I've not heard of it before."

"And if it is him?"

"Then it isn't coincidence," Corinna decided. "It's connected."

"The house and the woods?"

"I was running through the woods, Ness. In that vision I had."

"*You* were?"

Corinna was as surprised as Ness to hear herself say this. "Yes," she eventually answered, swallowing slightly. "I got this feeling in my chest, like I was breathless. It was actually me."

"And how were you feeling?"

"I was terrified."

"Any idea what you were running from?"

She shook her head. "It was all just...darkness."

"I see," Ness replied. "Have you ever had visions before?"

"Only as a kid."

"At Blakemort?"

"Yeah. But something's changed in me, you know, since Blakemort was destroyed."

"I do know, yes. The lid has been lifted, so to speak."

"I shut my abilities down for so long, but now it's as if they're taking on a life of their own."

"You're very gifted, Corinna. Even so..."

"Even so, what?" Corinna prompted when Ness fell silent.

"This is no ordinary case. I think we both know that now."

"Which is gonna upset Ruby."

"We don't need to tell Ruby about it. She doesn't want to know, remember?"

"Yeah," Corinna said, somewhat forlornly.

"As for Theo, I'm worried about her and her health. Her hospital appointments seem to be on the increase."

"Are they?" Although Corinna hadn't known this, she found she wasn't surprised. Dealing with Blakemort had caused Theo to have a near heart attack, landing her in hospital. She'd recovered but not fully; there was still a weakness there. "So she needs protecting too?"

"As do we," Ness said, "as do we. But what we know about, we can't simply...*unknow*."

"And so we have to deal with it?"

"Yes, we have to find out what's really at the bottom of the message Jess Biggs gave us, how far-reaching it is. Meanwhile, we ramp up the white light."

"To the max."

"Most definitely."

There were only a few minutes of the car journey left

before they parted ways, for today, at least. "So what's our plan going to be?" asked Corinna, eager to know.

"Warrington said Tom Witcher was moving in with immediate effect."

"That's right."

"And we need to know if it's your Tom Witcher or if it's just one coincidence too many."

"*My* Tom Witcher sounds odd. I mean, I don't even know the bloke."

"You know what I mean."

"Yeah, of course. So what are you suggesting?"

"I'm suggesting we wait 'til he's moved in. Which is sure to be in the next few days."

"Uh-huh."

"We then take another drive to Lindfield."

"Right."

"And, pretending we're local, we knock on the door, homemade cake in hand, and welcome him to the village."

Chapter Seven

"I must say, this is all a bit aggy, isn't it?"

Ness's expression was one of confusion as she looked at Theo. "What do you mean? 'Aggy'?"

"Aggravating, dear, annoying, a pain in the proverbial."

"So why not say that in the first place?"

Theo rolled her eyes, looking perky enough, no sign of the cold she'd professed to have developed, much to Corinna's relief. "The reason I didn't say it in the first place," she explained, "is because I'm down with the kids. All my grandchildren say 'aggy', even the toddlers!"

The thing she'd referred to as aggravating was Psychic Surveys' most recent case. Whilst lounging on the sofa at Presley's flat after visiting Low Cottage on Thursday, still feeling really quite drained from all that had happened, Corinna had decided to check her emails. One had come in via the Psychic Surveys website from a woman called Daisy Parker, requesting an urgent visit. She wanted the team to investigate her house in the village of Barcombe Mills, which was just outside Lewes, a bit further into the countryside.

In the body of the email, she'd explained that she and her family had only recently moved in there and their dog was acting strangely, staring at the ceiling in a corner of their living room, sometimes barking, sometimes whining. Confused by this, Daisy had asked her husband, Mike, to climb up into the attic to see if there was anything in that corner.

To their surprise – and horror – he'd found a bundle of old-fashioned clothing stashed there, seemingly belonging to a child, and each and every item charred to varying degrees. They'd removed the clothing, bagged it up and, not knowing what else to do with it, stowed it in the garden shed. They thought this might solve the problem or, rather, calm their dog, at least. But it hadn't. The dog's behaviour had become even more erratic, barking, howling, and growling, going nowhere near the shed but remaining in that same spot in the living room.

The Parkers had kids, Bea, who was six, and Scarlett, who was eight, and they were beginning to get freaked too. "They just want their dog to go back to normal, and so do we, but something's wrong here, really wrong, and I want it to be right. This is our dream home, out in the country. We've poured what savings we had into it. Please help, please come as soon as possible."

Corinna had rung Daisy rather than reply by email, and a morning visit had been set for the next day, Friday. She'd been worried she'd lie awake again, the mystery of Jess Biggs' message, what had happened at Low Cottage, and the vision she'd had of herself running away from something – be that in Rayners Wood or somewhere else – weighing heavily on her mind. She'd slept deeply, however, and dreamlessly, ready to tackle the Barcombe house firing on all cylinders.

Which was just as well, as it was no ordinary job either, with no quick resolve to be had.

The house the Parkers had moved to used to belong to a railway worker, and, being station architecture, it was a Victorian red brick property that had been extended in recent times, overlooking where the old tracks used to be, which were now grassed over. All three women had gone into the cottage and introduced themselves over the obligatory cup of tea, explaining procedure to Daisy and Mike. The couple had then retrieved the bag of clothes from the shed, and the team examined them. They comprised a couple of jackets, long trousers, shorts, and a selection of shirts, which were indeed old-fashioned – 1930s or 1940s, Theo thought – and not badly burnt either, a sleeve on the jacket singed, the collar of a shirt, that kind of thing.

"As if someone was playing at setting fire to them?" suggested Ness.

Theo agreed. "And then hiding the evidence. I think the child who wore these was around seven or eight, but of course it's hard to tell; he might have been big for his age or small, especially during wartime when food was rationed. Corinna, Ness, I'm not getting much information from the clothes alone, are you?"

Ness shook her head, as did Corinna. "They seem really quite benign."

"Indeed," Theo said, "but something in the attic *isn't* benign, not if the family dog is anything to go by. Oh, if only Jed were here with us, he might be able to help."

"Ruby *and* Jed," Corinna murmured.

"Of course, darling," Theo appeased, the sadness of her expression matching Corinna's.

Daisy and Mike agreed to let them 'get on with it', whilst they went off for a walk with their dog. Their children were at a friend's house, so no need to worry about them.

Getting on with it, though, was proving, as Theo had said, aggy.

There was a spirit at the old railway property for certain, but whoever it was remained stubbornly distant, blocking any psychic connection as much as he or she was able to.

"Could it be a child?" Corinna asked, standing in the spot the dog favoured in the living room and looking up at the ceiling.

"The clothes do suggest that," Ness replied.

"Not necessarily," Theo denied. "It could be a guilty parent, sister, sibling, cousin—"

"Okay, okay." Ness quickly grew haughty. "We get your point."

"I don't feel as if it's a dark presence," Corinna said. "You know, I feel okay."

"Not like you're about to throw up?" Theo questioned, referring to what had happened at Low Cottage, which they'd briefed her about – some of it, at least. "You know," she continued before Corinna had a chance to reply, "I can sense well enough you're trying to protect me concerning that case, which is not just aggy, but a little bit patronising."

"It's not a case, Theo, not yet," Corinna tried to appease.

"We haven't yet established any connection between Low Cottage and the Bow family house," Ness added.

"But you intend finding out," Theo countered. "I know you do. So, keep me in the loop, okay? Don't shut me out. Without Ruby, well, we need to stick together more than ever. Right," she said, clapping her hands together in a decisive manner, "back to the business in hand. No use standing here in the living room, as comfortable, light and airy as it is – they really do have very good taste, the Parkers. I think we have to actually go into the attic, the scene of the crime, as it were."

Corinna and Ness agreed, and all three left the living room and ascended the stairs to stand under the loft hatch on the landing – a very small loft hatch, for a very slim person.

"Oh, for God's sake—" her hands on her hips, Theo sighed "—could it get any worse?"

"Looks like you'll have to stay down here, Theo," Corinna said, stating the obvious.

Ness pointed to a chair. "We can drag it over, position you close to the hatch."

"Go on, then. I'll sit here and do what? Twiddle my thumbs, I suppose."

Once she was seated, still bitterly complaining, Corinna opened the loft hatch, lowered the ladder and began to climb, Ness behind her. Glad she'd worn leggings today rather than a skirt, Corinna stepped tentatively onto the attic ceiling joists, reaching behind to help Ness, who was grunting slightly, making sure she was okay before endeavouring to find the light switch, which was on a joist to the left of her, half buried beneath the pink fibreglass insulation.

The light, when it came on, was weak as, in her experience, all attic lights tended to be, with a yellowish cast to it – one that reminded her of the light in the attic at Blakemort; it was just as sickly. *Don't think of that place!* No, she wouldn't. There was no need. There, she'd entered the attic with a sense of dread, and alone, a young child, maybe even the same age as the child possibly grounded here. In it, she'd found things that had horrified her, boxes and chests full of things pertaining to the dead, including photographs, terrible, terrible photographs, some from the Victorian era, some more recent than that... She had to rid her mind of those as well, although it was hard. Ness had said when you knew something, you couldn't unknow it. With the photographs the same principle applied – she couldn't *unsee* them. All she could do was stow them away on a shelf in her mind, far, far back.

Ness had broken away from her and was slowly creeping around various items and boxes to the seemingly afflicted corner. Corinna followed her, taking in all that had been stored here, items surplus to the needs of this house, most of which wouldn't make it down again until the next moving day, and maybe not even then, but left just as the clothes had been.

"Ness, what can you sense?"

Ness halted and inclined her head to the right. "I'm not really sure. There's something or, rather, someone. I feel as though they're watching me...assessing me."

"Trying to work out who we are?"

"That's right, and what we want."

"Shall we start the address?"

"Yes, of course."

Corinna arrived by her side, having to crouch because of how low the beams were, noticing too they were white with powder, thick, stringy cobwebs decorating them. Good job Theo hadn't made it up here. As hard as she tried to deal with her phobia of spiders, she wasn't always victorious.

Ness, who'd crouched too, turned to look at Corinna. "Do you want to do the honours?"

Normally, it was Ruby who'd take the lead, but in her absence the youngest member of Psychic Surveys was being encouraged.

"Okay," she replied, taking a deep breath, repeating what were now such familiar words, those designed to offer comfort. "My name is Corinna Greer, and this is Ness Patterson. We're not here to harm or upset you in any way; all we want to do is help. We can't see you, not yet, probably because you don't want us to, you're blocking us, but we can sense you well enough. Ness and I are psychics, which means we're able to tune in to what is spiritual as well as material. With you I'm sensing...I'm sensing..." Briefly she looked at Ness, who nodded her head. Further encouraged, she continued. "I'm sensing you're young, aged between seven and nine, that you've...erm...been here a long time, too long. There's something to do with fire. Did the fire hurt you in any way?" In truth, these were all clues gleaned from the Parkers' discovery of the clothes, but, she reasoned, any port in a storm... You had to use what tools were available. "I mean it when I say we only want to help you. The darkness...it's no place for a child."

Was it her imagination, or had Ness stiffened beside her?

"You okay, Ness? Have you sensed something?"

"I'm fine." Her stern voice surprised Corinna. "Carry on."

"Oh, okay. I'm doing all right, aren't I?"

"Yes." Again, she was curt. "Don't break the connection."

"Sweetheart"—so often this was the term Theo used to address a spirit, good, bad or otherwise—"why don't you step forward and let us see you? We won't be frightened, we won't turn our backs, no matter how you present yourself. We're here to work with you, to send you to the light, which is home, your true home, because it's not here, not anymore."

There was no response, and yet something had changed,

the atmosphere becoming slightly heavier. Hope surged in Corinna. "That's it, come forward. Your time in the shadows is done. Tell me who you are, your name, perhaps. We can...we can start with your name."

In truth, there was no movement in the shadows but a sense of bewilderment. What was the matter with this child? What had happened to...*him*? The clothes suggested a boy – shorts, shirts, jackets... Why had he tried to burn them? What reason?

Above her, the light from the bulb dimmed a little, the spirit leeching energy from it, perhaps, or it was a cheap bulb. She took a shuffle forwards, instinct telling her to crouch further, to kneel, to make herself as small as the child. "Tell me your name."

Immediately a name came to mind. *David*. Corinna was about to speak, to say thank you for this information when another name popped up, this time more ferociously. *Christopher!*

"What?" Corinna muttered.

From beside her, Ness spoke too. "What is it? What's the matter?"

Corinna turned her head. "Did you get that?"

"Get what?"

"A name, two names."

"Two?"

"Definitely two. First David and then Christopher."
Christopher!

There it was again, that same insistence. And then what sounded like a sob. *David*.

If the spirit was confused, so was Corinna. Was it actually one child present or more than that? Given the clothes were all the same size, could it be...twins?

"Is that it, you're twins, and you're trapped here?"

"Twins?"

Ness's voice was slightly breathless as she repeated the word, Corinna remembering Ness's own twin, the one who'd died at birth, the confession she'd made about her before they'd gone into Blakemort, telling their deepest, darkest secrets to each other, what tormented them. Doing so in order for there to be nothing hidden between them, nothing the house could latch on to and use against them. Ness had also told them about another child, Claire, from the woods...

"Ness, I'm wondering if they're twins. I'm, like...sorry, I know it's a bit sensitive—"

"Don't. Focus on this case and nothing else."

"No...I mean, yes, yes, of course. I... Are you twins? David *and* Christopher?"

Afterwards, so many things happened at once, that Corinna couldn't be sure if she was pushed by an invisible hand or simply lost her balance, but she toppled sideways, colliding with a stack of boxes and suitcases that, in turn, crashed to the ground, making a racket.

A scream rang out, not hers, not David's or Christopher's or whoever it was. It belonged to Ness and not just Ness — there was another screech, so loud, so piercing, it was earsplitting. Inhuman, that's what it was, Corinna still busy trying to shield herself from further damage as she turned to look. A creature...there was some kind of creature on Ness, something black and clawed, the thing that had screeched, tearing at her, as if trying to rip flesh from bone.

"Ness! Ness! What the hell is that? What's going on?"

"Good God!" Ness continued to scream. "Get it off me!

Get it off!"

"What's going on up there?" Theo's voice, full of horror, added to the cacophony. "I'm coming up. Damn it, I'm coming up."

The creature on Ness sent her sideways too, more boxes toppling over and the sound of breaking glass.

Corinna quickly scrambled back to a crouch. "Ness, it's all right, I'm here. Oh, Ness!"

"Get it off!" Ness was frantic, and who could blame her? "Get it off me!"

"What the fuck?"

That last voice belonged to neither Ness nor Theo.

"What's all this chaos?"

A head appeared through the hatch, not Theo as she'd promised, which brought with it only a partial sense of relief – even with her friends in trouble, how had she thought she was going to squeeze through? – but a man, the owner of the house, Mike Parker, absolutely furious.

Chaos, it was that, all right. *Carnage* might be another word he could have used.

"Mr Parker," Corinna began, still fretting about Ness, who was still batting at her now empty chest. "Something...erm...attacked my colleague. Something black."

"Something black?"

Corinna nodded her head avidly. "Yes, it came out of nowhere. We were just making contact, and then...and then...this creature—"

"Creature?" Mike Parker was fully in the attic now, still glaring at them as he bent forward.

What was he doing? Corinna wondered. He seemed to

scoop something up into his arms – something they'd broken, perhaps, when the boxes had toppled, something beloved or of great value? When she saw what it was, however, her eyes widened. It wasn't something broken but very much intact. Something that was mighty pleased with itself, that was purring.

"This creature, as you called him, happens to be my cat."

"Your cat?" Corinna breathed. "You never said you had a—"

"Why should I?"

"Why? Because…because…"

Ness was back on her feet, crouched with her back to the slope of the rafters, and if looks could kill, the creature would be a goner.

"A cat!" she muttered. "It's a bloody cat!"

Corinna made an effort to be more contrite. "We're so sorry. We thought…we didn't know…we were making contact, two boys—"

Again, Mike interrupted. "You know what? I don't care. This is a shambles. A sodding shambles. God knows what you've broken. I thought you were professionals. I thought you were quite cool, actually, you know, levelheaded. The testimonials on your website suggested you're levelheaded. I'm not so sure now, though. I mean, look at you both and the state you're in. Professionals, eh? Yeah, right. I mean, who the hell's frightened of a cat? Come on, Walter, let's get you a few treats, calm you down a bit. I think it's you who's had the shock, not them."

As Mike turned, Corinna and Ness shot each other a look. *Walter!*

Corinna caught Ness's thought and the sheer disgust in it.

A beast like that and they call it Walter!

If she wasn't so embarrassed, Corinna might have laughed. As it was, she could barely summon a smile. They were being chucked out, might not get paid for their time either. Worse still, they'd failed at cracking yet another case – the second in as many days if you counted the Bows, which right now she did – tarnishing their good reputation, their almost perfect track record.

Sod it! She and Ness followed Mike and Walter down the ladder and back onto the landing, where a wide-eyed Theo was waiting. As Corinna caught the older woman's gaze, she shook her head. To coin a phrase, the day was turning out to be very aggy indeed.

Chapter Eight

"YOU could have warned us!"

Theo remained indignant. "I didn't see the damned thing scoot up there!"

"You didn't see it? Seriously? It was huge, Theo, not a cat, a panther!"

"Well…erm…he was a big boy, I have to admit, but…"

"You fell asleep, didn't you?"

"Asleep? Absolutely not!"

But Ness could always tell when Theo was lying and, for that matter, so could Corinna, who was driving them away from the Parkers' home in Barcombe Mills and back to Lewes, only six or seven miles away, thank goodness. Any longer with the warring pair and she'd scream.

"Look," she interjected, "it doesn't matter now what went wrong, only that it *did* go wrong and we've got to try and claw it back somehow, maintain our good reputation. If only for Ruby's sake."

"Corinna—" Theo began, but Corinna cut across her.

"I know, I know what you're going to say about Ruby, but…it just…it means a lot to me to keep up the good work she started, to build on our reputation, not ruin it."

"We haven't ruined it," Ness denied.

"We haven't done it much good, though, have we? Mike Parker practically chucked us out of his home, and we're still trying to work out what Jess Biggs meant too at the Bows' house, and...and... Oh crap, sorry, I know I need to get a grip, not get so disheartened."

Or overexaggerate either. They hadn't been chucked out of the Parkers' house, but Mike had clearly been unimpressed with what had gone on.

"So what's this connection you said you'd made?" he'd asked as they stood in the living room, all eyes not on each other but on the dog that, sadly for the Psychic Surveys team, was just as transfixed on the corner spot of the living room as ever, growling up at the ceiling, waggling his bottom from side to side in an agitated manner and occasionally barking too.

"I got the name of a little boy," Corinna replied. "Two names, actually, David and Christopher—"

"*Two* ghosts?" Daisy, who was standing beside her husband, was horrified.

"Erm...that's the thing, we're not sure. We were just getting somewhere when...when..." Walter was nowhere to be seen. The devil's spawn, as Corinna had mentally dubbed him, had wrought havoc and then sashayed off into the wild blue yonder with probably not so much as a backwards glance. "If your cat hadn't startled us, we could have perhaps got further with this."

Theo was clearly tiring of having to provide an explanation. "We'll do more research. We have a name to go on, a first name, at least – two of them, it seems. We can check census records, house deeds, birth and death certificates, etc., find out what we can. The more information we have, the more likely we are to find a solution, encouraging who's grounded here to move on."

"Well, that's what we hired you for." Mike's expression was still anger-tinged. "I thought you'd come and, you know, get it sorted. It's what they say in the testimonials—"

"Not *all* the testimonials." Ness was clearly fed up too. "Some cases are straightforward, and others aren't. They can take time, and they can take effort. We're good at what we do, let me assure you of that, despite a few hiccups on occasion, including those of a feline variety."

Here, she'd brushed pointedly at the blouse she was wearing, which had several pulled threads, and rubbed at her hands, which were bloody with scratches, stopping any further comment from the Parkers and actually causing them to look rather shamefaced.

"Our cat," began Daisy, "he…erm…can be a bit temperamental at times."

Ness raised an eyebrow. "A bit?"

"Look, do your research," Mike quickly continued. "We'd appreciate it, but we can't be expected to pay you for that, surely? Only the work you do in-house."

"That work contributes to the work we do in-house, as you put it," Theo informed them.

Corinna butted in now. "We can agree on a rate that suits everyone."

Theo snorted and muttered something under her breath. Something Corinna was sure was along the lines of 'we're not a sodding charity, you know', but, luckily, the dog emitted a loud bark, ensuring it reached no other ears but her own.

Back in Lewes, Corinna dropped Ness off first, frowning as she watched her walking to her front door – not walking, actually, but limping. Quickly she wound down her window.

"Ness, are you okay? I didn't realise you'd hurt your ankle."

"I'm fine," Ness replied, only half turning. "It's nothing."

"Too stoic for her own good, that one," Theo remarked, sighing.

"Make sure to put some ice on it," Corinna called again, just before Ness disappeared inside, "and keep it elevated."

As she pulled away into the traffic, she heard Theo yawn loudly.

"Still tired?" Corinna asked. "Despite your nap earlier?"

Unlike Ness, she was being tongue-in-cheek about it, but it caused only a slight smile from Theo. "You know, darling, I *am* tired. All the time lately. It could be the new meds I'm on; in fact, I'm sure it is them, but…it's a bore, you know? Feeling your life force drain."

"Theo!" Turning up High Street, past some of Lewes's most-loved shops, including boutiques and bakeries, Corinna couldn't help but admonish her. "You've got more life in you than anyone I know. Christ, who does as much as you do at your age? Nobody I know, that's for sure. You're out there rescuing spirits, investigating case after case, sleeves rolled up, piling in… No, Theo, you're amazing. Sure, you're tired, but that's all it is, tiredness. Your life force is as strong as ever!"

Theo was chuckling away. "Dear Corinna, you do me good, you really do. You're the daughter I never had but wished for, although Lord knows I love my three boys well enough. Don't worry about me. I'm feeling sorry for myself, is all. Seventy-two, eh? It's a ripe old age, but hopefully there's more years left in me yet. As for Psychic Surveys and Ruby, don't keep worrying about them either. You're doing a grand job keeping the company afloat, as is Ness, and whether Ruby returns to the helm or not, we have to remember what will be, will be. You can't force the issue, no matter how much you want to. Acceptance is a wonderful thing, darling, one of the greatest lessons we can learn in life. Give Ruby time and, as for you, carry on being the joy that you are."

Having stopped the car outside Theo's house, Corinna subsequently turned to her friend and hugged her. "I don't know what I'd do without you, you know."

"You have me, darling, and always will."

As they pulled apart, Theo glanced at the clock on the dashboard. "What are you up to for the rest of the day? Got a shift at the pub?"

Corinna shook her head. "I might head back to The Keep, see what I can find out about David and Christopher."

"Oh, really? Do you want me to come with you?"

Although she did, she also couldn't deny that Theo did indeed look tired, her peaches-and-cream complexion not as bright as it usually was, the shadows beneath her eyes more pronounced. "It's fine. I'll get the ball rolling. If I find anything, I'll let you know, okay?"

"Sounds like a plan, Stan," Theo said, opening the door and climbing out of the car.

Putting that plan into action, Corinna gave Theo a final wave, fired the car back up and continued onwards through Lewes, past the prison and onto the A27 towards Brighton. The Keep was located just off the A27 on the left-hand side, close to the University of Sussex. Easily, she found a parking space, then decided to send a quick text to Ruby to see how she was and whether she was up for another meeting sometime soon.

Still feeling dreadful, was the almost immediate reply. *Iron levels are really low now. They think I'm anaemic. Blood pressure also a cause for concern. Again it's low, which is apt, cos I feel like one of the walking dead! Honestly, Crin, I'm never going through this again! Hendrix — yes, we are calling him that, for now, anyway — is definitely going to be an only child. How are you?*

Corinna gave her a brief rundown of what had happened at the Parker house and said she was just about to go into The Keep, try to get some more information on the house.

Okay, good, sounds interesting.

Corinna read between the lines: it sounded ordinary, that's what she meant.

Sorry not up for meeting at the moment, Ruby continued, *but soon, yeah? I'll be in touch.*

For a while, Corinna sat staring at that last message, missing her friend more than ever. An ordinary case, maybe. But what about the other case and the link with Low Cottage? Had Tom Witcher moved in yet? Should she go and see, just…check it out? She could visit The Keep in the morning instead, before her afternoon shift. It was an idea that both unnerved and attracted her, to go straight to Lindfield now, so much so that it was with surprise she noted she'd turned the engine on, as if something was drawing her again… Obsession, was that it?

Christ, she thought, putting Plan B into action, *I'm as bad as Witcher!*

* * *

There it was, coming into view…Low Cottage, squatting, like Blakemort used to squat.

Stop comparing them!

Corinna sighed. That little voice in her head was right: nothing compared to that other house and the sheer base nature of it. This house, though, its name suited it. It *was* low, she felt, and base too. Was that the reason she was fascinated with it, not just because of the strange visions and sickness she'd experienced whilst there but because it reminded her of Blakemort? It was familiar, better the devil you know and all that? The thought was an uncomfortable one that almost had her turning her car back round and heading home – or to Brighton, into the arms of Presley, who'd soothe her and tell her it wasn't so, because…because…it *wasn't* so, truly. She had a case to solve, courtesy of Jess Biggs, the spirit who'd talked of another house, a bad house, where things had happened and must never happen again. She'd lingered for so long to get that message across – she'd stopped time because of it.

This house had to be the one Jess was talking about, now occupied by Tom Witcher, *the* Tom Witcher, the man Corinna had recently read so much about.

Taking all this into account, she didn't turn the car around but parked it a few metres from the house, intending to walk the remaining distance. Once on the pavement, she smoothed the sleeveless black top she was wearing, then, with her fingers, sorted out her long red hair; strands of it had become plastered to her face, as she was so hot. After this, she'd head into the village and buy an ice-cold drink from the Co-op, down it in one.

Rather than take another step, however, she hesitated.

90

Was this really such a good idea, returning alone? She was only going to check if Witcher had moved in, though, nothing more – peer over the gate as surreptitiously as possible to see any signs of life within, whether new curtains had been put up, that kind of thing, or if any lights were on. She might even be able to catch a glimpse of the man himself, berating herself for not checking his book out on Amazon already, as there might be an author picture there. Perhaps she should do that now; it'd only take a minute or so.

Still obscured from sight, she called up the Amazon page on her phone and typed in his name, *The Demonic Link* appearing straightaway, a plain-looking book with a black jacket and white lettering. Currently, it was out of print, but several used copies were available. To be fair, there was very little to tempt the reader to buy it – there was no blurb available, no author photograph as she'd hoped, and no author biography either. There were a couple of reviews, and, in the absence of all else, she read those.

One simply said the book was 'okay', but the other was a little more erudite, talking about how well it described satanic rituals being carried out in deepest, darkest Sussex, that Witcher was clearly a man 'in the know', a man to be taken notice of. It was so glowing, in fact, Corinna wondered if the man himself hadn't posted it! Priced a penny under thirty pounds for a copy, Corinna baulked before deciding, sod it, it could go against tax. Pressing the 'buy' button, she typed in Presley's address for delivery rather than her home address, just in case her mother opened the package – the last thing she wanted to do was worry her. Although her mother never spoke of Blakemort, it had scarred her too; Corinna was well aware of that. And her brother, Ethan, whilst not a recluse, was very much an introvert. Hopefully, the book wouldn't take long to arrive.

Right, no more stalling. Get on with it, Corinna.

Obeying her own command, she finally reached the gate, sweating even more, feeling really quite hot and sticky and in dire need of a cold shower as well as a cold drink. Only briefly she glanced up – the sky was beautiful, a canvas of pure blue, no clouds to temper the sun, to give them a break. Her eyes back on the cottage, they remained there, ignoring now the sound of cars behind her and an echo of birdsong from high above. She felt...*absorbed* by the atmosphere that surrounded Low Cottage, that drew her closer still.

What is it about you? she wondered. *What happened here once upon a time?* There'd been so many changes of owners, and the current ones, the Wintertons, rented it out rather than lived there. Would Paul and Julie Winterton be willing to talk to her about their decision, or would they simply slam the phone down on her? Corinna feared it'd be the latter, and who could blame them? If some stranger rang up and asked her about such private matters, she'd do the same. That was the trouble with psychic investigation; there was no official police badge that compelled people to give them information, plus once they heard it was to do with psychic matters, many didn't want any truck with it at all. Maybe Witcher would know more... Considering what he was into, maybe he'd be willing to talk...

Still standing by the gate, she began to feel nauseous again, a wave of it that washed right over her. Thankfully, it passed quickly enough, although it was a reminder to reinforce the white light she'd surrounded herself in, to make it as strong as could be. She was *not* going to be sick or let whatever resided here get to her in that way, be it an actual spirit or a deluge of negative energy, something residual that tainted the very ground the house was built on.

What was it built for? How that question nagged at her. *And for what kind of people?*

Acting almost as if on autopilot, Corinna pushed open the gate and stepped inside, an invisible cord still tugging at her. *What do I say if I get caught?* Mentally, she shrugged. She could say anything, that she was lost, that she'd got the wrong address. *Or you could tell the truth. This is Tom Witcher, after all; he'd understand.*

The windows were so dark despite the brightness of the day, glass panes complicit in hiding something, a secret, perhaps, a world within a world, one she was not privy to, that she should stay away from – follow the path more ordinary. Still, she was moving forwards, towards one of those blackened windows, her hands coming up to shield the sun's glare so that she could see inside, get a grip on what was happening…

"Hey! What do you think you're doing?"

Every bone in Corinna's body froze. She'd been caught, like this, peering into a window at Low Cottage. Whatever excuse she came up with wasn't going to cut it.

The truth, remember? Confess.

God, she felt sick! The nausea was back more viciously than ever.

"This is my property," the voice continued. "I want to know what you're doing here."

He sounded stern, angry, and rightly so.

Just tell him the truth!

She had no choice, tearing her eyes from the windowpane

but not before noticing how dark it was inside too, as if the sun was afraid to encroach, with no boxes anywhere, as you might expect from someone who'd so recently moved in. Instead, the kitchen was exactly how it had been when she'd first seen it – empty of everything except shadows.

Lowering her hands, she turned, slowly, measuredly, bolstering herself all the while, taking advantage of every second to do just that. *I'm not a criminal, and I won't be treated as one.*

"Mr Witcher," she began but stopped the minute she laid eyes on him. "Oh!"

He, too, expressed surprise. "It is you!"

She'd convinced herself to tell Tom Witcher the truth because he'd understand, but how could she do that now? This was the man they'd met when first setting eyes on this place, when Ness had made her stop the car, feeling the pull of it every bit as much as Corinna did now.

Not just Tom Witcher, he was also the man who'd threatened them.

Chapter Nine

"HOW do you have your tea?"

"Oh, black, please, not too strong."

"Right. Hope this is okay. I didn't leave the tea bag in too long."

"It's fine, honestly, it's great. Thank you."

Whatever she'd expected of her impromptu visit today, it wasn't this, to be sitting in the kitchen of Low Cottage with *the* Tom Witcher making her tea – no Ness with her, no homemade cake, as they'd planned – just her. Both being civil to each other, his anger at having caught her acting the Peeping Tom somehow diluted by his recognition of her.

He'd threatened her, and not just her but Theo and Ness too, and yet, the minute she'd faced him, she could see how curiosity had replaced surprise. His eyes had narrowed, his head had come forward slightly, his tongue darting out to lick lightly at his lips.

"I thought it was you," he said, bringing the mugs over to the table and taking a seat opposite her, "because of your hair. I also had a feeling you'd return."

"Did you? Despite your threat."

"My threat?" Tom Witcher looked surprised, and then

clearly the penny dropped. "Ah, yes, I remember what I said."

"About us having to keep away if we value our lives."

"That wasn't a threat. That was…a warning."

Corinna stared at the mugs. Her tea was black, but his was too pale, too milky, prompting a third wave of nausea. Having managed to beat it back down on two other occasions, she had to do so again now. She should drink; it might help her to feel better. She hoped so, picking her mug up and sipping, trying not to wince, as it had a strange, slightly bitter taste. Perhaps the teabag used had been an old one, knocking around in a tin somewhere, the only thing that had stayed put in the cottage over recent years, the one constant. Forcing it down, she took another sip, and another – wishing she'd just asked for plain old water. She also mulled over what Tom had just claimed. It hadn't been a threat he'd issued but a warning. Really? It kind of made sense.

"Okay," she said, "if it was a warning, then why? What's there to warn me about?" When there was no immediate reply, she had to prompt him. "Mr Witcher?"

"Oh, call me Tom, please," he said at last. "How much do you know about this house?"

"I know it's changed hands several times, that it was built in 1900, that it has history."

He leant forward, his prominent features once more reminding her of a hawk. "But what *kind* of history, do you know that?"

Corinna swallowed. How much should she tell him? She'd already decided on a little of the truth, but she also needed to be prudent, tread carefully; they might be on the same page, but he was still a stranger. "Tom, I'm what you might call…sensitive. There's a feeling here…"

"A dark feeling? A dark history, as one of the women you were with the other day said. But if that's so, why would you want to live here?"

"We weren't serious about wanting to live here. We'd just stopped outside to have a look."

"We?"

"My coll—" Just in time she managed to stop herself from saying 'colleagues'. "The other two women I was with...my, erm...my aunts."

"They're your aunts?" One arched eyebrow lent him an almost comical look.

"That's right."

"And you and your aunts have an interest in history?"

She nodded.

"Dark history."

"Well...history, full stop. Tom, I could ask you the same question. If you agree that the history of this house is on the dark side, why is it you want to live here?"

Witcher reclined in his chair, his tea remaining untouched although Corinna still sipped from hers, still seeking to quench her thirst. "It's not that I want to live here, far from it. It's more I *need* to, in order to understand." Expecting him to elaborate, Corinna was stunned when he pushed his chair back, which in turn seemed to screech in protest, and stood up. "Why don't I show you around?"

"Yeah...sure..." He wasn't to know she'd actually been inside the house and on a tour already.

"If you're as you say, perhaps you can tell me what you sense. It could prove useful."

Her chair screeched too as she stood, Witcher leading her back into the hallway, through a series of rooms to a living room at the far end of the house – the main living room, Corinna presumed, one with a large open inglenook fireplace in which an empty metal grate stood.

"There are no boxes," she said, standing beside him.

"Boxes?"

"Yeah, boxes. You seem to have unpacked already." Although had he? Because, aside from a sofa, a table, and an armchair, all period pieces that had already been in situ, the room was as empty as it had been before, as were the rooms she'd passed through.

"I tend to live lightly," was his reply. "What do you think took place here in the past?"

"Here? In this living room?"

"That's right."

"It's just a living room."

"*Just* a living room," he repeated, a trace of sarcasm detectable. "Let's go to the study."

Corinna's heart sank. The study was one of the rooms she'd felt particularly sick in. The mere thought of returning... And what if he asked her the same question in there: *What do you think took place here in the past?* How would she answer? What could she say? *I don't know, but something bad, bad enough to ground a spirit elsewhere in this village, one desperate to impart another warning, besides yours, that told me things happened in another house, dreadful things, and I think it's this house she meant, Low Cottage.*

"I can't." The words were out before she could stop them. "I can't go in that room again."

"Again?"

Damn it! She'd have to come clean.

"Look, Tom, I've actually been inside the house too, with

98

Greg Warrington, the estate agent. In fact, you phoned whilst we were here, Ness and I. She's…she's one of the aunts you saw me with originally, the one with dark hair. We were here when you rang him, when you secured the place. And I can't go in there because…because…I'll be sick if I do."

"Sick?" Witcher was aghast.

"Yes, and I'm not joking. I was sick before. This house…what I'm sensing…it's so dark…"

His expression didn't change; he was stunned by what she was saying and confused too.

Although she didn't want to touch the wall beside her, she leant against it, in need of support. "I don't know what happened in this house, but I know who you are. You're…you're *the* Tom Witcher, the one who wrote about the Devil's Triangle, about Rayners Wood in particular. And now…well, now you're renting this house. It seems…I don't know…such a coincidence."

"A coincidence," he repeated, more to himself than her. "If you've been here before, then, okay, no need to go over old ground, let's return to the kitchen. You're all right in there, are you?"

"Yeah, yeah, I'm sure I will be."

Once back where they'd begun, and although she neither asked or wanted him to, Witcher made Corinna a fresh mug of tea, or as fresh as it could get with stale teabags. Once in front of her, she wrapped her hands around it, glad of the warmth, at least, not having realised until then that she was shivering. The height of summer outdoors, in here it was midwinter.

Tom Witcher was peering at her, as if trying to read her. Was that possible?

"Are you psychic?" she asked.

He shook his head. "No. Unfortunately. Are you?"

"I've told you I'm sensitive."

"You're more than that."

"Perhaps."

"What, then?"

"Psychic," she said eventually, "and there's not just something wrong with this house, there's something...dangerous, and you know it, hence your...warning. I have no idea in what way it's dangerous, not yet, but, Tom, are you really intending to stay here?"

"I've told you, I have to."

"Why?"

"Because it's linked."

"What is?"

"This house and the Devil's Triangle. All my research points to it. There's a link of some sort with Low Cottage and those woods, with past residents, perhaps one in particular."

Leaving her mug and the bitter tea alone, she sat back, surprised, not to hear what he'd just said but to realise that he was right and that on some level, she'd suspected it too. A triangle within a triangle, it was the devil at play or, rather, those that worshipped him.

"Whatever you can sense, if there's any information," Witcher continued, his eyes hazel in colour, although tending more towards brown than green, "you have to tell me. This is my life's work, unearthing the crimes of the past, the *criminals*. People have been murdered."

"Why, though?" Corinna breathed. "Why are you so—" she hesitated, not wanting to say the word *obsessed*, thinking

100

of an alternative "—interested?"

He straightened his shoulders. "I have my reasons. Good reasons."

Reasons that were also private, clearly.

"I specialise in spirit release," Corinna confided, still keeping her 'aunts' out of it. "That's why I came back, with the aim of releasing any spirits that are grounded and sending them to the light."

"Are there any spirits here?" He was leaning forward now, only just stopping himself from reaching out, Corinna suspected, and taking her hand in his. "Can you commune with them?"

Commune? "I can sometimes make contact. I can hear them, what they're saying—"

"Can you see them?"

"Sometimes."

"Actually *see* them?"

"Only on occasion." And not for many, many years, thanks to Blakemort.

"Then we do need to take that tour, visit every room, see what you can sense…or see."

"NO!"

She hadn't meant to shout, but she really couldn't do that just now, not alone. She might as well admit it: whatever was here frightened her. She wouldn't be coerced into dealing with it without her team. She needed them by her side – all of them, preferably, but at least Theo and Ness.

"I'm sorry," she continued. "What's here is strong, and I need to…prepare."

Thankfully, he nodded, seeming to understand. There was a moment of silence, and then he began to speak. "The reason I'm so interested…" Quite suddenly he hung his head.

"Tom?" Corinna reached out. "What is it? What's the matter?"

He assured her he was fine but to give him a minute. Eventually, he raised his head. "Over the course of recent history, three people have been found dead in Rayners Wood."

"Yes, yes, I know."

"One of them was my daughter."

Corinna was stunned. "Your daughter?"

"Samantha Lawrence."

"Oh God! She was the last victim, wasn't she?"

"Yes, she was found dead there in 2001."

"I'm sorry. So sorry."

"Not as sorry as I am, believe me." He wiped at eyes that had become moist, before continuing. "I'm going to be honest with you here, Corinna. My daughter and I were…estranged." Again, he seemed to be in so much pain admitting this. "My wife and I had divorced, and, as often happens, she took our child. Gradually over the years, she managed to turn Sam against me. You see, I've always had an interest in the paranormal; my wife, not so much. I was fascinated with Rayners Wood. So much has happened there over so many years: dogs go missing, and there'd been two bodies found there prior to my daughter, plus talk amongst villagers of strange beasts roaming the woods, aliens even, alleged UFO sightings reported."

"I do know something about it all, about Chanctonbury and Cissbury Rings too, where devil worship has also allegedly taken place. You mentioned something about a cult…"

"Yes, in my book, *The Demonic Link*, the Cult of Badb."

"That's it, that's right."

A slight frown marred his features. "Have you read my book?"

"No, I haven't. I have ordered it, though, off Amazon."

He nodded. "Ah, right, I see. I talk about the Cult of Badb, expose them, if you like, this…this…sordid little cult full of sordid little people." If Samantha Lawrence was his daughter, Corinna could understand the vitriol in his voice. "I've even met someone who claims to be head of that cult, as a result of threatening to expose them. No way he was the head, he was a lackey, just a lackey, sounded more like a kid than a grown man. He came to meet me in the woods, although whoever it was kept their face covered, wouldn't let me see him, stood at a distance and told me to back off, to leave them alone, that they weren't responsible for my daughter's death or the other deaths and to never mention them publicly again or they'd come for me, and then…well, then murder *would* be done. I turned to face him, even though I'd been instructed not to, but he fled, and in those woods…those gnarled old woods, I couldn't see which way he'd gone. The man got away. But I'd spooked him and, I hope, by proxy the rest of them, bunch of amateurs. Bunch of liars too. Someone's responsible for Sam's death, and it all points to them and their followers."

"That your daughter died in Rayners Wood, it seems…"

"You're going to mention the word 'coincidence' again, aren't you?"

"Well…"

Again, her voice trailed off, but, thankfully, the silence didn't stretch on for long.

"My daughter was troubled," Witcher continued. "My wife isn't…*wasn't* the easiest woman to live with. She…" He tapped the side of his head to indicate mental health issues, perhaps depression. "Sam and I were estranged, as I've said, and, well…maybe that hurt her as much as me, deep down. Maybe that's what drew her to the woods, my involvement with them. Sometimes I think that. I even draw comfort from it, that she was trying, in a way, to connect with me. Other times I rage inside. If only she'd kept away from those woods, contacted me directly. Oh God!"

A sob burst from him, Corinna completely at a loss as to how to comfort him. What could she possibly say that didn't sound trite in the face of such a terrible revelation?

"I'm so sorry——" she repeated, but Witcher wasn't done.

"*That's* why I'm here, at Low Cottage, to find out more about what the link is, to explore every nook and cranny of this place, to experience it in order to understand the minds behind the murderers. Not because I want to, but because I intend to have my vengeance."

Before Corinna could answer, try to soothe him further, he asked, "Have you been to Rayners Wood yet?"

Quickly, she shook her head. "No, not yet."

"It's not far away, less than twenty minutes by car."

"Yes, yes, I know that."

"Do you want me to take you there? Explain more?"

Did she? She couldn't deny her curiosity was growing. "Well, yeah, but when?"

As he'd done before, he stood again, an abrupt action. "There's no time like the present."

"Now? But it's late in the afternoon."

"It's also summer. It won't get dark for a long while. We'll just go for a walk, nothing more, see what you can sense about the woods too." He shrugged; it was a sad gesture, pathetic somehow. "Maybe it's no coincidence we met. Maybe you can help me. You said you specialise in spirit release. What if—" he swallowed hard "—what if my daughter is still in those woods, her spirit, I mean. Tormented still?" A tear raced down his cheek. "That's a thought I can't bear. We *have* met for a reason, I know it. So we can work together, so you can help me."

Was he right? Is that why she'd felt compelled to come here today? A simple case like the Bows' had expanded and become so much more. And she, Corinna, could make a difference, do as Jess Biggs implored and put an end to what was bad, expose it as Tom Witcher was trying to expose it, drag it out of the darkness and into the light.

It was 4.30 p.m. He was right, it wouldn't be dark for a long while. Just a short walk and a chance to glean more information from him, to help him in his fight in whichever way she could.

She pushed aside her second mug of tea and smiled at him. "Do you want to drive, or shall I?"

"You've got your car outside?"

She nodded.

"Let me grab a few things, and then take your car," he replied. "It'll be...easier."

PART TWO

Ness

Chapter Ten

THE darkness...it's no place for a child.

That's what Corinna had said, crouching in the attic of the Parkers' home in Barcombe Mills, staring into a corner of the roof space, addressing one, possibly two boys, twins even.

Ness had run a hot bath and sunk into it, her nerves shredded as much as her clothes had been by Walter the cat, her ankle pulsating with pain from the fall she'd suffered. She was trying to relax, force her mind towards stillness, focus only on the warmth of the water and how it caressed her, but she was failing dramatically. Inside, she remained as cold as ever, a hole bang smack in the middle of her, at the bottom of which resided longing and regret.

"Damn!" she swore, eventually admitting defeat, heaving herself upwards and out of the bath, grabbing a towel off the radiator and wrapping it around herself. The water had been too hot anyway, and the scent of the bubble bath she'd used cloying. There was no chance of relaxation, not tonight, her mind too active for its own good.

Before she left the bathroom, she glanced in the mirror, having to lift a hand to wipe steam from the glass. Old, that's what she looked. A woman in her mid-fifties, she saw instead a crone, and not a wise one either, the weight of past mistakes etched deep into the lines around her eyes.

She sighed, and, with one hand clutching at her towel, she left the bathroom, making her way across the landing to her bedroom, noticing how gloomy it was as the evening began to close in. Her hand outstretched, she was about to grasp the door handle when a noise from the spare bedroom caused her to pause and turn her head in that direction.

The house she lived in, that she owned, modest but comfortable and close to everything in the town of Lewes, was devoid of any spirit but her own. Okay, yes, it was perfectly possible to bring home attachments from certain jobs – those that would cleave to you rather than move on, desperate to remain in this realm rather than face the unknown – but for two things: Ness knew how to detect them, even those adept at riding the backs of others, and so she could easily remove them before setting foot over the threshold, and she'd set up a white-light barrier, making these bricks and mortar impenetrable. It wasn't many people who wanted to bring work home with them at the end of a busy day, and in that regard, she was no different.

And yet, accompanying that creak she'd heard from behind a closed door was a subtle change in atmosphere – it had become more charged.

Lyndsey?

No sooner had she thought about her twin than she heard the slight echo of a giggle.

Almost slipping on the floorboards, she was moving so

fast, Ness flew across to the spare room, grabbing that door handle instead and thrusting it open. Standing there, transfixed, she peered into the room, scanning it from top to bottom and side to side. Gloom was prevalent in here too, *empty* gloom, with no sign of anything in it, no outline, no shape, no twin of her own. But the atmosphere remained altered, indicating that something was going on inside her house.

Focus, Ness.

She inhaled and then exhaled deeply, evenly and several times over, opening her mind and praying too. *Let it be her. Let it be her.* A mantra that repeated in her head.

"Lyndsey?"

She called her name as she'd done so many times. Would she get a response?

"Lyndsey, is it you?"

Nothing could cross the threshold into her private domain unless she'd invited it, and Lyndsey she *had* invited, over and over.

"If it is you, let me know. I'm here. I'm waiting. You know I am."

Houses made all sorts of strange noises, especially whilst 'settling' for the evening. As a paranormal investigator, she knew that – it was one of the first things to discount when working on a case, along with rattling pipes or the keening of the wind as it soughed through the eaves. By that token the creak was accountable; the giggle, however, was not.

"Don't do this, don't…mess with me." She'd only just stopped herself from saying 'torment', even though that was precisely what it felt like, a thought that gave rise to another fear. Was her twin only doing so because she herself had been in such torment for so long, trapped in a spiritual hell that Ness had confined her to? Was it the only thing she knew how to do now? *The darkness…it's no place for a child.*

"Enough!"

Before guilt could overwhelm her, Ness backed out of the spare room, then padded across to her own room, although one concession she made was to leave the spare room door open, just in case it was Lyndsey and she wanted to follow. That hope never died.

If it was Lyndsey hell-bent on teasing her, then let her continue, because anything – *anything* – was better than no contact at all.

As she dried herself, nothing more happened, nor as she pulled on a pair of sweatpants and a tee shirt. She'd call Lee later, perhaps, and see how he was. Not her *boyfriend*, if such a word could apply to a grown man – actually, she detested that word, along with *girlfriend* – but *partner* didn't sit well either; it was a little too intense. Their relationship was exclusive, but it was also relaxed, and had been for more than two years now. Both led busy lives: he was an investigating officer in the Sussex Police Force, and she had cases of a paranormal nature to occupy her. But they got together often enough, taking it forward slowly, tentatively.

Two years, Ness? You can certainly call that slow!

Towelling her hair before combing it into place, Ness allowed herself a small smile. Yes, it was indeed slow but safe too and secure. They enjoyed each other's company. They had an understanding – or, rather, he understood her and her background, that she found it difficult to open up, to trust implicitly, that, in short, she had her demons. He never pushed her for more commitment, but there was love between them, and respect. Maybe one day…

Another creak! A stronger sense that something was upstairs in the house with her.

Not hesitating, not for a second, she swiftly returned to the spare room, venturing deeper into it this time and standing there, her head turning from side to side, her eyes straining to make out something, anything. "Lyndsey, if it's you, that's fine. I *want* it to be you. So much. God, I miss you! I feel incomplete without you. If it's you…oh, please, let it be you."

Her heart shattered further when only silence answered.

* * *

Later, with a glass of red wine poured and her laptop fired up, Ness started her own research on the Parker house. Cross-referencing various websites to which she had access, she found Barcombe had been rechristened Barcombe Mills in 1885 and the Parker house and several others had been built just a few years before, modest two-up two-downs like her own house, with none of the extensions that were prevalent now. The village attracted anglers, who came via train to fish in the nearby river, but, as was the fate of many a rural station in England, the station was closed due to the Beeching cuts in 1969, the main building becoming a restaurant but now given over to more accommodation.

Railway stations fascinated Ness – that whole concept of going on a journey, consisting of a start point and an end point. All the stations stopped at in between represented various stages of life, perhaps, as sometimes you sped from one to the next with barely a glance at the scenery, and other times you disembarked the train and lingered awhile. Disused stations had an even curiouser feel to them, of journeys no more, that had come to an abrupt end, as Lyndsey's had...

Not everything's about Lyndsey!

It wasn't, and yet...it seemed to be. Everything came back to the twin that never was, that should have accompanied her stage by stage. How different it might have been if it were so, even Ness's own relationship with her mother might have been different, so much easier.

She mustn't get distracted. Right now, she was trying to find out more about David and Christopher, two boys who might be twins or not related at all. Census records could be useful, but the 1931 census for England and Wales had been destroyed by fire in 1942, and no census was taken in 1941 because of the Second World War. A register was taken in 1939, however, so she could check that.

Sure enough, in 1939 – the year that fitted their suspected timeframe – John and Betty Jackson had lived in what was now the Parkers' house. There was no mention of a child, though. Not that this deterred Ness. Clicking on another site she had access to, she viewed John and Betty Jackson's marriage certificate – they'd got hitched a decade earlier, in 1928. Taking a sip of wine, she savoured its strong, rich flavour, then continued to delve deeper into online records, finding a birth certificate, not Betty's or John's but that of their child, David, who was born in 1929. Sadly, she also found his death certificate; the child had died in 1937, aged eight, just before the start of the war.

Despite such sad news, Ness yelled out, "Bingo!" and was

reaching across to take another sip of wine when her glass tipped over – away from the laptop, mercifully, but its contents coated the rug below, a beige rug that now looked as if a massacre had taken place upon it.

"What the hell—"

Christopher!

As the name resounded in her head, she jumped to her feet.

"What? Who said that? Who the hell is in my house?"

She'd brought back no attachment from the Parker house, she was sure of it. She'd been a psychic all her life, she'd know if something had cleaved to her, she'd just…she'd know.

There'd been nothing – absolutely nothing. Whatever spirit occupied the Barcombe house remained there. That being so, was it her own hand that had knocked the glass when she'd stumbled on David's name? Certainly, it had been close to it, closer than she perhaps realised.

Whatever had happened, she had a mess to clear up, practicality taking over from shock. And maybe, just maybe, a spirit to address too.

When she was sure she could speak calmly and evenly, she began. "When we were in the Parker house, we got two names, David and Christopher. Records confirm, however, that only David may have lived there, although I'm prepared to accept that records are sometimes incomplete or wrong. Who's Christopher? You seem keen I keep his name in mind. Why?"

Once more, Ness had to contain her frustration at receiving no immediate answer.

"There is no Christopher mentioned on record," she reiterated. "If you want to help me, you're going to have to tell me more. Is there one spirit at the Parker house?"

Silence.

"Are there two?"

Yet more silence.

"Are David and Christopher...twins?"

When the glass had been swiped from her hands, it hadn't shattered; it had lain on the rug, on its side. But now another sound filled the air – not a reply, nothing like that but, rather, the crunch of glass, as if it had been stamped on.

Refusing to be intimidated, however, she spoke again.

"That is NOT an answer. Whoever you are, deal with me respectfully or not at all." God, the life of a psychic, it certainly had its peculiarities! Although usually they happened outside the house, not in. *Always* they did. So who'd got the hump here? Who felt about the boys this strongly?

"I've asked this once, but I'll ask again. I want an answer. Are David and Christopher twins?" When there was no reply or any further display of temper, she dared to elaborate, aware of a feeling in her chest, not shock this time, but excitement. "Lyndsey, are they twins?"

There was an echo of an answer in her mind, as if reaching her from across a great divide.

No.

Chapter Eleven

HI, I can't take your call right now. Leave a message, and I'll get back to you.

It'd been the fourth time Ness had rung Corinna, and each time it had gone straight to voicemail. Sitting at the small table in her kitchen, light streaming in through the window, she poured herself a second cup of coffee and munched her way through another slice of hot buttered toast, the excitement of the previous night fuelling her appetite rather than quashing it. Surprisingly, she'd also been able to sleep well, waking to feel refreshed. The voice she'd heard, the one insisting David and Christopher were not twins – and certainly there'd been no mention of a Christopher living at that address on any of the records she'd explored – was not either of those boys. She remained convinced of that. So could it be…?

Don't get carried away, Ness.

She'd said that recently to Corinna, and now she said it to herself. Even so, she prayed that her fervent pleading had finally moved her sister to act. The Parker case might have helped too. If anyone could identify with children being trapped in the dark, it was Lyndsey.

Tread carefully. Go slowly.

She mustn't rush into anything or try to force the issue. If Lyndsey was responsible for what had happened last night with the glass, she had to wait patiently for her to make more contact. She also had to work hard to solve the mystery of the two boys in the attic, make another appointment to visit the Parker house as soon as possible, early in the week, perhaps, as today was Saturday and most likely the Parkers had weekend plans. *Oh shit!* Because of all that had happened, she'd completely forgot to phone Lee the previous night or even text him. She'd do that now, then phone Corinna again, wanting to tell her all that had happened since they'd last met – that it wasn't twins in the attic, just one boy, David, who was somehow Christopher too.

She picked up her phone and punched Lee's number in. Although at work, he answered quickly enough, and plans were made for him to call round that evening and have dinner with her, Ness busy contemplating what she could cook, some fish, perhaps, new potatoes and a salad – something light, anyway. She'd also buy a good bottle of wine, splash out a bit, and why not? Inside, it felt like she was celebrating, *cautiously* celebrating, knowing that if it turned out she was wrong, disappointment would be like a tidal wave, not just overwhelming but crippling her.

With breakfast finished, she rose from her seat and made her way upstairs to the bathroom, her phone still in her hand and calling Corinna once more en route. Again voicemail. She'd already left a message so didn't bother to leave another. Instead she'd phone Theo before jumping in the shower, just in case Corinna had checked in with her.

At the top of the stairs, glancing in the direction of the

open door to the spare room, Ness heard Theo pick up.

"Hello, Ness."

"Morning, Theo, how are you? You sound a little groggy."

"Ah, I see you're your usual charming self this morning."

Ness rolled her eyes. "I was only saying, that's all."

This was how it was between them, affectionate but edgy too. It always had been, ever since they'd worked their first case together in a village called Thorpe Morton in the North of England about twenty years ago, and no doubt it would remain that way, the rhythm of their relationship cast in stone.

"So, to what do I owe this pleasure?" Theo continued.

"Have you heard from Corinna?"

"Corinna? No. Why? Is everything all right?"

"Yes, I think so. It's just I've phoned her several times, and it keeps going to voicemail."

"It is Saturday morning, Ness."

"I'm perfectly aware of that, Theo."

"She's probably busy with that man of hers. Try her this afternoon."

"I will. I'll do that. Theo…"

"Yes?"

"You are all right, aren't you?"

"Me? You're worried because I sound groggy?"

In truth, yes, there was something missing from Theo's voice, her usual spark. She might be on the large side, but Theo had always had so much energy up until…well, up until Blakemort. To see that energy on the decline was, in Ness's opinion, concerning.

"You mustn't worry," Theo said, "you and Corinna both. There's life in this old dog yet."

Ness couldn't help but smile. "I know there is."

"Good. Was it the Parker case you wanted to discuss with Corinna?"

"Uh-huh. I was doing some research on it last night and I found a reference to a David who'd lived there but no Christopher."

"I see. Corinna went to The Keep after she dropped me off, so it'll be interesting to compare notes."

"Oh, did she? Yes, very interesting indeed. We need to arrange a return visit to the Parker house as soon as possible."

"I'm game for that. Anything else interesting happen last night, by any chance?"

Ness closed her eyes, part amazed by Theo's intuition, part annoyed. What else had happened was only conjecture at the moment, plus, standing there on the landing, a few feet from the spare room, talking about it so openly might prove insensitive to a certain someone if she was listening. Ness shut Theo down, deciding that was the safer option.

"Nothing else. Look, I have to go, but if you hear from Corinna, let me know."

Assuring Ness she'd do just that, the call ended, both of them getting on with their day.

* * *

It wasn't only her local supermarket Ness visited in order to get food and wine for that evening. Prior to that, she'd popped into various shops in Lewes, browsing and making the most of some free time. As someone who'd lived in the town for many years, she'd often bump into people she knew or those who ran local enterprises, so today she took the time to stop and chat with them, the excitement of what had happened the previous night responsible for lifting her mood, putting a spring in her step. Would there be any more signs of Lyndsey tonight? Was it best if she put Lee off visiting and just sat at home and focused? Although she considered doing that, she decided against it, not wanting to make a big thing of it, even though it *was* a big thing. It was huge. It was also delicate, and she worried too much enthusiasm might frighten her sister away. If *it's her, Ness, if...* So many times she had to remind herself to hold back.

Finally heading home, she was surprised at how much time had passed. Then again, Lewes had plenty to keep a person occupied, including several antique stores and a very intriguing flea market. Stepping inside its doors was like entering a different world, with so many unusual objects for sale from so many eras, their history still tangible, someone like Ness able to read it...

Having negotiated a busy road, she was now on a quieter side street a few feet from her house. Lost in thought, only half acknowledging she was actually enjoying the heat today rather than cursing it, the way it soaked into her skin to warm her bones, it took a moment to register that someone was calling her name.

"Ness! Oh, Ness, thank goodness! There you are! I've tried phoning you several times. Why didn't you answer? And not just me, Presley's been calling too and no doubt Ruby."

"What? You've been trying to call me? What is it, Theo? What's wrong?"

Theo, as fast as she was able, closed the gap between them, her mobile phone in her hand, waving it at Ness as if in further accusation. "You've been out of contact for hours!"

"What?" Ness said again, confused. Placing her bag of shopping on the ground, she opened her shoulder bag and rummaged through it. Sure enough, there was no phone; she must have left it at home. She hadn't missed it either, her mind on other things and simply…relaxing, which she now felt guilty about. For Theo to be outside her home, waiting for her to reappear, for others to be trying to contact her too, Ruby, Presley even… She could feel the blood drain from her face.

"What about Corinna? Has she been trying to phone me too?"

Theo's complexion wasn't just pale but waxy. "Let's go inside. I'll fill you in."

Fumbling for her keys now, her hands shaking, Ness opened the front door, and they made their way through to the kitchen, where Ness dumped her bags on the table.

"Tell me everything," she said, turning to Theo, not even bothering to pull up a chair.

"Corinna didn't come home last night. The last person who saw her face-to-face was me."

"What?" Ness's voice was barely above a whisper. "She went to The Keep!"

"*I* went to The Keep," Theo told her, "as soon as I found out she'd gone missing. The staff were kind enough to check CCTV for me – well, I insisted, actually, wasn't going to move until they had, and sure enough, she'd turned up there. The car park, anyway. She sat in the car for a while, on her phone. Ruby said she texted her around that time, but it was just general chitchat, told her she was at The Keep, intending to go in. At some point, though, she changed her mind and drove off."

"She's gone missing?" Ness repeated, that fact sinking in. "Shit! When was the alarm raised?"

"A few hours ago, just before noon."

Ness shook her head in further confusion. "But you said she didn't come home last night, so why wait until noon today?"

"Because...because of damned crossed wires, that's why!" Her worry and frustration clearly mounting, Theo had to sit as her breathing became more pronounced.

Her own legs feeling as if they were about to give way, Ness sat too. "Theo, take a deep breath, calm down. We can work this out, work backwards. She can't have just...disappeared."

Theo took her advice, something that alarmed Ness further, highlighting the fact she knew as well as her friend did the toll that stress could take on an already weakened heart. "The thing is," she began, her breath still coming in gasps, "Presley thought she'd gone home to her mother's for the night; apparently, she does spend two or three nights a week there, and she and him hadn't arranged anything. By the same token, Helena thought she was at Presley's. Presley and Cash were involved in rehearsals for their band last night and weren't getting home until late anyway. Corinna knew that. No one checked with anyone else, not until earlier today anyway. Everyone just...assumed."

"I see," Ness answered, growing as stricken as Theo, her breathing a little shallower also. "You said you've also spoken to Ruby."

"I have, yes, that's how I found out Corinna had texted her, just before she took off. I originally rang because I wondered if Corinna had stayed the night there, being as Cash was out too, but no such luck. Ruby's as worried as us, but she's also suffering so badly; her sickness is back with a vengeance. She knew I was coming to see you and wanted to come with me, but I said no, to stay put. I assured her we'll keep her informed every step of the way, although, again, being honest, I think Cash is going to have a hard time restraining her, despite how terrible she feels. Ness, she said there's talk of her being hospitalised if her blood pressure falls much lower."

"Shit!" Ness said, having to stand again to pace the kitchen floor. "Shit! Shit! Shit!" Coming to a halt, she faced Theo. "There's no chance Corinna's gone to stay with another friend?"

"And not tell anyone? Not get in touch with Presley or her mother, even, since last night?"

"No, no, of course she'd get in touch. Sorry…" Ness wiped at her brow, which was soaked with sweat. "I'm finding it difficult to think straight. What about the police? Have they been informed?"

"As soon as Helena realised Corinna was missing, she phoned the police. I think she's at the station now, in Brighton, going through all the necessary stuff."

"Right, okay, Lee, I can phone him. I don't know…maybe he can get involved, fast-track this. He has to. My mobile's upstairs, I'll go and grab it."

Ness rushed from the room and flew up the stairs, her knees protesting only slightly at the effort she exerted. Where was her phone, exactly? In her bedroom? It must be, on the chest of drawers there. Entering the room, she spied it immediately and headed over to it, noticing, as Theo had said, just how many missed calls there were. About to unlock it, she came to an abrupt halt.

Also on the chest of drawers, beside the phone, was a framed photograph. It was nothing fancy, simply a portrait of a place she'd visited a while ago now with a friend, a local National Trust garden. The season was autumn, and the trees were magnificent, a plethora of greens and golds. It was the reason she'd kept the photograph and had it framed. She was in the picture too – her friend had taken it – although she was in the distance. For a moment, however, she thought she'd seen *two* people in the photograph, someone else standing beside her, someone who was the same height, with the same look, the same...everything. She looked again and blinked hard. It was just her. There was nothing different about it at all – and yet...for a moment...

She grabbed her phone and called Lee, got the engaged tone, swore, and left a message for him instead. *Call me as soon as you can. Urgent!*

With that done she was about to turn around to go back downstairs and rejoin Theo, but once more she stopped, picking up the picture this time rather than scrutinising it from afar, having to convince herself that it was only her in it and no one else, certainly no one...special.

"Lyndsey..." she began, before reminding herself that Corinna was the issue here, *only* Corinna. Dread joined panic.

You'd better be all right, Corinna. You'd better be.

Chapter Twelve

THE old saying had some substance to it: just when you thought things couldn't get any worse, they did. A missing persons investigation had been set up for Corinna, and, although Lee wasn't able to oversee it, he'd agreed to keep an eye on it, making sure everyone and anyone connected with her was interviewed. Meanwhile, the doctor had insisted Ruby go into hospital for tests despite forceful protests that she wanted to get involved in the search.

"You have to think of the baby," Theo had said to her on the phone, managing against all odds to adopt that famous soothing tone of hers. "Corinna would be the last person to want anything to happen to you or your boy because of her. Let them run their tests, stabilise you, and then we can take it from there. Right now, sweetheart, it's one day at a time, for all of us."

It wasn't even that, in truth. They were living hour to hour, praying their friend would somehow miraculously turn up with an explanation to hand. So far, however, every avenue had drawn a blank – there was no trace of Corinna or her car either, which police were also searching for. Helena was being comforted by other members of the family, and

Cash was dividing himself between Ruby and Presley, doing his utmost to be a rock to them both.

All other work, private or on behalf of Psychic Surveys, had of course been put on hold.

It was Sunday morning, and Theo was once again at Ness's house. The previous night, neither had been able to sleep a wink. Lee had arrived at Ness's close to midnight, but he'd seemed agitated too. He didn't have to tell Ness the reason why; she knew well enough, thinking back to a case she'd worked on with the police many years before, that of two missing girls much younger than Corinna, just children, everyone so desperate to find them that they'd called in a psychic to help. Ness had eventually led the police to the girls, who'd been lying cold in a grave deep in the woods. That case had tormented her and, indeed, caused her to end any future work with the police because it'd been so harrowing and tormented her even now, especially as she'd only been able to release one of the children from the shock that kept them grounded. The other girl, Claire, had simply refused to come forward – another child lost in the dark, who remained there still.

As it always did, the memory of that case prompted tears, and Lee had held her last night, remaining silent rather than doing her the discourtesy of fobbing her off with false words of hope. Almost three-quarters of missing people were found within twenty-four hours. The more time that passed, however, the slimmer those chances became. When her tears had finally subsided, Lee had assured her again the police were doing everything they could, and she believed him. Lee was a good man, he cared about people and getting results, and although he wasn't in charge of the case – it wasn't his department – he'd pull a few strings and ensure no stone was left unturned. As psychics, however, she and Theo had to do their bit as well, which was why Theo had arrived so early on Sunday morning, just as Lee was departing, her eyes as bloodshot as Ness's own.

Together, they were going to try to reach Corinna on a psychic level. Since the demise of Blakemort, their friend's psychic abilities had developed enormously, with Theo teaching her how to catch thoughts, something she and Ness were adept at, Ruby not so much. Corinna, though, showed great promise. Not able to achieve it all the time, she could manage it on occasion. Maybe, just maybe, if they projected hard enough, she'd catch their thoughts now, regardless of whatever distance was between them. She'd be trying to reach out too, surely, maybe equally as desperate as them for communication?

The fact that she *hadn't* communicated yet was a good sign – or, rather, Ness chose to see it as such, because if Corinna had, it could mean something else entirely, that she was dead, grounded, couldn't move on, just like the girls in the wood, traumatised. And so, like everyone else who knew and loved Corinna, they held on to hope, because right now, it was all they had.

Ness offered Theo water, but she declined, eager to get on with the task they'd set themselves. As they'd done the previous day when the news had broken about Corinna, they sat at the kitchen table, opposite each other but within hand's reach, the blinds at the window closed, and the kitchen door too. Yesterday, shock and grief had effectively disabled them, overnight both had had to work hard to prepare themselves for the task ahead.

The pair took several deep breaths before reaching out to clasp each other's hands and closing their eyes. The aim was to combine their energy and strength, to reach out for Corinna beyond the boundary of their bodies, their minds probing the space between them, to find her, to get some inkling as to why she'd disappeared so suddenly.

Corinna? Are you there? Corinna…

Aside from thoughts, total silence filled the room, an air of expectation having developed. Already Ness could feel Theo's mind probing: *Darling, it's Theo. Answer me if you can. We're here, and we're doing our utmost to find you. We will find you…I promise.*

Ness tensed at those final words, at the wiseness of using them.

You have to believe, Ness. We all do.

Theo was addressing her now and, in response, Ness squeezed her hand, albeit gently. She was right, belief was everything; they had to drag Corinna back out of the void she'd fallen into. Like Claire and Lyndsey, she didn't belong there. They couldn't fail, not this time.

Corinna, where are you? Try to reach us. We're here, we're waiting, we're listening out for you. Try your hardest, Corinna, we know you can do it. It's not impossible. Nothing's *impossible.*

"Wait!" It was Theo, her hands squeezing Ness's now. "I think…I think…"

She didn't say anything more, probably afraid of breaking whatever link she'd forged.

Are you there?

And if so, if she was reaching out in this way, there was both hope and despair – hope because she was alive and despair because something bad had happened to her.

Corinna?

Ness sent every ounce of energy she possessed into the ether, imagining it increasing in strength, dividing like strands of golden thread, continuingly growing in length. White light surrounded each and every one, a means of preventing them from connecting to anything else lying in wait, that space in between never empty but a sanctuary for some, those able to mimic…

Corinna!

She had to work hard to subdue the panic in her, to emulate Theo and her cool, calm demeanour. Damn, but how did the elder woman maintain that in such circumstances?

Because I have to. Panic doesn't help.

Theo's answer flew back at her, and she was right. Panic would attract precisely the energies she was trying to avoid, those that belonged to a much lower level, that were forever seeking nourishment, that would probe at those strands of golden thread and attack them.

Corinna, where are you? Come on, reach out, get in contact. We're all so worried…

A flash of something! Ness was sure of it. Not a thought as such, but something, a vision, an image, barely seen or understood but enough to capture her breath.

"Theo, I saw—"

"Yes, I know." No longer as calm, Theo's voice held urgency.

"Whatever it was, was fleeting. Did you see it too?"

"No. But I sensed well enough that you did. Focus, Ness. She's there, trying to reach out. She'd never do this to us, torment us this way, not deliberately. Reach out, Ness. Try again."

At Theo's words, Ness briefly opened her eyes, noting the pain etched on her face, how deeply this unexpected loss had marked her. She noticed too that, although gearing up to be yet another blistering day, there was a chill in the air – in the kitchen, at least – the gloom that surrounded them thanks to the blinds having been shut developing a thickness to it.

Closing her eyes again, she took more deep breaths, harnessing the light, going one step further than before and imagining herself leaning forward in essence rather than body, traversing the in between, reaching out to Corinna, calling for her, begging her, promising her, as Theo had done. *We'll find you. We are going to find you!*

Oh, it was dark in the in between, far gloomier than the kitchen. Having to force progress was akin to wading through treacle, her eyes wide, her head turning from side to side as she searched. She was no longer able to feel Theo's energy; instead, she was alone on her quest, although she knew better than to be certain that was the case. People were *never* alone, despite so many thinking and feeling that way. There was always something lying in wait, ready to come forwards, to attach itself, to sink its teeth in and feast on all that was negative in a person. Such were things that waited in the darkest part of the shadows, the umbra – *nameless* things – patient things, some half-formed, some fully fleshed, reflections of ourselves, comprising our deepest, innermost thoughts, those we rarely acknowledged because to do so was shocking.

Everything was energy – it was important to realise that, the sum total of us all. Although venturing into the darkness, it was essential that Ness remain in the light, to weave it around herself, as thick as a blanket and tougher than steel.

Corinna, I'm coming for you.

She continued to forge ahead, her body remaining static at the kitchen table, her hands still in Theo's but only barely able to acknowledge the softness of them. Theo was her protection too; she'd pull her back if things became too much, if she sank too deep…

The landscape, such as it was, was beginning to change. In the darkness were darker things, long and twisted, spindly sometimes, reaching upwards and outwards. A smell assailed her, one she was familiar with, earthy but with an underlying sweetness that could choke you.

"Keep going, Ness."

Theo's voice told her that she knew her colleague was on to something. Her eyes remaining firmly closed, her nose wrinkling, Ness readily obliged, any fear or confusion she felt remaining firmly under wraps. She was in control of this situation – *they* were, she and Theo – she could continue or wrap it up at any stage. Knowing that gave her both comfort and courage.

The woods. Of course it was. The ground not hard beneath her feet but soft and uneven, something scraping across her face, sharp and capable of drawing blood. A branch, perhaps?

Corinna, are you here?

The long, twisted shapes were indeed trees, and they were becoming denser the further she roamed, obstacles beneath her feet too, stones, twigs and roots that threatened to topple her.

What the woods had to do with Corinna, she didn't know. What they had to do with herself, she knew all too well. *Be careful, Ness.*

"Be careful."

Theo echoed her thoughts, likely sensing how her physical body had tensed.

Hateful woods. The ones she'd visited over and over, where not one but two graves had resided, such a grim discovery causing even the most hardened detectives to seek counselling.

A doubt surfaced. Could Ness trust what she was seeing? Did it have anything to do with Corinna, or were her own fears being played upon, dragged to the surface?

Did she know these woods? Were they familiar at all?

She couldn't tell. All woods looked the same in the dark, with silhouettes of tall giants towering over you and branches forming webs. But now she remembered. Corinna had talked of the woods recently, Rayners Wood, part of the Devil's Triangle in Sussex. She'd talked of them, and she'd had a vision of herself in the woods whilst at Low Cottage, running there terrified. Running from what, though? When Ness had asked her, she'd answered that it was as if the darkness had solidified, taken shape, grown wings, perhaps, in its quest to capture her – a devilish thing.

Ness shook her head, reined it in, tried not to embellish all she saw, not letting the memory of what Corinna had said mislead her. In the thick of it now, her mind tried to reach Corinna once again. *Tell me what I'm doing here. Am I meant to be seeing this? Is this where you are?*

Ness...

Hearing her name called, she came to a halt.

Corinna, is that you?

Ness...

It was a faint reply, barely above a whisper and impossible to tell if it was Corinna or not.

Ness turned on her heel, looking all around her, scouring this strange, apocalyptic landscape that was drenched in darkness. *Corinna, it's me, it's Ness. Where are you?*

Ness...

Corinn—

Ness!

The voice, such as it was, became more strident. Ness started to walk again, having to protect her face with her hands as more branches clawed at her.

Corinna, keep calling. I'll find you.

Damn these trees! They formed a shield wall of their own, a realisation that made her breath hitch. Darkness like this knew how to hide itself.

Corinna! I'm here.

Ness! Ness!

As suddenly as they'd become dense, the trees cleared, as if an invisible hand had swept them away. She was in some kind of clearing, the space not circular but...triangular?

What was happening? Was she being toyed with here, played like a fool? And this clearing, so similar to another, had it been plucked from her mind by mischievous fingers?

At a standstill yet again, her chest was heaving as she scanned all that was in front of her, trying to see when really all she wanted was to snap back into her body, have this over and done with. But what if the voice calling did belong to Corinna? She couldn't abandon her.

Corinna, is this you? Answer me!

As though her voice were a trigger, the ground beneath her started to vibrate, causing her to throw her arms out in order to achieve balance and stay upright. From overhead there came the thunderous sound of clashing, as if mighty shields – the light and the dark – were colliding. She felt hot, like she'd developed a fever. Not just shaking, the world was spinning, the landscape she was trapped in shunting her from side to side, her eyes still open, still trying to scan what was in front of her, to make sense of it, to ascertain whether it was a mockery or a message.

Ness! There it was again, her name being frantically called.

Still trying to stay upright, she called back, but it was as if her voice was snatched from her throat, the rumbling overhead deafening now, threatening to split her head asunder.

Ness! Ness! Help me.

I'm here, I'm trying to. Where are you? Tell me.

Ness!

Yes! It's me! Corinna, is that you?

Another clash caused her to fall to her knees, her hands out in front and sinking deep into mud, deeper still, finding something harder than mud, something solid that grabbed at her.

Immediately she tried to withdraw her hands, but whatever held on refused to let go. She wouldn't give up trying, though, noting how cold that something was, wishing instead for Theo's soft skin. This had no skin. It was bone against her flesh, and it was desperate.

Let go of me. You're not Corinna, you're not!

She'd been duped, the darkness having turned on her, sending its own tendrils out, those that searched eternally, devouring secrets, shame, and regrets before regurgitating them.

She couldn't release what was in the ground or even bear to look at it.

Claire or Lyndsey, which one would it be? Perhaps both, bone white, wretched things that would glare up at her, revealing so much helplessness and, worse still, so much blame.

You bitch! Worms would spill from their mouths as they spoke. *You left us alone in the dark.*

Ness shook her head as she imagined all that would unfold, still trying to untangle her hands, to break such a terrible connection. *I'm sorry, so sorry.*

Still she could hear what their voices would say:

You're failing us again, leaving us in the dark, all *of us, to rot.*

Chapter Thirteen

IT seemed to take an age for Ness to calm down, persistent tremors so violent that on occasion water would spill from the glass she held in her hands, which Theo had insisted she drink. Eventually, she had to admit defeat and place the glass of water back on the kitchen table, her head sinking into her hands instead. The shutters had been opened, and sunshine poured into what had become a bleak space, the kitchen warming but only by degrees.

Theo was back sitting opposite her, sipping at her own glass of water and wearing a very grave expression indeed as she tried to make head or tail of what Ness had told her.

"The darkness turned on you, you're right about that," she said, sighing. "No surprises there, I suppose; it's so damned predictable. This thing with the woods, though, whether it was a message or a mockery, as you say, could be significant, particularly regarding the fact that Corinna herself had a vision of being in the woods, running and terrified."

Ness lifted her head, still exasperated. "That's right, she did, whilst we were at Low Cottage. She'd been reading about Rayners Wood, which forms part of the Devil's Triangle—"

"Along with Chanctonbury Ring and Cissbury Ring, Crowley's old stamping ground."

"Him and numerous other occultists."

"Genuine or wannabes, depending on your take on things."

"Precisely. Even so, it could be significant – we can't ignore that. I can phone Lee, feed him through the information. Tell them that…she seemed to have a bit of a fascination with Rayners Wood, or an interest, at least. Get the police to go there, and not just them, us as well."

Theo nodded in agreement. "But, Ness, rewind. That voice you heard, before things got all twisted, can you be sure it was Corinna?"

"I'm sorry, Theo. Because of what happened at the end, I can't be sure of anything, no."

Theo sighed heavily and then raised a hand to thump at her chest. "She's not dead, Ness. I'd know it. I'd feel it in here."

"So what's happened to her? Is someone keeping her against her will?" There was a moment of silence before an idea occurred. "We were going to return to Low Cottage, Corinna and me. A man called Tom Witcher is renting it out. We wanted to see if it was the same Tom Witcher who'd written a book about Rayners Wood."

"Okay. And?"

"We thought he might know something about Low Cottage, its history, I mean, which in turn might lead us to solve the mystery of what Jess Biggs was trying to tell us."

"Ah, the riddle of Ms Biggs."

"Maybe the Bows' house, Low Cottage, *and* Rayners Wood are all connected somehow. That connection might also give us some clue about what's happened to Corinna." As that theory gained traction, Ness stood, her eyes on her phone, which was on the kitchen worktop in airplane mode. "I've got to call Lee, tell him about Rayners Wood, get a search party organised as quickly as possible. Shit, Theo, there've been deaths there, three of them—"

Theo stood too, reached out to stay Ness as she almost dived towards her phone. "Ness, please. Stop breathing life into thoughts like that. Corinna is *not* dead."

"I'm sorry, I didn't mean—"

"But yes, go ahead, call Lee. Do it now."

The minute she put her phone back online, it rang, Presley's name appearing on-screen.

"Presley!" she said, quickly answering it, putting it on loudspeaker as she turned to face Theo, whose eyes had widened in anticipation. "Is it about Corinna? Have you got news?"

There was a slight pause before he spoke, the crack in his voice evident. "No, no news, nothing at all. I'm going mad here, Ness. Where the hell's she gone?"

Theo looked as deflated as Ness felt. "Presley, I wish I knew. I…" Damn it, her voice had a crack in it too. *Don't crumble, Ness.* "The police are doing everything they can—"

"I know, I know."

"We are too. Theo and I have just been trying to connect with her on a psychic level."

"Have you? Did you get anything? Any clue?"

"Erm…we've only really just begun, but, Presley, the good news is we feel strongly that she's alive. If she wasn't, if she were…" Ness didn't want to elaborate further. "She's alive, Presley, and we'll find her," she said instead, perhaps with more conviction than she felt.

Thankfully, Presley seemed to buy it, although he remained distraught. "Ever since I realised she was missing, I've been out, either walking the streets or on my motorbike, in town, out of town, down tiny rural roads that no one ever goes down, back to where that house was, you know, Blakemort. There's nothing there, though; it's a burnt-out shell, it feels...hollow. Then this morning I thought I'd spotted her out near Ringmer, where she works. There was this woman with red hair, the same as hers, and I called out. My heart was, like, hammering in my chest. She turned around, and I could hardly breathe. But it wasn't her, of course. It's noon on Sunday, Ness. She's been missing since Friday afternoon – where's she gone?" he repeated. "Where?"

"Oh, Presley," Ness murmured, swallowing. "Is someone with you?"

"Cash was, but he's now with Ruby at the hospital."

"Of course, yes."

"The reason I rang," Presley continued, "besides just wanting to talk to you, is because a book arrived for Corinna today from Amazon. She must have ordered it a day or so ago."

"What book is that?"

"*The Demonic Link* by Tom Witcher. You heard of it?"

"I've heard of him, yes," she answered, her blood running cold.

"I don't know if it's just a research book or whether it's...more than that."

A clue. That's what he meant.

"It's a bit of a battered old copy, obviously well read by whoever had it before – some pages have a few sentences underscored, that kind of thing. I can drop it round, if you like."

"Yes," said Ness, "please. I think we'd better take a look." That and pay a visit to Low Cottage, as she and Corinna had said they would, to see if it was the same Tom Witcher as the author. If there *was* a connection with Corinna and the woods, then he might be able to help them. In fact, a visit to Low Cottage had been essential even prior to getting the book. She'd head there straightaway after speaking to Presley and then to Lee, to see if the latter could get that search party underway – covering all angles, no matter how tenuous they might be. It was clutching at straws, perhaps, but clutching at anything was better than thin air.

"I'll come by this evening," Presley told her, and Ness agreed, certain that she'd be back by then and could tell Presley all about it, if indeed there was anything to tell. Best not to forget that the route she was travelling down might prove a highway to nowhere.

After saying goodbye to Presley, Ness was about to tell Theo about Low Cottage and the visit she'd upgraded in her mind to urgent when a text came through from Karen Bow. All Psychic Surveys cases were on hold, she and Theo had agreed on that, but the message she just received chilled her blood when she'd thought it was cold enough already:

We wanted to give you an update. It's not just in the kitchen that clocks won't work – they've stopped in the living room too and one of the bedrooms. They've gone stone-dead.

* * *

They'd visit the Bows. Ness had already phoned to tell them they were on their way but not before they swung by Low Cottage, despite Lee having warned against it on the phone.

"Ness," he'd said, "if there's anything suspect about Tom Witcher, let the police find out."

"But when?" Ness had replied, unable to quash her rising frustration. She'd already told him about Rayners Wood and her fears surrounding it, but because they weren't fears grounded in fact, not yet, anyway, she also knew the reality of it – that organising a search party there would take some persuasion on his part. And now here he was, telling her to hold off calling on Tom Witcher. She wouldn't, she couldn't, something Theo agreed with.

"It may be frustrating for us sometimes that we work outside the parameters of the police," the older woman had said, "that when it comes to the general public, we don't hold sway, but it's also liberating because at least we don't have to suffer the restrictions of protocol and red tape."

Nonetheless, Lee had reiterated that the police were cracking on with the case, Ness almost willing him to say that CCTV footage had at least picked up a sighting of Corinna's car, but no such news was forthcoming. She'd rung off from their conversation, refusing to give him an answer either way about her intention to visit Low Cottage. And now she and Theo were almost there, that same sense of dread in her chest when she'd first noticed the house.

Corinna had already provided some information about Low Cottage prior to her disappearance, Ness relaying that to Theo as they sat in Ness's car a few metres from the property, their windows wound down to let the air in, although it remained scant, hardly circulating at all.

"The cottage was built in 1900 and was occupied by Phyllida Hylands from 1901 to 1962. After that, there are gaps in the records as to who lived there until the early eighties, when there was a series of owners, lots of them, right up to current times. Paul and Julie Winterton are its most recent owners, who quite possibly bought it as a buy-to-let. I'm not sure they've ever lived there."

"Letting it to Tom Witcher."

"That's right."

They also Googled Witcher's book on Amazon, primarily to see if there was an author photo, but there wasn't. Having done that, they Googled his name. The man had plenty to say for himself about the Devil's Triangle but was clearly camera-shy, as there were no mugshots. Further checks revealed there were no Facebook, Twitter or Instagram accounts that fit him either.

"A mystery man indeed," Theo had murmured, glancing again at articles on Rayners Wood, Chanctonbury and Cissbury Rings, her expression darkening as she read the content.

En route to Lindfield, Ness had also brought her up to speed regarding Corinna's triangle-within-a-triangle theory, with Low Cottage and Rayners Wood both positioned on the low point of each triangle, and the village being the smaller triangle within the larger one.

"Well, if it is the same Tom Witcher, better hear what he has to say about that," Theo remarked.

Leaving the car, they walked towards the gate set between tall hedges. To Ness's surprise, Theo didn't remain there but instead pushed it open and continued boldly along the path that led towards the front door. There was to be no hesitation there either, Theo grabbing a wrought iron knocker that graced the door and rapping it hard against the studded, splintered oak. She'd brought herself up to her full height, just over five foot but appearing much taller than that, adopting an air of superiority – or the 'glamour', to give it its ancient description, whereby you injected so much energy into your presence that few would dare to question or intimidate you. It was clear to see Theo believed in herself, in what they were doing, and this was her physical representation of it, driving home the ethos at the heart of Psychic Surveys: belief was everything.

We will find you, Corinna.

As she repeated these words in her mind, Ness drew herself up to full height too.

The seconds passed, the door remaining shut. Theo rapped again, but there was still no reply.

"Mr Witcher appears to be out," she remarked.

"In that case"—Ness moved towards a window to the left, where she knew the kitchen to be—"he won't know if we peer through his windows."

"Needs must when the devil drives," Theo said, moving to the right and the window there.

Both had to bring their hands up to cut out the glare of the sun, which, beating down upon the windowpanes, made them feel lava hot. It was dark inside the kitchen, almost unfathomably so, Ness wondering if Theo was finding the same regarding the living room.

It's dark, all right. Ness caught the thought Theo fired at her in response. *And rather sparse too. Has he actually moved in yet?*

Apparently, Ness fired back. According to Greg

Warrington, Witcher had been insistent on moving in straightaway, but if that were the case, then Theo was right, it *was* sparse inside. In fact, it looked exactly as it had when Warrington had showcased it to them, no items apparent that might be considered personal to its new resident. Feeling slightly confused, Ness joined Theo and peered in through that window too, into yet more darkness.

"It's like a warren in there," she informed her. "Rooms lead into other rooms, with no real order."

"Who was the architect, do you know?"

"No, but Corinna had a suspicion it was Phyllida Hylands who commissioned the build, the lady who lived here such a long time."

"Perhaps she commissioned the newer wings of Blakemort too."

Ness frowned as she glanced at Theo. "Seriously?"

"I'm joking, but... This house is highly unpleasant. Things *have* happened here, Ness, although I've no idea what—"

"There's nothing on record. Lee's already checked that."

"You know as well as I do, plenty goes unrecorded."

"True," Ness replied, her voice grave even to her own ears. "There were two rooms in there that Corinna and I felt particularly unsettled in, well...to be honest, Corinna more than I. The master bedroom and a smaller room towards the back of the house, a study."

"Was there a window in the study?"

"Yes, there was."

"Let's go around to the back of the house and peer in there instead."

Ness hesitated. "Theo, we're trespassing."

"Ness, Corinna's missing. If there's any link to be forged here, we explore it."

Ness quickly nodded. "Of course."

"Besides, if the worst comes to the worst and we're caught red-handed, that boyfriend of yours will be able to get us off the hook, I'm sure."

Ness couldn't help but scowl at Theo's use of the word *boyfriend*; the woman knew damn well how much she hated that term, but nonetheless Ness dutifully followed her colleague around to the back of the house, along a bricked path that had an assortment of cottage flowers bordering it, most of them wilting, however, the heat and the lack of rain perhaps only partially to blame. As they approached what Ness guessed was the window to the study, her unease, if not Theo's, increased. There was something about this house, about the very land it stood on…

"It's like the darkness in my vision."

"Hmm? What is?" Theo questioned.

"This house. It's well practised at cloaking itself."

"I wonder what sort of reputation Hylands enjoyed," mused Theo.

Ness shrugged. "A wealthy widow? Very likely she was regarded as a pillar of the community."

Theo agreed. "Very likely indeed."

"Ah, look," said Ness, pointing, "that must be it, the window to the study."

It was smaller than the other ones and looked older, a relic from another property, perhaps, its lead lining cracked in places and the glass slightly mottled.

Thankfully, there wasn't as much glare from the sun this time as they looked inside.

The study had a small desk pushed up against a wall, with a Tiffany-style lamp on it, a chair on which to sit at the desk, another armchair in the corner, and walls lined with shelves upon which you could place book after book. There *were* no books, however, and, again, no possessions of any kind that could be considered personal to the new owner. All was exactly as it had been the first time Ness had seen it, although she hadn't lingered in there, none of them had, barely entering the room halfway, Greg himself appearing quite happy about that.

Ness shivered. "Something's wrong in there, very wrong."

"Oh, I don't deny it, but what's it got to do with Corinna?"

"I don't know." Ness's voice was tight with frustration. "Like I told you before, we'd planned a second visit here, the pair of us, to find out if it's Corinna's Witcher—"

"Don't say that!"

Ness was surprised by the anger in Theo's voice. "Theo?"

"Don't say he's Corinna's anything. He's not."

"No. You're right. Sorry."

"Where is the wretched man?"

Wretched? So Theo was making that judgement of him already?

"Theo, what is it? What are you sensing?"

"Danger," was her frank reply.

Ness could only nod her head at that, beginning to rear back from the window to perhaps check a few others out, look for any signs of life within, when Theo's hand shot out and grabbed her.

"Wait," she said.

"What is it?"

"There. Look."

Ness did as she was asked, squinting into the gloom.

"Can't you see?"

"See what?"

"There's a shadow of some sort?"

"A shadow?"

"I don't know. Something. Just look."

"Is it Witcher?"

"I don't know...don't think so, no one living and breathing, anyway. It's in the corner, just by the door. Whoever it is, it's like they're...straining to get out, to—" Theo swallowed hard "—escape."

"I don't—"

"Focus, Ness! I'm not imagining this. Something's there!"

The dark corner beside the closed door had no shelves, and the walls were painted the dullest shade of grey, very stained in places, evidence of a heavy smoker, perhaps, constantly breathing nicotine into the air. She could almost imagine that person, not a man but a woman, maybe even Phyllida Hylands herself, sitting in that chair, opposite that desk, back straight but head lowered, reading one of the books that had lined the shelves. What kind of book, though?

Her eyes returned to the corner. Was there a shadow there, as Theo insisted? It was so dark in that corner, almost pitch. She couldn't see a shadow, but the wall, was it bulging in some way? The plaster being the thing that was straining. She blinked hard, twice. The wall was normal, nothing wrong with it, her imagination possibly taking over, embellishing the scene because she wanted so much to see something, craving a clue, any clue whatsoever.

Corinna, where are you?

"Corinna!"

Theo's voice made Ness jump. Quickly she turned to her. "What? Where is she?"

"Gone. Damn, she's gone!"

"Theo, what are you talking about? Where's Corinna?"

Theo's expression was one of confusion too. "I think I saw Corinna in there. I saw a girl, definitely, reaching out."

"Really? Then we have to get in there, get—"

Once again Theo had to restrain her. "She's gone, Ness. Whoever it was has gone."

"I don't understand, was it Corinna or not?"

"I...I thought so, but now I don't know..."

"Theo, you're not making sense."

"I only saw the figure for a second or two; it really wasn't much more than that. It looked like Corinna at first, but then...like someone quite different. Another girl."

Ness was still confused. "Does it...? Could it mean...?"

"No!" Theo was emphatic. "Corinna is not dead! But she came here, Ness, after dropping me off on Friday. I'm certain of it. She went to Low Cottage without telling any of us."

Chapter Fourteen

BUSINESS was business, and they were professionals. They'd made an appointment to go see the Bow family, and although both of them were still reeling from Theo's revelation, they had to keep it. But not before calling Lee, telling him, *insisting*, that a warrant be issued for entering Low Cottage.

"On what basis?" he'd asked, torn between wanting to do as Ness wanted and knowing their reasoning wouldn't be considered valid. "Psychic instinct doesn't always cut it."

He was right. It didn't. Ness was known to the police because of past collaborations, but that was all a long time ago. According to Lee, the magistrate required cold hard facts to issue a warrant. "Plus, we've so few resources," he continued, but Ness refused to let that cut it either.

"We've got to get in there and follow up on this, Lee. Corinna's life might depend on it!" And the clock was ticking, worse than that, actually – the clocks were stopping, in the Bow family house, at least, Jess stepping up the urgency of her message, perhaps, reaching out too?

She'd ended the call but not before telling him they *were* going to get into Low Cottage, one way or another. "It's all connected. Corinna, Witcher, Low Cottage, and Rayners Wood."

"Okay, okay, fine, I understand, really I do, but if you break in, you'll be arrested, so I'm going to pretend I didn't just hear that. I'm due into a meeting soon; don't do anything until I'm out of it, okay? I can have a check run on Tom Witcher, see if there's anything about him on our databases. Once it's all done, I'll come and find you."

"You'll come to Lindfield?"

"Yeah."

"Bring your badge."

"I will. But promise me, Ness, you won't do anything until I get there."

"How long will you be?"

He sighed. "These meetings tend to run on. It'll be at least an hour or so, plus the time it takes to run the check. Just be patient. I understand what you want to do and the reasons why, but don't break the law and, more importantly, don't put your life in danger. Please."

He was right, she knew he was – his warning compounding that of the mysterious stranger when they'd first encountered Low Cottage: *If you value your lives, keep away.* Who was that man? Would he return? How could they possibly trace him?

All of those burning questions and more were put on hold as soon as Karen Bow answered the door to them, a smile on her face but one that was a little strained.

"What is going on with all this?" she said as she ushered the pair of them into the kitchen.

Theo glanced at Ness. *If only we knew...*

Over a cup of tea, Karen reiterated how all clocks and

watches were beginning to stop elsewhere in the house now. "I'm still not scared," she professed, "even though you've told me there's a woman grounded here, Jess Biggs. That doesn't bother us, but this clock thing, it's annoying."

Theo checked where Karen's husband was.

"He and the kids are visiting his parents. It's just me here today. Oh, and Petra's asleep in the living room, as per usual. Where's your colleague, the young woman, Corinna?"

Because Theo faltered, Ness took over. "She's otherwise engaged." Not the truth but not exactly a lie either. And then aware of every minute ticking by – ironically – she asked if they could carry out the task they were here for.

"Yes, of course. I'll take my tea and go and wait with Petra."

Alone in the kitchen, the two women followed a procedure much the same as they'd done in Ness's own kitchen, although they stood side by side rather than remaining seated at the table.

Theo kick-started proceedings. "Jess, we've met before, although you connected with our colleague, Corinna, rather than us. Corinna's…not here. I'm going to be honest with you, Jess, we don't know where she is. She's missing." There was a slight pause, Theo having to work hard to collect herself. "Basically, Jess, we need your help. And what's more, we think you *want* to help us. The fact that you're stopping more and more clocks in this house tells us something, hopefully that time hasn't run out completely, but—" again, she took a deep breath "—that it *is* running out. We're doing everything we can to locate her, but, Jess, if you know anything, if you've got another message, tell us and tell us straight. No riddles, nothing that we have to work out, just…tell us."

When there was no reply, Theo prompted the spirit further. "Jess, we're desperate. If you do know anything about Low Cottage and Corinna, you have to let us know."

Ness held up a hand. "Theo, wait. I'm sensing her. It's as if…as if she's trying to connect. She's doing her best, but there's like a…a wall, something that's trying to block her. That's the impression I'm getting." Addressing the spirit, Ness continued. "If there is something preventing you from fully presenting, remember this: it's only energy. Pit your own against it, it's just as strong. Don't think otherwise. Please, Jess, you've waited a long time for someone to notice you, to listen to what you have to say. Push against it and tell us what's going on."

Girl… Danger…

From the horror on Theo's face, she'd clearly heard exactly what Ness had.

Corinna? she mouthed. There was only one way to find out.

"What girl?" Ness asked. "What danger?"

Poor girl… Innocent…

"Who was innocent?"

Theo asked this time, the frustration in her voice evident. It was important not to assume, however, that this *was* Corinna being talked about. Ness sincerely hoped not.

Girl…

"Are you talking about Corinna?" continued Theo.

Girl…

Theo shook her head. "We're getting nowhere fast with this."

"Just be patient." Taking over from her, Ness asked what

Jess thought was blocking her.

Dark...

"The dark? What does it feel like?"

Cold...

"Okay. Jess, we're here for you, we're sending light towards you, an abundance of it. Light is so much stronger than the darkness – it'll devour it. You have to believe that."

Cold...

Ness changed tactics. "Why have you stopped the clocks?"

Change...

"But change what? You have to help us understand."

Discover...

"Discover what?"

Girl... Change... Discover.

Her voice faded to a silence that was stark.

"She's gone," Theo muttered.

Ness nodded. "For now."

"Leaving us without answers, just more questions."

"That's the way it works sometimes, we know that. Jess is trying, she really is."

"*Trying's* the word," Theo replied, in no mood to be charitable.

Behind them the door opened, and Karen poked her head round. "Is everything okay? I just thought I'd check. Is it...you know...fixed?"

Yet again, they had to tell a client no, it wasn't fixed, not yet. Karen took the news well, considering, although Ness could see she was frustrated too. Most people just wanted a normal house; very few were happy to live alongside the dead, but, like before, they assured her Jess Biggs was not someone to cause mischief for the sake of it.

"It's just…she has a message to convey," Ness informed her, "and our task is to try and understand what that message is."

"And that's what you're having trouble with?"

"Clearly," Theo said, a little acerbically.

Ness quickly intervened. "We'll continue to work on what we've received so far. Get to the bottom of it."

Karen raised an eyebrow at that, and who could blame her?

They left her house, promising to return very soon, hopefully with the means to receive clearly the message Jess Biggs wanted to impart, thus encouraging her to move towards the light. How this would be achieved, they had no idea, the frustration of their situation almost at breaking point – for them, anyway. Karen, on the other hand, had accepted their explanation readily enough.

Outside, both checked their phones – there was a message from Ruby wanting to know if there'd been any developments and swearing she was going to cut loose from hospital, come and join them, that she couldn't just lay there going mad with worry.

Both had received exactly the same message, causing them to look helplessly at each other. Ruby had to stay away, her health and that of her baby depended on it, but what could they tell her? There were no real answers to anything.

"Let's leave off replying for now," suggested Theo, "and head to that tearoom."

"You can eat at a time like this?" Ness was appalled.

"Oh, for heaven's sake, what's the use in starving ourselves? We need to be in possession of all our faculties, and food is fuel, so we eat, we drink, we keep ourselves going and, whilst we're at it, we try and work out what the hell Jess Biggs was trying to tell us."

"What if the poor girl she's referring to—"

"You know we mustn't assume it's Corinna. I saw two girls, remember? But yes, it's…very unsettling, I agree. Come on, my poor legs won't tolerate much more of this standing around."

Leaving the car where it was, they wound their way through the lanes back to the high street, Ness's phone indicating more messages were coming through. Quickly, she checked. There was one from Presley and one from Lee. Checking Lee's first, he told her the meeting was over and he was on his way to Lindfield, and also, regarding the check on Witcher, there was nothing on him, not so much as a speeding ticket recorded – he was essentially 'squeaky clean'. Before replying, she switched to Presley's message. He was out and about on his motorbike, and he had the book Corinna had ordered with him – should he drop it off at Ness's house in Lewes?

"Hang on, Theo," she said, stopping just outside the tearoom. "You go inside and sit down. I'm going to make a quick call to Presley."

With Theo doing as instructed, Ness began the call, Presley answering straightaway. Clearly, he was still on his motorbike and on Bluetooth.

"Hey," he said, "thanks for replying so quickly. Are you in?"

"I'm not, actually. I'm in Lindfield with Theo."

"Lindfield?"

"Yes, we've been to Tom Witcher's house."

"And?"

Should she tell him what Theo had seen? Not knowing how he'd react or, indeed, how to even read what Theo had seen, she decided against it. "He wasn't in," she said instead.

"Will you still be in Lindfield for a while?"

"Yes, we're just about to go into a tearoom in the high street, perhaps wait a while and then try Witcher's house again, see if he's returned."

There was a slight pause before Presley replied. "Okay, I'll head there instead of Lewes."

"Really? Oh, I—"

"I want you to have a look at this book, Ness."

"Okay, I see. Have you looked through it already?"

"Yeah, 'course. This Witcher, how can I put it, he's a bit of an oddball. Look, this place you're going to, this tearoom, is it easy to find?"

"It's on Lindfield's high street and it's the only one, lots of bright pink cushions in the window, so yes, easy enough."

"I'm on my way."

Just as she finished, another call came through. It was Lee this time.

"Where are you? Still at Witcher's place?"

"Erm…no, no, we're at a tearoom in the high street."

"Stay there, then. I'll see you within the hour."

Chapter Fifteen

"I see what you mean," Ness said as she too scanned big chunks of text in the book Presley had brought with him. Theo was leaning in close to her, spectacles in place as she also read along. "I'm not sure about being an oddball, but there's another way to describe him, certainly."

"Obsessed," offered Theo. "The man's obsessed with Rayners Wood and all that's happened there." She wrinkled her nose. "And whoever read this book was clearly obsessed too, underlining things all over the place, probably taking notes. There you have it, you see, obsession breeds obsession, on and on it goes, around and around in circles." At this, she gave a shrug. "Or in this case perhaps triangles might be more apt, the silly buggers."

A bit nonplussed by what she'd said, Lee also shrugged, quickly taking a sip of tea from a china cup adorned with flowers before commenting. "You can't deny, though, it is interesting what's happened there. Three deaths. No obvious cause and no perpetrators ever found."

"Three deaths years apart, that may or may not be linked," Ness further commented.

"This is what's really interesting…" Presley, sitting beside

Lee and opposite Theo and Ness, took the book from Ness's hands and thumbed through it. "Here it is. Not sure if you've noticed this bit yet, but it's about a cult that uses Rayners Wood for their rituals, according to Witcher, anyway. He says he *demanded* a meeting with them, threatening to expose them if they didn't."

Looking at the text rather than at them, he started to read: "'I'd written extensively about the cult in articles online, repeating my desire to meet with them. I wanted, amongst other things, to find out if they'd had anything to do with the deaths that had taken place there and with the disappearances of so many dogs. What did they use those poor, unfortunate animals for? As sacrifices? It took many, many months, with me repeatedly posting the same thing, that I wanted to meet, that it was *essential* for us to meet, until I eventually received a reply from someone who claimed to be a cult member. That person agreed to meet with me, in the woods, at night, in a clearing that lies towards the centre of them. I was to come alone, and I was to swear I wouldn't look upon their face, that if I did, it would be to my detriment. A clear threat if ever there was one!'"

"Excuse me." A stout woman, with dyed yellow hair and a pinafore also adorned with tiny flowers, came over from the counter to stand at their table. "Fancy another pot of tea?"

Ness guessed they were all feeling a bit awash with tea by this time – this next round would make it their third – but they couldn't keep sitting without ordering, and so all four duly nodded, and the woman retreated, but not before Theo got in an order for a slice of Victoria sponge cake as well. Clearly regarding Ness's gaze as reproachful, she muttered, "Fuel."

"So, what happened?" Ness asked Presley. "Did Witcher go ahead and meet the cult member?"

"Yeah. Shall I read some more?"

Ness agreed, as did Theo, but Lee leant forward, said to carry on but also keep his voice down. Despite there being people at a few other tables, it had grown quiet in the tearoom, the air expectant, almost, not really the sort of place to discuss a satanic ritual or two.

"Look, I'll tell you what. That lady hasn't started on the teas yet," Lee decided. "Why don't we split, pay up and head to the Bent Arms just up the road. It's bound to be busier in there, noisier. We can carry on without being heard. Plus, I could murder a cold pint."

They all agreed, Theo lamenting the loss of her cake all the while.

The Bent Arms – a former coaching stop, as Corinna had previously informed Ness – certainly looked ancient inside, with its low ceiling supported by gnarled beams. A round of soft drinks was purchased, Lee knowing full well he couldn't have a pint if he was driving, and the four retired to a cosy corner where there was no risk of being overheard. Before he continued to quote from the book, Presley sank half the contents of his glass.

"'It was a chilly September night'..."

Lee laughed. "Sounds like a ghost story around the open fire."

Ness shushed him and reminded him they were trying to find Corinna. As Presley repeated the opening sentence, Lee looked sheepish.

"'It was a chilly September night when I headed to Rayners Wood, alone as was agreed, the moon and whatever stars there were in the sky covered entirely by clouds, the darkness as I entered the woods far denser than it had ever been before, as if it was impenetrable'—"

"Ooh, loves a bit of drama, doesn't he?" Theo interrupted, a look of complete derision on her face. In fairness to her, Ness could only agree, signalling for Presley to continue.

"'The clearing that had been mentioned is a space I know well. A truly resplendent and ancient oak tree lies at the heart of it. Surrounding the clearing is a ring of less majestic trees that, to my mind, form something a barrier. The oak tree is significant; it's a place where I believe the cult meets and where rituals are conducted, today as well as historically, and heaven help you if you stumble upon them whilst in the throes. All hell will break loose.'"

"There he goes again," Theo muttered but more to herself this time, "with his purple prose."

Presley drank the rest of his lime and soda before returning to the book, Lee's eyes, Ness noticed, agog. "'I reached the clearing, the only guiding light I had courtesy of a small torch I'd brought with me, which I now switched off, again as agreed, to wait there in absolute darkness. There wasn't a sound to mark the night; it was perfectly still, perfectly silent, and remained that way for what seemed like an age. Inside, I could feel the first stirrings of anger as well as frustration. Was anyone going to show up? Had I been duped? Made a fool of? The group that met here were indeed a cult, as I had called them many times before, a cult of cowards! If I'd been duped, the lambasting I would give them! They were a secret organisation, but I had a following too. I could do damage to them and their reputation, and they knew that. They knew also that I was working on finding evidence to connect them with the deaths that had occurred in these woodlands over the years, deaths with nothing but mystery attached to them.

"'I continued to stand there. Was not one of them willing to meet me, a lone man, and hear what I had to say, provide at least some answers to my questions? A cult of cowards, as I said. I walked away, my boots crunching against twigs and bracken. No need for my torch now. I knew these paths, I'd walked them enough times, plus my mood suited the night. It was as dark.'"

Still Lee's eyes were on stalks as Presley's smooth voice continued to recite. Theo, however, was fidgeting.

"Bored, dear girl," she whispered to Ness. "This is utter tripe."

She'd kept her voice low, but Presley heard her all the same. "If you want me to stop—"

"Don't you dare!" Lee instructed. "Get to the end of the chapter at least."

Ness smiled. Dear Lee, in his mid-fifties like her, was a well-constructed man, not overly tall but solidly built, with broad shoulders and dark hair kept short. His face could be described as craggy, but in it sat a pair of eyes almost navy in colour. Although a down-to-earth man, he had a great respect for all things spiritual and, clearly, a fondness for purple prose, as Theo had called it. Presley did as he asked, mentioning there wasn't much more to go.

"'Just as I was about to leave the clearing, I stopped. I'd heard a sound, the crunch of twigs again, this time not made by my own feet. I swung around. "Who's there?" I shouted. "Identify yourself! You've shown up at last, have you, or have you been there all along? Watching me? Thinking I'd quake with terror at the prospect of meeting you. If so, you're wrong. I'm not frightened of you at all." There was silence, but only for a heartbeat. Eventually someone spoke, a voice that floated towards me. I couldn't tell where from, what trees there were guarding the man as if colluding with him. He spoke – he threatened me, basically – and then he fled. His last words ringing in my ears.'"

Presley paused. For dramatic effect? wondered Ness.

Lee looked fit to thump him. "Come on! What were his last words?"

At last Presley obliged. "'If you value your life, keep away,'" he answered before adding, "Someone's underlined that bit as well."

* * *

With all glasses drained, the four of them sat back in their chairs in the corner of the pub, digesting what they'd recently learnt. Ness then pointed out the obvious, to Theo, at least.

"Those words – 'If you value your life, keep away' – that's what the man said to us outside Low Cottage."

"What man?" said Presley.

Ness shrugged. "I don't know, a stranger. The first time we went to Low Cottage, the three of us, Corinna, Theo and I, we stopped outside it because…because I had a feeling about it, compounded, perhaps, by what Jess Biggs from the Bows' house had just said about another house, basically a bad house, a house where things had happened in the past, dreadful things. Whilst we were standing there the pavement, looking at it, a man came up to us and asked us what we were doing. He told us the cottage was available for rent, and when we said we might be interested in it, he replied, 'If you value your lives, keep away.'"

"A threat?" said Presley.

"Possibly," Theo answered.

"Or a warning?" suggested Lee.

"Possibly again," replied Theo. She held out her hand for Presley to hand over the book. All sat patiently as she leafed through it, except Lee, who asked the name of the publisher. Theo duly checked the inside cover and the acknowledgements. "Ah, here we go. He says he published the book himself on Amazon 'for the benefit of other concerned individuals'."

Lee nodded. "Or because an established publisher might shy away from such matters?"

"Maybe," Theo agreed, returning to the section she was studying before declaring, "Got it!"

"Got what?" asked Ness, frowning.

"The name of the cult."

"And?"

"The Cult of Badb."

"What?" Lee was also frowning.

"*Badb*?" repeated Presley. "There's no such word, is there?"

"There is." Theo was performing the glamour, sitting up straight, shoulders back, daring anyone to contradict her. "In Irish mythology, Badb refers to a war goddess, the Morrigan, who's rather fond of adopting the form of a crow, hence another handle she goes by is Badb Catha, 'battle crow'."

Presley was impressed. "How'd you know all this?"

Theo tapped the side of her head. "I've lived a long time,

my darling, and knowledge like this builds up. The Morrigan is associated with war and fate, with the foretelling of doom. She's able to strike fear into the hearts of her enemies, and quite effortlessly too."

"So, this Morrigan malarkey," Presley continued, "is this a female cult or something?"

Ness shook her head. "Not necessarily. A lot of cults name themselves after subjects steeped in myth and legend, just as the Morrigan is." She rolled her eyes. "It's on-trend."

Theo nodded. "And let's not forget that Witcher reports it was a man that spoke to him."

"And that was all he said?" Lee checked.

"According to what's written in the book," Presley replied.

"You know, this Witcher person," Theo added, "seems to be baiting the cult."

"Both online and in his book," Ness said.

"Not really the sort of thing you want to do with a satanic cult, really, is it?" murmured Lee.

"Not if it's a genuine one, no," said Theo, "because if it is genuine, then they're not to be taken lightly. What they do, these people, is draw upon energy, negative energy, and then they spread it. And, as we're all aware, negativity can be very powerful; it incites fear in people, and when fear gets a grip, it can wipe out common sense entirely."

Again, they all agreed.

"Lee, when you ran a check on Tom Witcher, did you get a prior address for him?"

"Uh-huh. He was last registered at an address in Brighton."

"We might need to pay a visit there too, as well as Low

Cottage."

"It does look as if we need to talk to him. By *we*, I mean the police."

"Oh, it's vital," Theo said, before deciding to inform Lee and Presley what she'd seen at Low Cottage, a girl reaching out, one who'd briefly resembled Corinna.

Presley gripped the edge of the table. "What the fuck? What's that supposed to mean?"

"We've no idea," confessed Ness, still withholding what had happened at the Bows' house, or what it suggested, at any rate. It seemed Theo agreed, as she glanced at Ness and nodded, a slight gesture that only she caught. Neither of them wanted to cause Presley more distress than he was already feeling. She reached across the table to squeeze his arm. "We want to go back to Low Cottage today. With everything we've found out about Witcher and what's been seen and experienced at Low Cottage too, we need to get in there." Turning her head towards Lee, she added, "Even if he hasn't returned there yet."

Lee sighed.

Presley, on the other hand, was as keen as mustard. "So we bust the mystery man?"

"Hang on, look," Lee said, holding up his hands to placate Presley. "Tom Witcher is a line of enquiry, I agree, but that's all. There's no crime in simply being mysterious."

He was right, causing Ness to rein in her eagerness too. Could she really complain if someone else strove to protect their identity? It was wise of Witcher to do so, considering he'd made a career out of provoking the occult. There could be serious repercussions to that, as Theo intimated, people deeply entrenched in that lifestyle believing the hype, in the power that demons invested in them, considering themselves above the law, capable of anything, murder included.

Even so, they couldn't just sit around. Ness was about to say that when Theo spoke again.

"You know, the name Low Cottage has always bothered me."

Ness frowned. "Why?"

"Because I don't think it's the correct name. Not amongst certain circles."

"Certain circles?" Clearly, Presley was also confused.

"The kind we've been talking about, dear boy, satanic." How blithely she pronounced that word, and Ness admired her for it, for refusing to entertain fear in the slightest.

"Still got no idea what you're talking about," Lee admitted.

Theo leaned forward. "Then let me enlighten you before we wend our less-than-merry way. As we know, cults use all kinds of mythological beasts and brethren to name themselves. We also know Low Cottage is a very dubious place, that it sits at the low point of a triangle, the Bows' house being at the top at one end, Old Place and the hunting lodge at the other. Of them all, Low Cottage is the worst, the hunting lodge being a tad dubious as well but not really in the same league, home in the past to dabblers rather than those who threw themselves into demon worship in a wholehearted manner." She paused. "Or should I say a blackhearted manner, that'd be more apt, don't you think? Anyway, I digress.

"In contrast, the Bows' house is a place of happiness and love, the home of a very happy family indeed. But it's connected to the other two nonetheless, I tend to think by default, and maybe because of that connection, Jess Biggs was more aware of what went on at both addresses, Low Cottage in particular, which I'm now absolutely sure is the house where dreadful things happened. There *is* something about that house, undeniably, and Jess has hung around, for a long time, in fact, wanting to tell someone exactly what it is, trying to attract attention by tampering with clocks. Unfortunately for her and for us, that message is not easy to convey, as if there's an energy preventing her from talking in anything other than snatches. Are you all with me so far?"

Ness was, but she couldn't vouch for Lee and Presley, both of whom were frowning.

"Good," continued Theo, oblivious. "Before Corinna went missing, she did some research on Low Cottage. We know how often it's changed hands in recent times, people initially attracted to the idea of a quintessential country residence but actually finding it impossible to live in. Corinna herself had a terrible reaction whilst there, and you felt unsettled too, didn't you, Ness?"

"Yes, in certain rooms especially."

"The master bedroom and the study?"

Ness nodded.

"There's also a gap in its history, dating from sometime in the sixties to the early eighties."

"That's right, from 1962 it all gets a bit sketchy," Ness elaborated.

"Lord knows what went on there during that time"— Theo raised an eyebrow—"especially in the swinging sixties, a bit of a wild time for all of us, to be fair." She smirked as she said this but quickly grew serious. "Records from back then, before the widespread use of computers, are often incomplete, and so it's the case with Low Cottage. Convenient, really, as I've no doubt there's a history there that prefers to go undetected, a history we may be forced to find out."

"Forced?" Presley queried. "Odd choice of word."

"Not really," Theo denied. "You see, when I say it's the name of the cottage that's been annoying me, I've worked out why. I think it's an anagram."

"An anagram?" Lee murmured, and even Ness was surprised.

"Yes, rather a simple one. Rearrange the word *low* and there you have it: *owl.*"

"Owl Cottage?" Ness said, quickly sitting up straight and testing it on her tongue, agreeing with Theo that, yes, it felt...*exactly* right.

"Sorry for being thick, but I'm really not getting this," Presley once more admitted.

"You will in a moment," Theo assured him. "When I was saying earlier that cults often adopt the names of mythological creatures and brethren, well, an owl is no exception."

"But it's an actual creature," he argued.

"It is, both actual *and* mythological," she replied. "And as much as I love them, especially the snowy variety, they're also associated with death, sorcery and the dark underside of life."

Ness, aware that her mouth had fallen open, not least because she'd failed to make this connection, quickly closed it as Theo continued talking.

"The Bible goes one step further. In Leviticus it declares the owl to be an *unclean* bird, and, as such, it's the perfect symbol for a cult or secret society. It's my opinion that Low

Cottage was built for a purpose, as a meeting place for occult members to carry out their dastardly deeds and, I'll wager"— she turned to Ness—"the lady who lived there for the longest span of time?"

"Phyllida Hylands," Ness answered.

"That's it, Phyllida Hylands. I'll wager Corinna's hunch was right and she was the one who commissioned it to be built. If so, and if she was involved in the Cult of Badb, she might even have been at the head of it, the Morrigan made flesh, so to speak, with an entourage of devoted disciples. From the eighties onwards, however, for whatever reasons, the cottage then fell into the hands of the uninitiated. By then, however, all damage was done, and the house was tainted."

"Christ," Lee exclaimed. "It's all a bit far-fetched, isn't it?"

"Not in the least," Theo contradicted. "And as I say, on some level, Corinna was aware of it all, hence her talk of triangles and triangles within triangles. God, that girl's senses are developing and fast! In order to find out what's happened to her, it's imperative we discover how it's linked."

"You know, Theo," Ness said, "as much as it galls me to say it, you're a bloody genius."

Before there could be any reply to that, smug or otherwise, Presley stood up with so much force the glasses on the table in front of him rattled slightly.

"We need to go to Low Cottage right now," he said, his dark eyes flashing. "And if this Witcher bloke isn't in, then I'm sorry, Lee, whether it's a crime or not, I'm knocking the fucking door down!"

Chapter Sixteen

"STILL no response."

Lee had rapped on the door long and hard, Tom Witcher proving as elusive as ever.

"You know," said Ness, "considering he wrote the same words as the man we met here said, that threat or warning or whatever it was, I'm beginning to think they're one and the same."

"Do you think Witcher's gone missing too?" Presley's dark eyes were full of agitation.

"Let's not jump to conclusions." Lee had issued a warning of his own but not one that held any weight with the rest of them. Sensing this well enough, he dug out his mobile.

"What are you doing?" asked Ness.

"It's abundantly clear we need to talk to Tom Witcher concerning Corinna and get an idea what he looks like too. The case officer can possibly get that from the Passport Office or the DVLA, but, Ness, that doesn't mean it'll be shared with you or even me, for a whole host of legal reasons. What I can do, though, is dispatch a couple of officers round to his Brighton address."

"But he rents this cottage," Presley pointed out.

"Doesn't mean he doesn't have a second home," Lee reasoned. "Look, we give it a go. It might be he doesn't have a connection to the Brighton address anymore. We'll have to see."

"What about this house?" Presley said, taking a deep breath and squaring his shoulders. "Corinna could be in there, imprisoned. And that's why he's not answering his door."

As she'd done in the pub, Ness reached out a calming hand. "If she was in there, she'd have let us know somehow. Her…energy wouldn't be faint; it would be strong."

Whilst Lee stepped aside to make his phone call, Theo elaborated on Ness's words. "It's not in any doubt anymore, not in our minds, at least, that this house and/or Tom Witcher is connected with Corinna's disappearance in some way."

"Then we have to get in there—"

"We will," she assured him. "We are. As soon as Lee's off the phone."

A few minutes later, Lee was back, his request having been acted upon.

"We've got to get in there," Presley reiterated, again looking for all the world as if he was going to break down the door to Low Cottage in spite of how sturdy it looked.

Lee was agitated about the situation and began to pace. Gradually he came to a halt, his gaze on Theo. "Earlier, you said you saw Corinna inside Low Cottage."

"I thought I saw a figure that resembled Corinna but not necessarily a physical—"

"I'll ask you again. Are you officially telling me, a police officer, that you saw Corinna, the missing person, inside this house?"

Clearly, Theo now realised what she was being asked. "Yes," she answered. "I did."

He approached the front door again and resumed knocking on it, announcing very clearly it was the police at the door and to open up. As quickly as he'd begun, he stopped, telling them to follow him as he took off round the path to the back of the house.

"Where are we going?" Ness asked him.

"If we're going to break in, kitchen doors are usually more amenable."

She'd expected this – for them to break in if necessary – but even so, Ness couldn't help but inhale at the prospect, glancing at Theo as Presley caught up with Lee.

Ramp up the protection, Ness.

She caught Theo's thought clearly enough.

I am. I don't need to be told.

This house, whilst maybe not as bad as Blakemort, was certainly what its true name suggested: *unclean.* They needed to maximise their protection, surrounding Lee and Presley in light as well. Going into Low Cottage a second time was a far from enticing thought. If she were honest, Ness wanted to turn tail and get the hell out of there, take heed of Ruby's advice to Corinna and crack on with more normal cases, leave the others well alone.

Not an option.

Again, Theo had read Ness's mind.

Ness glared at her. *I don't need to be told that either!*

The sound of breaking glass drew her attention. Lee had covered his arm in the light jacket he'd brought with him and, with his elbow, broken a pane of frosted glass in the kitchen door. His hand then reaching through the cracked pane, he managed to unlock the door, holding it open before addressing them all in a serious manner.

"I'm advising you all that you are to stay outside this property. This is a police matter, and you are not permitted to enter, as it's not considered safe for you to do so. I trust you understand this? I also know that alone, I'm unable to stop you, but there may be consequences if you go against what I'm asking. I'll have backup here when I call it in. And I *will* need to call it in…eventually."

Despite how trepidatious she felt, Ness smiled. The arrangement she had with Lee might be somewhat relaxed, but lately, as recently as the last couple of days, in fact, it was becoming something more. She trusted him, and because of that and their mutual respect for each other, their bond was intensifying. Something that both pleased and frightened her. But also something not to be contemplated, not right now, standing outside the kitchen of Low Cottage.

As they all entered, Lee resigned to the inevitable, Ness gazed around her. She'd thought it earlier, and she thought it again: if Witcher had moved in, it didn't look like it. The place was exactly as it had been before, apart from one thing.

With Lee having ventured deeper into the house to check for signs of Corinna, Ness crossed over to the sink and saw two mugs placed deep within it, mugs that had been recently used. Psychometry – the ability to handle objects and gain an insight into their history – was a bit hit-and-miss with her. Even so, and despite knowing that this was a crime scene and she shouldn't touch anything, she couldn't resist picking up first one mug and then the other, Theo drawing closer, picking up the one Ness had put down and trying to read the object too.

"One of these belonged to Corinna," Ness said. "I'm sure of it."

"Yes, but again, if so, her energy is weak. It's this one," Theo said, holding up the mug she had in her hand. "*Why* is it weak? That's what I want to know."

"She didn't feel threatened, I think that's why."

The relief on Presley's face as Ness answered was obvious; it was also short-lived. Whether Corinna had felt threatened or not whilst here didn't cancel out that she was missing. Something had happened to her, something against her will. Theo had seen her reaching out, imploring...

Carefully returning the mug to the sink, Theo addressed Ness. "Want to lead the way?"

The remaining two followed Ness as she led them through the kitchen door and into the hallway, which in turn led to several different rooms, a confusing jumble, nothing orderly about the layout at all, often taking surprising twists and turns. It was disorderly and, in nature, unclean. Why would Tom Witcher want to live here? Was it a way of riling the Cult of Badb some more?

"Hang on a moment," Theo said as they entered not the study but a living room, the main one, Ness presumed, as it was a large room complete with an open fireplace. The entire cottage had a smell about it, but in certain rooms it was more prevalent, this being one of them – musty and unpleasant, the stench of all things old. Although there was no light fitting overhead, there were sconces on the wall, what light they gave out – Presley had already flipped the switch – scant.

Theo had closed her eyes and inclined her head.

"What is it?" Ness asked, curious.

"This room was definitely a gathering place," she replied. "I get a sense of people milling about in here, and then…and then…standing still, in a circle, their hands linked. Oh, here we go, yes, yes, it's as we imagined – they're calling upon dark energy, trying to summon something from the depths, the usual bloody demon worshippers. They're all a little tedious, really, aren't they?"

Lee was back, having checked the house, clearly with nothing to report. "You're sensing something?" he asked.

"Absolutely," said Theo. "Phyllida Hylands, I think. A small woman, petite. Can't see any detail, it's just an impression. Small but powerful. A lady who knew about the glamour."

"The glamour?" Presley queried.

"Think of it as adopting a no-nonsense demeanour, in her case fuelled by sheer arrogance."

"Do you want us to tune in too?" Ness checked.

Theo nodded. "Let's see if we can get more of a sense of this lady, a term I use in the loosest sense."

With Ness ushering them into a circle, they joined hands.

"I hate to point this out," Lee began, "but as Ness knows, I don't have a psychic bone in my body."

"Doesn't matter," Theo told him. "It's your energy we want, yours and Presley's, *good* energy. It'll help to bolster our own."

She then closed her eyes, and Ness duly followed, imagining the other two doing the same.

"Phyllida, love," Theo said, no affection in her voice but, rather, uncharacteristic sarcasm, "what were you and your deluded cohorts guilty of here? Do any of you remain? Are you spending the afterlife counting the errors of your ways?

Come on, what happened? There's something wrong with Owl Cottage. What is it?" It was no error she used the cottage's true name, doing a little baiting of her own.

Only a brief span of time passed before she spoke again. "Gatherings. Yes, we – for want of a better word – have gathered that. A group of you from hereabouts, not just the village of Lindfield but the villages surrounding it too, London, even, and further afield. Such ambition! Amongst a fair few of you, anyway. Such greed! The quest for money and power really does corrupt a man, and a woman too, of course. Gatherings such as those at the hunting lodge—"

"Ah, the hunting lodge," Ness interrupted, also beginning to get a sense of times past.

"Go on," encouraged Theo. "Tell us what you're seeing."

The atmosphere had become denser. If she opened her eyes, Ness guessed it'd be darker in the room too and nothing to do with the ineffectiveness of the wall sconces. She took a deep breath and exhaled slowly. "I'm seeing a group break away from the gatherings that took place at the hunting lodge. As you say, Theo, it was a far more ambitious group."

"The kind that won't stop at anything?" Lee questioned.

"Bastards!" breathed Presley.

"Ness?" questioned Theo. "Anything more?"

"This place was built by one of those people, a friend of Hylands'? An admirer? And its location was no coincidence either, Jess Biggs' house the only blight, although…hang on. There was another house there before Jess's, a modest one. I don't know who it belonged to. I want to say a witch, but…I hate that term; it's unfair, derogatory. A woman, though, one who was…scorned in her time, a woman that both Hylands and the architect knew of, who didn't scorn but admired her."

"I thought Jess Biggs' house was supposed to be a good place?" queried Presley.

"It was. It replaced whatever was there, and Jess, who was clearly a good woman, a *wise* woman – the antithesis of the one before – brought the light back, whether determinedly or unwittingly, I can't tell. More likely the latter. A blight, as I say, but one that nobody took seriously. Biggs wasn't seen as a threat, not whilst she lived, anyway. In death, it's perhaps a different story. Her house is neutral nowadays. Old Place and the hunting lodge are also neutral. But no light, metaphorically speaking, has ever been able to penetrate Low Cottage; here the darkness remains. The people that contaminated this place, they walked amongst others, they passed the time of day with them, were regarded as friends, invited into other people's houses to eat and to drink with them. No one suspected a thing."

"In that respect, nothing changes," Theo mused, echoing what Jess Biggs had said.

Ness's insight was fading. "Are you able to sense anything more, Theo?"

"No, as with you, the connection's gone. Time to move to the hotspots."

"The hotspots?" repeated Lee.

Ness opened her eyes and loosened her grip on Presley and Lee, causing them to do the same. "She means the master bedroom and the study."

Theo nodded. "Let's head upstairs first, might as well save the worst 'til last."

"The master bedroom?" Lee repeated. "Phyllida's bedroom?"

"More than likely," Ness replied. "Although don't worry, I don't think she went as far as cutting the necks of young virgins and drinking their blood."

"Don't you?" Theo commented as she brushed past her, making her way out of the living room and to an oak-carved staircase. "I wouldn't be so sure."

Just like before, Ness felt nauseous as she reached the top landing, the air stifling. She could feel sweat envelop her, managing to wipe it from her forehead, at least. Although the bedrooms were undoubtedly beautiful to look at, some of them with low oak beams and oak panelling, none had an enticing air about them, the most repellent being the master bedroom.

"My, oh my," Theo commented. "Phyllida, old gal, you really did have a questionable appetite."

"She was a widow when she moved here," Ness told Lee and Presley. "Lived here with staff only. I get the impression she was…restrained before her husband's death, or kept restrained. When he passed, leaving her well off, she was free to be whomever she wanted."

"A mistress of the dark," Theo said, derision evident in her voice still. "She took it to the nth degree, didn't she? Walked a long, long way down a dark, dark path. She and so many others like her, all vying to be the ultimate baddie, trying to prove it to themselves as well as to others. Ugh! What's taken place in this bedroom, the sheer depravity of it, not just Phyllida but after Phyllida too, many years after her. You'd have to be very dense not to sense it."

Lee looked at his shoes, whilst Presley examined his hands.

"Oh, boys, surely to God you can sense it!" thundered Theo. She moved across to the far wall, various lumps and bumps making it look like the surface of the moon, and, raising a fist, gave it a good thump. "These walls have seen it all," she declared. "They soak up everything." She faltered for a moment, her expression darkening further. "They…incubate."

Presley's expression changed from sheepish to stricken. "What the hell has Corinna got herself involved with? This is bad, man, fucking bad."

Unable to comfort him, not on this occasion, Ness turned on her heel, leaving behind the master bedroom and the imprint of whatever antics had gone on in there. "It's time we went to the study," she said, having to brace herself, knowing that Theo would be doing so too.

God, every fibre of her being railed against returning there, but there was to be no escape, the other three duly following her. Once fully in the room, Presley pushed the door closed, effectively trapping them further. Ness had to swallow furiously; the smell in here, the stink, was worse than ever.

"Ness—"

"Can you smell it, Lee?"

He shrugged. "There is a smell, but…it's not having the same effect on me as it is on you."

"This room," she said, "it's the worst one in this entire cottage. It's…" Without saying another word, she went over to the corner Theo had seen Corinna reaching out from, where she herself had seen the wall bulging. "Merciless."

Lee came up behind her. "Ness, what are you talking about—"

Swivelling on her feet, she faced him. "This house needs to come down!"

"What? I don't understand—"

"This house needs to come down. This...wall"—as Theo had done upstairs, she banged on it—"needs tearing down. We have to make that happen, Lee! Somehow. Some way."

Theo also stepped forward. "Take a deep breath, Ness. Tell me what you're sensing."

"It needs to come down!" Christ, she was becoming hysterical, couldn't stop herself.

"Ness, listen to me, to my voice and my voice only," Theo continued, having reached out to hold both of Ness's arms. "Tell me calmly and rationally, what are you sensing?"

"A body." Ness swallowed as bile crept back up her throat. "Behind that wall is a body!"

Chapter Seventeen

IT wasn't Corinna's body. Ness had to repeat that several times over to Presley, who was also on the edge of losing his shit, actually going over to the wall and thumping it too, not once but several times, as if beneath his fury and frustration, it would cave in to reveal all.

"It's not Corinna!" Ness said again. "It's not her energy I'm sensing, and this wall isn't recent. Stop it, Presley, stop doing that. This has to be handled properly. I think I'm right when I say there's a body there. A girl."

Lee had gone over to stop Presley, having to work hard to secure his arms by his side, although he spoke gently enough. "Ness is right. *If* there's a body behind that wall"—and Ness heard the doubt in his voice as he said it—"then we have to go about this in the right way, the *only* way. Get a team in, forensics, find out who she is." He paused. "How long she's been here."

"Oh God." Feeling her legs give way beneath her, Ness had to reach out to hold on to the back of a chair, another wave of nausea washing over her.

Theo was beside her in an instant. "What is it, Ness? What's happening now?"

Ness closed her eyes briefly and took a few deep breaths. "Theo, are you sensing anything?"

"Not as intensely as you are, sweetheart, not in here. I know this is hard, but go with it. We need as much information as we can to find out what we're up against."

Words began to form in Ness's mind, nothing to do with Theo and definitely not her own. They belonged to Jess Biggs. *Girl. Dark. Cold. Change. Discover. Girl. Dark. Cold.*

"Damn!" she said, her head hanging low as tears filled her eyes.

"Ness?" Now Lee concerned himself with her, not Presley.

"Why does it always have to be dark and cold? Why? And these girls trapped there! My own sister…"

Pulling the chair out, she sat on it, her hands reaching up to cover her face as her body shuddered. When Theo had said upstairs in the master bedroom that these thick walls soaked up things, they incubated, Ness hadn't realised just how close to the mark she was.

Lee was also by her side, kneeling whilst Theo continued to stand, Presley quiet now, no doubt stunned further by the scene unfolding in front of him.

"Hey, Ness, come on." Lee did his utmost to soothe her, his arm going around her back, his familiar scent overriding the other smell that persisted here, affording a moment of comfort when she felt so bleak. "We'll get to the bottom of this, I—"

"Don't do it," she warned. "Don't make promises you can't keep!"

"Ness—"

"I've made promises, so many of them. Good promises, bad promises, useless promises." Her heart felt like pulp instead of something solid. "In the end they're all bloody useless!"

There was no stopping the tears; everyone seemed to realise that, not just Ness. It was a while before she was able to speak again. "Lee, I've worked with the police before—"

"Yes, yes, I know that."

"There must be some in the Force that still remember me. They and you need to believe me when I say this house, if not torn down, needs to be...examined."

"I do believe you. And I'll do everything in my power to make that happen. It's just...you know what it's like, the procedures that have to be followed. This isn't even my case."

"There's no time to waste!"

"But if the girl's already dead..." His voice trailed off, although perhaps what was left unsaid was loudest of all. *This* girl, the one behind the wall, was dead, but what about another girl, Corinna? It was her death they needed to prevent.

"Corinna's alive," Ness continued. "She's alive, but she's somewhere cold, somewhere dark, somewhere..." Ness also came to a halt, remembering again Corinna's vision of running from something, terrified. She also thought of the mugs in the sink – the faintest residue of their lost friend clinging to one of them.

Ness gently pushed Lee away from her and stood up, heading to the kitchen, taking a wrong turn and cursing, then having to double back and take another. Once there, she crossed over to the sink and picked up the mug that Corinna had drunk from, sniffed at it again.

"This held tea in it," she said. "Corinna doesn't do dairy; she drinks hers black."

"And?" Lee questioned.

"It doesn't smell right. It smells…bitter."

"Bitter?" Presley questioned, but realisation dawned on Theo's face.

"You think she was drugged?"

Ness nodded, placing the mug back down before picking up the other one and sniffing that too. "This one doesn't really have that smell, or, I don't know, maybe just a hint of it. It could be why Corinna's residue is faint, because she's been drugged. I've no idea what with or to what extent, but, Lee, forensics need to test this. If I'm right, she needs to be elevated to high risk."

About to reply, Lee's phone rang. He retrieved it from his pocket whilst pointing to the mug in Ness's hands. "If that's true, then you need to put it down," he said before excusing himself.

"What are we going to do next?" Presley asked. "I can't just go home, to…emptiness!"

Before either Theo or Ness could think of an answer, a way to calm him, Lee returned. "That was one of my officers," he said. "They've been over to Witcher's Brighton address."

"And?" said Theo.

"There's no sign of Witcher there either. It's a studio in an old Victorian building, one of several. My officers knocked on doors and asked neighbours if any had seen him recently. He does come and go regularly, as you'd expect, but no, nobody's seen him for a while."

"Since when, exactly?" Ness enquired.

"Since around Friday. The same day Corinna went missing. My officers were also able to check with his landlord as to whether his tenancy has ended. It hasn't. The studio might be tiny, but he's obviously got money."

"Either that or he'd been saving up for an opportunity with Low Cottage to present itself," suggested Ness. "Biding his time. Waiting."

There was a brief silence before Presley, still agitated, spoke again. "What's our next move?"

Ness's reply was instant. "Rayners Wood."

"What's your reasoning, Ness?" Theo queried.

"We know from his book and from Corinna that Witcher's obsessed with Rayners Wood and what he thinks goes on there. Corinna had also developed quite an interest in the woods, one that had come out of nowhere. We also know that instead of going to The Keep, she came here, precisely because she was so interested. And then she just…disappeared. Corinna and Witcher went to the woods, I'm sure of it. In fact…" She shifted her body sideways to another spot and closed her eyes for a moment. "This is where I think Witcher stood, when he asked her to accompany him to the woods, whatever she'd been given making her more compliant, perhaps – there was something that made her agree, anyway. And we have to go there too. Now."

* * *

"'The woods are lovely, dark and deep,
   But I have promises to keep,
   And miles to go before I sleep,
   And miles to go before I sleep.'"

183

Ness shot Theo a look as she softly recited the words of a poem by Robert Frost, 'Stopping by Woods on a Snowy Evening', a beautiful poem – if it weren't for the bit about promises.

They'd taken Lee's car, and he was driving, Presley beside him, Theo and Ness in the back. Theo knew what the look Ness had bestowed on her meant and reached out to pat at her hand.

"Darling, you've failed nobody. Don't think that, please."

That she was using sentiments such as *darling* and *sweetheart*, the kind she normally reserved for Ruby and Corinna, wasn't lost on Ness, and quite suddenly she felt like a child again, but one graced with a loving parent rather than one who despised her.

"We're going to find Corinna," Theo continued, a soft smile on her face. "Okay?"

Words failed Ness, and so she simply nodded.

"And we must remember not to assume anything either," continued Theo.

"What do you mean?"

"There's a chance that Witcher may be a victim in all this too."

Presley turned around from the front seat. "What about the mug, though? You said only one smelt strange."

"That's right, but nothing's conclusive at this point. It's best we keep an open mind."

Lee's colleagues had now been asked to file a missing persons report on Tom Witcher too, naming him, despite what Theo had said, as the main person of interest in Corinna Greer's disappearance, and asking for search warrants to be obtained for both the Brighton flat and the Lindfield house.

He'd also informed Theo, Ness and Presley about the official position regarding Low Cottage.

"I've called it in, reported a possible sighting of Corinna at the property. Theo, you'll be required to make a statement as such. The house will be made secure and the agent and owners notified. We'll also get forensics on the mug. We need to talk with the owners to see if they'll cooperate with a non-destructive endoscopic investigation of the wall cavity, although I haven't got a clue how we can explain our suspicions. For once I'm glad I'm not the case officer for this. I've already tried to call Warrington because I wondered if we could get a description of Witcher that way. Couldn't get through to him, so I called his boss and spoke to him."

"And?" said Ness.

"He's on a lads weekend in Amsterdam, either out of range or too stoned to answer messages. Look, Ness, don't expect much of this to kick in until tomorrow, okay? But it *will* kick in. We are now officially interested in Witcher."

Tomorrow, though, seemed so far away.

There was silence now in the car as they continued to travel, except for Presley giving instructions as to where Rayners Wood actually was – not far now, just a few miles – the anxiety in Ness increasing as they drew closer. She sincerely hoped this wasn't a fool's errand they were on, a waste of time. But then again, what else would they be doing in their quest to find Corinna? What other avenues needed to be explored? The victims of Rayners Wood came to mind – the first having been found in the 1970s, almost fifty years ago. Would her kin still be alive? The woman's parents, maybe? The third and last death was in 2001, Samantha Lawrence. It was highly likely her parents or somebody related to her would still be alive, their details easily enough obtained via Lee. Possibly Tom Witcher's kin too. That was definitely another avenue that needed walking down. *Every* avenue did – in the hope it'd lead to Corinna.

"Here we go," Presley said. "Park where you can, looks like we walk from here."

Lee did as he was asked, and the four of them exited the car, both Ness and Theo craning their necks to see what lay ahead of them, trees in the distance interrupting a blue sky.

Rayners Wood was located right on the edge of a village called Rayner. As they'd driven through it, Lee had slowed the car down, all eyes searching for evidence of Corinna or a sighting of her car. Ness was tuning in, trying to get a feel for Corinna, Theo doing the same.

The houses they'd passed had been more cottage-like than anything, nothing particularly grand about any of them; certainly, there was no hunting lodge here as there was in Lindfield. None were similar to Low Cottage either, not in scale, anyway, although a few timber beams could be spotted here and there, signalling yet again how ancient Sussex villages were.

Was it possible that Corinna was being held captive in any of these houses, her car concealed in a garage somewhere? It was yet another line of investigation, with house-to-house calls having to be conducted at some point soon. Already, appeals on social media and the local press had been put out for anyone with information to come forward – so far no one had. All hospital admissions had been checked, locally as well as further afield, and CCTV footage was still being combed through. Corinna's mother had given police Corinna's laptop yesterday. Had they found any research on it yet concerning

Witcher and Rayners Wood? Or had all of that been conducted on her phone, which was missing alongside her?

"Ness, the police are doing everything they can. There's a clear line of enquiry now."

He was no mind reader, but it was obvious to Lee, to anyone, how anxious she was, how impatient. Corinna wasn't the only missing person in Sussex; the police had other cases to deal with too, but to her, Theo, Presley, and Ruby in her hospital bed, she was everything.

Theo had started to walk, her determined strides belying her age. Ness, Lee and Presley duly followed, the four of them making their way up a dirt track that had fields on either side of it. At the far end of one, a beautiful chestnut-coloured horse was drinking from a trough, and little wonder given the heat of the day, Ness glad they'd also furnished themselves with bottled water from a garage en route.

Although Theo had started off in such an impressive manner, she was now beginning to breathe heavily, and Ness could see her face was slick with sweat.

"Theo, take it easy—"

"I'm fine," Theo protested, causing Ness to hold back voicing any further concern. Instead, she opened her bottle of water and took a swig, hoping but failing to encourage Theo to do the same.

Quickly enough, the path veered to the left, the fields on either side replaced by an assortment of trees, their leafy branches reaching across the pathway and offering some respite from the sun at least, the temperature consequently dropping a degree or two. How big was this wood? Ness wondered. How easy was it to become lost within it?

As they ventured further, she took in every inch of

landscape, tried to commit it to memory as best she could. Would they come across any other walkers? So far there'd been no one. A coincidence? People would emerge later in the day, perhaps, when it was cooler. Either that or they were taking seriously the rumours that abounded about this stretch of land, the *facts* – the animals that had gone missing, the murders that had taken place – deciding to take their exercise elsewhere. This wood, this *renowned* wood, would only attract certain types: the ghoulish, the police and, of course, them.

The tracks ahead were clear enough, dividing into smaller tracks on occasion, which led into yet more greenery, the bluebells and wood anemones of spring having long since withered. In fact, there was very little in the way of wildflowers. Ness would have expected to see some harebells, perhaps, or cranesbill, offering a much-needed hint of colour; instead, it was all rather…drab, nothing verdant about them whatsoever. Woods where the atmosphere was heavy, and no birds called to one another.

It was silent. Deathly silent.

Lee stopped briefly to take a slug of water, wiping the sweat from his brow with his forearm whilst he was at it. "Needle and haystack come to mind," he muttered afterwards.

"Isn't every missing person case like that?" Ness replied, careful to keep her voice low.

"Some of them," he answered.

But not Corinna, please God, not her.

"Shit!"

Ness swung round to face Presley. He'd fallen to his knees, his hands splayed out before him.

188

"Are you okay?" she said, rushing over.

"Yeah, fine, tripped on a root, that's all."

Ness looked down at the ground, at the claw-like roots there, knotted and ancient things that bided their time before lashing out, to fell the unsuspecting...

Rein it in, Ness!

She would, she had to, not letting her imagination embellish an already awful situation.

Presley straightened himself up and dusted himself down. Checking again he was okay, Ness glanced at Theo, still worried about her. It might be cooler in the woods, but there was still very little air to draw on, and what there was felt far from fresh, as if whatever had played out here had drenched the atmosphere, trees able to soak it up every bit as effectively as bricks and mortar.

They were looking for a clearing – the supposed site of devil worship. They pressed forwards along the same path, deeper and deeper...

A groan from Theo brought them to a halt once more.

"Theo? What is it?" Ness asked, noting she was paler than ever, an expression on her face redolent of physical pain. "Theo," she continued, "I think we need to get you—"

"This place," she murmured, as if to herself, "this damned place."

Lee was alternating his gaze between Ness and Theo. Presley was too.

There was silence again, no rustle in the undergrowth, nothing, and then Theo abruptly turned.

"This way," she said, recovering something of her spirit. "Come this way."

Was it the clearing she was leading them to?

189

Now following a much narrower path, thicket rampant on either side, Ness would be very surprised if this led to any clearing. Narrowing further, it was becoming almost impossible to negotiate, branches and brambles relentless, but still Theo kept going, her hands raised to protect herself against any stinging scratches, her breath heavy, alarmingly heavy…

"Theo," Ness began, determined to call a halt to proceedings for now. They could deliver Theo home and come back here later, perhaps, or early the next morning without Theo – just her and Lee, depending on his shift, or her and Presley, performing a far more structured examination of the territory than they'd done so far, one that might yield better results. "Theo!"

This time, Ness screamed.

Chapter Eighteen

"STOP fussing! I'll be fine."

"Theo, you're not fine. You fainted."

"I did not!"

"Okay, okay, then. You *almost* fainted." Ness sighed heavily, torn between fear and frustration. "Look, you haven't been well lately, not since…well, since Blakemort——"

"I have!"

"No, you haven't. It's taken you a while to recover, and…who can blame you? It's taken its toll on all of us." She checked her watch. "It's just past two, but already it's been a long day, a stressful one. It's hot. It's…cloying in here. I think we need to get out."

"Not yet." And the way she said it caused Ness to quit any further begging.

"Theo, what are you sensing?"

Theo pointed to the ground, causing Presley to kneel, his hand raking over the area that had caused Theo to come to a sudden halt, to almost lose consciousness.

"Don't!" Theo ordered. "Don't do that."

"Why?"

"Because that soil," she uttered, raw disgust on her face, "has death clinging to it."

Her words had the desired effect, and, as if it was contagion that clung to it instead, Presley snatched his hand back, quickly rising to his feet. "Whose death?" he whispered.

Theo trembled as she endeavoured to answer him. "A woman, just a girl, a young girl. I...erm...I can't tell her name."

"Gaynor?" Ness prompted. "Or Samantha?"

"Yes, very possibly one of them. It's difficult to tell, that's the thing. It's like...there's a barrier, one that's very tall and very wide, a black energy that shields its own."

Lee had moved forward to support Theo, who, again, had started to sway slightly.

"I'm trying to connect too," Ness told Theo, but she agreed with what she was saying about a black wall of energy making any sort of headway difficult. If Corinna were here with them instead of missing, if Ruby were too, the four of them could have pooled their abilities and got further quicker. Never before had she missed her two other colleagues as much as she did in this moment, feeling small in the face of whatever it was they were up against.

She'd closed her eyes but only briefly, opening them to look at Theo. Her breath caught in her throat at the sight that met her. There were tears streaming down Theo's face, allowed to go unchecked. Seeing them, Ness's heart sank further as her anxiety heightened.

"Homeless," Theo said. "Of no fixed address."

"The girl?" asked Ness.

"Yes, the girl. Nowhere else to go. No safe place to stay."

Lee frowned. "Why come here, into the woods?"

"She thought it was safe," Theo replied. "The girl…" The older woman screwed her eyes shut briefly before turning her head to the side and reaching out to pat Lee's hand, seemingly grateful for his support during this time. "The girl was…damaged. Very."

"Drink?" Lee suggested. "Drugs?"

"Probably both," murmured Presley, and Theo agreed.

"Anything that could dull the pain," she said.

"Do you know yet if this is Gaynor or Samantha?" asked Ness.

"Gaynor. It's Gaynor."

Ness nodded. So it was the first girl whose body had been found here, Gaynor Sanderson, sometime in the '70s, the exact date of which they'd have to check.

"Poor Gaynor," Theo continued. "She camped here. That's right – she had some sort of makeshift tent, really very basic, tarpaulin and a few rods. It was hot weather. She…lived here. For a little while. Oh, there it is! A glimmer of happiness. She was content here, or as content as she could be. She was escaping everything and everyone, drink and drugs, her addictions. She wanted to get better, and these woods…dear Lord, they drew her to them."

"Drew her?" Presley commented.

"That's what I'm seeing," Theo told him, no more hope in her voice, just despair. "She was drawn here, she was encouraged, it was suggested to her, something like that."

"Encouraged?" Presley repeated. "By someone satanic?"

"Satanic!" Theo spat the word out. "It's bullshit, that's what it is. But it draws, it encourages, it suggests well enough. How many times must I say it? There are things that listen, that wait for an opportunity to connect, to break through, to rise up from subterranean depths to overwhelm us."

"Theo," Ness said, "was Gaynor involved in something satanic?"

Vehemently she shook her head. "No, no, no, not Gaynor, but coming to a place like this when you've enough demons of your own, it wasn't the sanctuary she hoped for."

"How long did she last out here?" Poor Presley was close to tears.

"Days. That's the impression I'm getting. Mere days."

A rustle behind them, amplified, perhaps, because it was so unusual, caused them all to turn. There was nothing there, not that they could see, but the air grew chillier still.

"What...what happened to her?" Lee said, turning back to Theo.

Because of Witcher, they all knew that Gaynor, like Jim Fowler and Samantha Lawrence, had been found dead with no evidence whatsoever of bodily harm, flat on her back, eyes open and staring upwards. That, at least, was different to the case Ness had worked on before in another area of woods. But was it a blessing or nothing of the sort?

"We need to keep walking," Theo said, stopping Ness's musings from developing further.

"Drink some water first," Ness insisted, relieved when Theo actually obeyed.

Unable to follow this particular path forwards, they backtracked, returning to the wider path. It felt more like trudging than walking, each step dogged. If there was a clearing, they seemed to be avoiding it, with Theo veering off again down another sidetrack.

"Why this way?" Presley asked. "Can you sense Corinna, anything at all? Whether she's been here, even? Whether this is actually..." His voice fell away shortly before adding, perhaps, 'worth it'.

"Presley," Ness answered as Theo was so absorbed in what she was doing, "trust Theo and what she's doing. And remember, right now, any information is better than none."

He nodded and, like her, like Lee, continued in pursuit of Theo, the four of them careful to lift their feet high enough as they crunched over more roots and bracken, bending low again to avoid the branches. Ness guessed where Theo was taking them, being drawn herself to a certain spot, that feeling within her intensifying with each step they took and so reminiscent of another time.

Ness tried hard to stop a tumult of memories from overwhelming her, but, as with psychic visions, there was sometimes no preventing them; they carried on regardless.

People went missing all the time. It was a fact of life. Some people *chose* to, but many did not – they were snatched, imprisoned, met with an accident in some distant place, or were murdered. When news had filtered through the media of two young girls, best friends, who'd gone missing, the world had sat up and taken notice. Strange, really, because so many incidents went unnoticed, but this one had captured the imagination of the people, it struck a chord. Not only had the world taken notice, it held its breath, people tuning in every day to TVs or radios to find out more news, praying they'd be found – Sarah and Claire. And yet all the world had known of them was their faces, two individual family snaps in which the girls were smiling, young, innocent and so full of promise. It was perhaps all the world had *needed* to know, because when it came to it, one child was the representation of every other, and a child missing was every parent's fear.

Eventually the girls *were* found, Ness had found them, doing as she was doing now, delving deeper into the woods. So many years ago, and yet it seemed like yesterday.

"Miss Patterson," the detective by her side had said, a young man, his baby face belying the important position he held, "are you sensing anything or…"

Or is this a wild goose chase, that's what he'd meant.

"I know you've combed every inch of these woods"— Ness had kept her gaze fixed firmly ahead rather than look at him—"but we also know the girls are here. We *have* to find them."

Technically, any psychic as well as a police officer must strive to remain objective when dealing with any case, to act in a professional manner. But every single one of them working on finding the girls had been in it up to their necks – the man beside her, Dave Jarvis, no exception. Ness doubted whether his strained expression would ever completely lift; he'd wear it forevermore, like a scar.

As Gaynor had been drawn deeper into these woods, as Theo was being drawn now, Ness had also felt the pull in those other woods. When the detective had spoken again, Ness hushed him.

Finally, a clearing had appeared, a small one, sun-dappled, with light bouncing off the leaves. A warm spring day, the trees overhead provided just the right amount of shelter.

A perfect place for a picnic…or a murder.

Tears had stung Ness's eyes back then, and they did so now. Such a pretty spot, secluded, there had remained a sense of people long before the murders. Those who had stumbled upon it had been delighted, wicker baskets in hand packed with food, ready to immerse themselves in nature, to inhale its fresh green scent whilst listening to birds trilling overhead. People had laughed, confided in each other, they'd kissed. Happiness still clung on there, but with increasing difficulty. Soon it would dissipate entirely, people no longer seeking that spot out but avoiding it.

Lawrence Gates was a monster, yet another who had sided with the darkness, who'd allowed it to eat him alive, consuming every ounce of humanity he'd been born with. He was also one of those who'd discovered that clearing on a prior walk, had formed plans for it...

From a few feet away, Ness could hear Theo grunting slightly. If only she'd listen to reason and stop awhile, drink some more water, but she was on a mission, just as Ness had been back then.

She had stood in that clearing in that other wood, her eyes examining every damned inch of it. The darkness in the form of Lawrence Gates, a tall, heavyset, shaven-headed brute who'd been barely even thirty, had swept in like a hurricane and overpowered the light.

"There!" Eventually Ness had lifted a hand and pointed to a space where several trees huddled together like old ladies gossiping.

"What about it?" Jarvis had asked warily, not that she could blame him. The ground below the trees had been perfectly level, no sign of any disturbance. Gates was canny, and he'd known how to cover his tracks, at least there he had, the girls' burial place. But later he'd slipped up, or perhaps it was arrogance that had been his undoing. He hadn't washed the blood from his clothes properly, a neighbour noticing the stain and informing the police. The story of the missing girls broke...

There'd been arrogance in his confession too; police officers told Ness it had been delivered with a smile, as if he was proud of what he'd done, as if there were others that would be proud of him too, for anyone who serves the darkness rejoices when the light is destroyed.

And now he was being held, incarcerated, separated from society with only himself and the darkness for company, for life. And he'd continued to laugh when he'd told officers they would never find the girls, that they were lost forever. Thank God for forensics, for police minds, who'd all worked together to trace his footsteps at the time the girls had gone missing, which led them to the woods, ones so beautifully named, Bluebell Wood in East Sussex. Thank God also that his expression changed when he'd been told, albeit for a heartbeat. Again, this was something later divulged to Ness – that for a second, a split second, there'd been shock, just when he'd thought he was so clever, so invincible, when he'd thought he could continue his torture from afar. Ness could imagine well that look and the reason for it. People who walked with darkness thought it would protect them, collude with them, reward them, but it never did. Carry out its sorry work, get caught, and the darkness abandoned you, turned its attention towards another fool, of which there were many.

Gates's expression had changed further still when he was told a psychic had been brought in to help find where the bodies were buried, one with an excellent reputation…

And eventually she'd found them, the exact spot, the detective setting the appropriate wheels in motion, the excavation beginning, Ness watching all the while.

The earth might have relinquished their bodies, but what of their spirits? It was as she'd suspected – they were grounded, still deep in trauma.

Hour after hour she'd spent trying to coax the girls forward, long after all tests and investigations had been carried out and the case closed, long after floral tributes laid at the site had turned to mulch, and the world had been captured by other news and yet more tragedies.

Ness had continued going to the woods to talk to the girls.

"I can't pretend to know how you've suffered," she'd say, "only that you have. But the longer you stay here, the longer that suffering will continue. And I don't want that. I want you to be free, to leave this terrible place and go where you belong, into the light, which is home – your true home – where nothing and no one can hurt you again. You can see the light, I'm sure of it. It's in the distance, perhaps, but not far. In it there are people you love and who love you too. They're waiting. Maybe one or two have come forward, have reached out like I'm reaching out to you now. Don't hide from them or me. Some people do bad things, but people like that can no longer reach you. It's only spirit that can reach you, and spirit is good, it's pure. Spirit will look after you."

Oh, how she'd pleaded with them, her body shaking with grief. She'd speak those words, all the while including Lyndsey too – *Don't stay in the darkness. You don't belong there.* And finally, finally something happened. Someone appeared, not Lyndsey, not Claire, only Sarah.

She was pale and delicate, wisp-like. To Ness's amazement and delight, she drifted forward from the gossiping trees, pausing only briefly to look at Ness, just a glance, no more, but one that entire volumes could be written about. There was despair on her face, bewilderment, anger, fear, hope and dread, but as she continued forwards, some of those emotions began to fade. Those that remained would also fade, once she was in the light, when peace wrapped its arms around her. Ness had been elated to see the girl, expecting Claire to follow her, to emerge from the shadows too. She'd waited…and waited.

But there'd been no sign of Claire. None.

Oh God – the tears that had stung her eyes earlier became a deluge, as she'd feared they would, more forceful than those she'd experienced in the study at Low Cottage. Claire had remained where she was; Lyndsey remained where she was. Both of them trapped, just as Corinna was trapped. Earlier, Ness hadn't been able to sense the grounded spirit of Gaynor, but right now she could detect *something*, and it was dark and frightening. *Don't leave me alone in the dark.* She hadn't meant to, she didn't want to, she'd tried to coax them forwards. But the darkness won sometimes. There it was, the bitter truth, and it was winning here.

"Ness! Theo!"

"Shit! What the fuck…?"

Both Lee and Presley were speaking at once, but, blinded by her tears, Ness could only hear them, not see them. There was alarm in their voices, and for a moment she wondered at it.

Another voice joined the panic – Theo's.

"This girl, this poor girl," she was saying, she was gasping. "What is it you saw? No! No! Don't show me. I don't want to see it. I can't! I can't!"

What was she saying? What did she mean? Quickly Ness lifted a hand to wipe at her eyes. "Theo? What is it? What's wrong?"

"Oh no, no, no. It's so…pure here. Not pure! What am I

saying? What the hell am I saying? Undiluted...pure... We have to get out. I can't breathe. Damn it, I can't breathe!"

Lee and Presley reached Theo before Ness could, catching her as she began to fall, both of them trying to stop her from tearing at her throat as if being strangled, her pink hair bedraggled, matted as it was with sweat, and her eyes bulging.

"Get her out!" Ness began to shout. "Get her out of the woods. Now!"

As all four began their desperate retreat, Ness noticed something: a liveliness when before the air had been so sluggish. Now, a slight rustle of leaves was as grating as nails being dragged along a chalkboard, as if...as if something was waking, something that rebelled.

There was no time to ponder it. Or fully register how much cooler it had got.

With Lee practically carrying Theo, Presley scouted ahead.

"This way," he kept saying. "I'm sure it's this way."

The paths they'd taken had become yet another puzzle to work out.

"This way," Presley kept muttering. "It has to be."

"No," Ness said, "I think it's this path. Come on, follow me."

There was no time to argue the toss – they had to act and quick.

"Hang on in there, Theo," Ness heard Lee say.

"I will," she responded weakly. "I'm trying."

This path they were on wasn't one they'd trodden before, and yet instinctively Ness knew they should continue down it – it would deliver them to safety, but it would also reveal something more: the clearing at last, just to the left of her, through yet another bank of trees. It was much larger than the sun-dappled clearing in the other woods, and at its centre was another tree, its size an indicator of just how ancient it was. Only she seemed to notice it, and she was thankful for that. Thankful because of what she saw in the clearing: dark figures, a mass of them – not human, that much was obvious – standing there and staring back at her.

The path they were on would lead them out, but what she'd seen, what they had *wanted* her to see, would continue to torture her. As would something else. Corinna was in amongst them, the merest hint of her, a glimmer, her hands reaching out as they had reached out to Theo in Low Cottage, a plea on her lips: *Time's running out. Help me! Help me, please!*

Chapter Nineteen

NESS led them out of the woods and back onto the path that was flanked by fields instead of innumerable trees. Theo was now sitting in the front seat of Lee's car and was still panting heavily but had thankfully regained a spot of colour in her cheeks.

Ness was kneeling so that she was at eye level with Theo, ignoring how uncomfortable the gravel was as it pressed into her knees. This would normally be the point where Theo would reject being fussed over, telling Ness to leave her be, that she was perfectly all right.

This time, she did nothing of the sort. Instead, there was an air of resignation about her, though not regarding the darkness; Ness didn't think that for one second. Theo would *never* resign herself to that. Oh no, it was to do with a far more down-to-earth issue: her health. No matter how young Theo was in spirit, her physical body was ageing badly. In her early seventies, overweight and with a heart problem, she was in mortal peril.

"Damn it," she was muttering to herself, taking a sip of water from her bottle.

"Theo," Ness asked, "what happened to you in the woods?

What did you see?"

Theo didn't answer straightaway. She simply continued to sit there, a solemn expression on her face. A few moments passed until she spoke again. "I saw victims, Ness."

"Gaynor and Samantha?"

"And no doubt the policeman too. What was his name?"

"Jim Fowler."

"That's it. No doubt he was in amongst them. There've been others, though, through the years, the centuries, probably. Way before Gaynor."

Lee spoke next. "How do you think they died?"

"I don't know, various ways. But the last three, the most *recent* three, their hearts just stopped, stone dead. That's why I suffered the way I did in there. I was empathising a little too much."

"Their hearts stopped dead?" Presley repeated. "How's that even possible?"

"Because, young man"—some of Theo's usual spirit was back—"what they saw or felt, or likely a combination of both, terrified them to that degree. Remember what I told you about the Morrigan, or Badb as she's also known? She was able to strike fear into the hearts of her enemies, her victims, and quite effortlessly too. That's the thing about this, it can all be quite effortless."

Presley swallowed. "Those people, those…victims, are they grounded?"

"I don't know, I couldn't tell," Theo replied. "Not necessarily."

Lee was shaking his head at Theo's words, not in denial but in wonder. "Bloody hell," he said. "There are more things between heaven and earth…"

Theo agreed. "Shakespeare was a very astute man."

"How does all this help Corinna?" There was a plea in Presley's voice.

Rather than answer him, Theo gazed at Ness. "What did you see? Or experience?"

Ness had to work hard to cloak her thoughts, aware that Theo was reaching out, doing her utmost to probe them. It wasn't that she wanted to keep secrets from Theo but that she was all too aware of how frail her friend had become in recent times, and she wanted to protect and preserve her for as long as possible, not cause her heart to overheat again.

"Ness?" Theo prompted, a frown on her face.

"Being in there, it reminded me...you know."

Theo nodded sagely at that. "Yes, I do know."

"I didn't experience what you did, because I think I was too preoccupied with...with the past." She hung her head low. "I'm sorry, I couldn't seem to think of anything else."

Theo reached out, took Ness's hand and squeezed it. "You're so hard on yourself," she said, and the sadness in her voice because of it almost drew more tears from Ness.

She took a deep breath instead. "We need to get you straight home. Lee, shall we get going?"

"Sure." Already he was heading towards the driver's seat.

"But what about Corinna?" Presley reiterated.

Ness stood to face him. "No one's forgetting about Corinna. She is first and foremost on our minds, our priority. In there, the woods, I got sidetracked. That won't happen again."

"Is that why you were crying?"

"Yes, Presley, it was. As I said, I...I won't let it happen again."

"Did you sense Corinna?"

"I…"

"Did you?"

"Let's get Theo home; she needs to rest. Once we've done that, we can talk. We can…plan."

"Okay," Presley said, and Ness sighed in relief. He seemed to grasp that she couldn't say anything more, not yet, not in front of Theo.

It was decided that Presley would return with Ness to her house. As he'd already said, he couldn't face returning to his flat alone, which everyone could understand, Ness also grateful for company as Lee was due back on duty soon. Having to travel via Lindfield so that Ness could pick up her car and Presley his motorbike, all three then followed in convoy to Theo's house, Ness having called one of Theo's sons, Ewan, who was going to be there waiting.

When they reached Theo's house in Lewes, located at the opposite end of town from Ness, Ewan was on the doorstep, anxious about his mother and what she'd endured. Ness helped Theo out of Lee's car, and together they walked up the pathway to her front door.

"Mum!" Ewan said, rushing forwards, a smile on his face that was clearly forced. "What've you been up to now, eh? No good, as usual."

Theo returned his smile, albeit weakly. "What I get up to, dear heart, is *always* for the purpose of good, let me assure you."

"Even so," he said, taking his mother's arm and leading her through the door into the hallway, "you'll be no good to anyone if you overstretch yourself. You know this. We've talked about this."

"Stop fretting, love," she replied good-naturedly. "Ness, come in too. I want a quick word."

Before she also entered Theo's house, Ness signalled back to Lee and Presley that she'd only be a few minutes. Waiting with their respective vehicles, both gave her the thumbs-up.

Inside the Lawson residence it was cool and comfortable, with plenty of light furnishings and space, the way Theo always said she liked it – 'sacred space', she called it, seeking to let the energy flow, 'positive energy, of course', she would add with a smile. As they made their way to the living room, Theo sat herself on a white leather armchair adorned with cushions.

"Ewan, sweetheart," she said, "be a poppet and put the kettle on, would you? I'd kill for a cuppa right now. Ness, what about you?"

"I can't. Lee…"

"Ah yes, yes, we mustn't keep the boys waiting. Even so, don't stand there, dear, take a pew. What I have to say won't take long."

Once Ewan had left the room, Ness did as instructed, sitting on a sofa opposite Theo, one that also held plenty of cushions. "What's the matter, Theo? What is it you want to tell me?"

"Actually, what I'd like is for you to tell me what you saw in the woods."

"Theo—"

"Because I know you cloaked your thoughts for a reason."

"It's just…I…"

"Stop floundering, girl!"

At this, Ness didn't know whether to smile or be indignant; she chose the former.

"I know why you don't want to tell me," Theo continued, "and to an extent I agree with your decision. You saw Corinna in the woods—"

"Theo—"

"You sensed her energy. And because you did, you have to go back into the woods. I know that too, and I can't come. I can't come because I've become a hindrance, not a help—"

"Theo, that's not true!"

"Oh, tell it like it is, for goodness' sake. A fat old lady like me can't go traipsing around in the woods on a hot summer's day, not with my heart in the state it's in. I'm bloody pissed off that I can't, make no mistake, but I also accept it. The last thing I want is to be a burden."

Ness hung her head. "Never," she whispered, a silence ensuing that sat between them, one that was as much of an old friend as they were to each other.

The creak of leather as Theo shifted in her chair and leant forward caused Ness to raise her head. "I can't go with you back to the woods," she continued, "not physically, at any rate. But, Ness, rest assured I'll be with you in spirit, every bloody ounce of it. My useless body will remain here, but everything else that is Theo Lawson will be by your side, okay?"

"Okay. Okay, Theo."

"And you won't go alone?"

"No, Presley...Lee..."

"And an army of police?"

"Lee's doing what he can, but it isn't his case, and he's already—"

"Red tape." Theo almost spat the words out. "God, I detest it, but it's a fact, one we can't deny. How soon do you

208

think you're going to go back, Ness?"

"Very soon."

"What about Ruby?"

Ness frowned. "Ruby?"

"Yes. What about her?"

"She's in hospital…the baby…"

"I know where she is."

"Well, then you'll also know that she *can't* come with me."

"Have you asked her?"

"No!"

"You can't go there alone, Ness."

"You'll be with me, you just said."

"I mean physically alone."

"I also said that Lee and Presley—"

"You need Ruby."

"I can't ask Ruby! She's in no fit state either."

Theo leant back into her chair again. What colour she'd regained had all but disappeared; she looked not like a woman in her early seventies but one who'd seen far more life than that.

"I wish there was some other way," she said, muttering at first before speaking more determinedly. "Regardless of whether a cult still operates at Rayners Wood, as Witcher believes, what we can be certain of is that it once did. I'm talking the real deal here, not wannabes, with Hylands at the helm, I'm certain of it – the Arch-Morrigan, if you will. She's long dead, of course, as are many of her followers, although there'll be current members in it still, but probably not as deeply. I guess there's far more available to excite a person these days besides the odd bit of devil worshipping.

Nonetheless, what was done in those woods, the corruption, remains as tangible as ever, as dangerous. Ness"—she sounded so pained to say it—"if you're ever going to find Corinna, you need Ruby by your side."

* * *

It was Sunday evening, usually a time to put your feet up and relax, watch something gentle on the TV, have a glass of wine, or a gin and tonic, and try not to think too hard about the coming week. For Ness, Lee and Presley, it was *all* they could think about – what to do next.

The three of them returned to Ness's house, filling the tiny living room with their presence, Ness only briefly glancing up the stairwell after entering, sending out a silent message to her twin. *Soon. It'll be our time soon.* Right now, though, it had to be about Corinna. She was in danger. *Mortal* danger. With Presley offering to make the tea, Ness was left alone with Lee.

Leaning into him, Ness whispered in his ear. "I saw Corinna in the woods, a vision of her, a strong vision. She's there, somewhere, Lee."

"Actually in the woods?"

"Yes. Don't say anything to Presley, not yet, but that's our hunting ground, right there. House calls to everyone in the village need to be organised, garages checked for Corinna's car, etc., etc. The police also need to comb every inch of Rayners Wood. She's alive, I'm certain of it, but for how much longer, I don't know."

"Ness"—Lee seemed torn between hope and despair—

"I'll do my best, but I can only put forward suggest—"

"Not good enough, Lee! It *has* to be done."

"Everything you're telling me, all the information, the suspicions, it's all being fed back and action's being taken, you know that, but…but…damn it, you also know I can't just click my fingers and get the entire Force to focus on it. If I could, I would, believe me. Look, I'm heading to the station soon. I'll check where we're at with it—"

"Here you go." Presley had reentered the room, carrying a tray of mugs. Placing it on a low table in front of the sofa, he handed Ness her mug and then Lee his before grabbing his own.

Rather than sip from his mug, Lee simply stared at it. Ness also held on to hers without drinking, something of its warmth sinking into her bones but only faintly.

A phone rang, not Ness's but Lee's.

"Sorry, Ness," he said, the one to leave the room now. Returning a couple of minutes later, he apologised again. "I can't delay it anymore. I've got to leave now."

"Corinna, though…" Presley began, but it was Ness who answered.

"Presley, we have to let him go." She turned to Lee, offered him the semblance of a smile before walking with him into the hallway, to the front door. Before she had a chance to open it, he took her in his arms, bringing her close and kissing her mouth, hard. Realising how much she needed his touch, she clung to him, the kiss finishing but their hug continuing.

"We have to find her, Lee," she murmured. "We have to pull out all the stops."

"We will. We are. We'll find her. Meanwhile, don't do

anything without telling me first, okay? Keep me in the loop, and I'll do the same with you."

Ness nodded and pulled apart from him despite not wanting to. It was early evening, but she felt exhausted, her head pounding because of stress. Sleep, however, was a long way off.

She opened the door, finally, and waved Lee goodbye before closing and leaning against it. Now what? Her mind was whirling, making it difficult to focus. *Deep breaths, Ness.* She had Witcher's book – it was time to plough through it some more, fire up the laptop also, dig deep regarding the Cult of Badb, and get Presley involved too. Keep themselves busy, basically.

In the living room, Presley was clearly thinking along the same lines. He was already re-reading Witcher's book, engrossed in it.

"Obsessed," he muttered. "The guy's definitely obsessed."

Whilst he was occupied, Ness switched on her laptop and typed *Cult of Badb* into the search bar. The first links to come up focused on a definition of Badb from Wiki as well as the Morrigan, compounding what Theo had said. Further down were links with the cult and extracts from Witcher's book as well as several interviews in which he'd mentioned the cult.

She clicked on one, picking up her tea at last and taking a sip, barely noticing it was tepid.

Various paranormal investigators were interested in Witcher. In fact, he appeared to have achieved a certain notoriety amongst them – the go-to expert on Rayners Wood, which, within the Devil's Triangle, was considered the epicentre. Clicking on another link, she began to read.

"And you're certain," one such investigator questioned

him, "that it's the Cult responsible for the deaths that have occurred there as well as the disappearance of dogs and other animals?"

"Yes," Witcher replied. "Extensive research I've undertaken all points to that being the case."

"The animals are, for want of a better word, used as sacrifices?"

"The humans too."

"Tom! That's quite some claim."

"One I stand by."

"But come on, of the three people found dead there over the past fifty years, none showed any signs whatsoever of bodily harm."

"That's right," acknowledged Witcher, "but there are many ways to achieve the same result."

"Tom," said the interviewer, and Ness could imagine not only the disbelief in his voice but, dare she say it, the amusement too, "don't you run the risk of upsetting people in the cult by accusing them of heinous acts so publicly? Aren't you afraid of becoming a target yourself?"

"As you know, I asked for a meeting with them. I wanted to hear their side; I agree with you that it's imperative we should. They sent one person, *one*, who wouldn't show his face but hid in the shadows, who went right ahead and threatened me. Cowards, that's what these so-called cult members are, but even cowards when they band together can prove dangerous."

"Have you taken your concerns to the police?"

"What's the use? Without evidence, they won't act."

"But you're determined to carry on with your exposé?"

"I am."

What the interviewer said next caused Ness to shiver. "Mr Witcher, do you consider yourself a crusader?"

That word – that *particular* word – was something the Psychic Surveys team used to describe themselves and their dedication. Witcher assured the interviewer that that was exactly what he considered himself. Should she be heartened by that? Was he going out on a limb because he truly believed this cult was evil and needed to be brought to account? Rather than the enemy, was he a brave man, someone on their side and right now in just as much peril as Corinna? Okay, he came over as obsessed, but sometimes obsession had its roots in good intent.

With this in mind, she carried on reading the article.

"Tom, so many villages in Sussex have historic links with witchcraft, with supposed devil worship. Would you say the county is something of a hotbed?"

"There's nothing supposed about it. It's everywhere, in every county in the UK and in every country in the world."

"Wow! Again, that's some statement."

"Why dilute the truth?"

"Why do you think it's everywhere?"

"Religion is everywhere, and it's the same thing. Because of power."

"Power? Can you explain more, Tom?"

"People want power, and they don't care about the price they have to pay to achieve it. Indeed, some believe there is *no* price to pay or, if there is, they'll be the exception, the devil's favourite, if you like, his right-hand man. Sometimes it seems God doesn't listen, but the devil does. Always."

Ness raised her eyebrows at this, wishing she could hear Witcher's voice, the way in which he'd said these things.

What are you? Friend or foe?

Taking a break, she lifted her head and looked at Presley. "Anything?"

"Nothing that's helping," he said, gazing back at her before averting his eyes to stare out of the window and into the blackness there. "You?"

"If only we could speak to Witcher," she said, sighing.

"But he's gone missing too."

"We *think* he's gone missing. He may not have. I guess that's what the police are trying to find out."

Presley got up and walked over to the window, continuing to stare out of it. "She's out there, Ness," he said, cutting such a forlorn figure, "out there somewhere and in trouble."

Ness also stood up, walking over to stand beside him. "I know, and it hurts me too. But Corinna's clever, she's tough. She survived Blakemort; she'll know how to survive this."

Presley disagreed with her. "The danger she's in now could be more immediate, couldn't it? Not necessarily supernatural but a human danger. Which right now seems worse."

He was right, a fact that only dismayed her more.

"Should we go back out?" Presley asked. "Head to the woods. Keep looking."

"We will go, but not tonight. Tonight's all about arming ourselves with more information, just like Lee and the officers working on Corinna's disappearance are doing down at the station, and then...then we'll go back, as soon as day breaks. We don't know the layout of the woods. If we go there now, at this time, we might endanger ourselves further, and that's no good to anyone, least of all Corinna. Presley"— she turned to face him—"we're doing our best to find

Corinna, and we have to keep the faith that she is also doing her best to keep herself as safe as possible in whatever circumstances she's found herself in."

With nothing more to be said, both of them simply stood by the window, staring out towards nothing. How many moments passed, she had no idea; time became skewed – she felt both suspended within it and as if it were racing away from her, such a curious feeling. *Who are you, Witcher? Who are you?* Those words – that threat, that warning, whatever it was – she'd had them spoken as well as read out to her. *Are you a stranger, Witcher, or...?*

A sudden bang from behind her made them both swing round. At the same time, Ness's phone began to ring. Rushing over to it, she saw it was Lee and accepted the call.

"Hi, Lee, what's going on? Have you found anything?"

"Ness, hi. I've got to go out, over to Saltdean. Some local teens think they're in deepest, darkest LA rather than a seaside town and are running riot. Before I go, though, I wanted to tell you, I've had a brief chance to do a bit more digging, and it seems Tom Witcher has no living kin."

"Damn," she said as Presley went over to the coffee table, no doubt investigating where that bang had come from, which had sounded like a mug had been lifted and then heavily replaced. If Witcher had any kin, parents, a wife, children, anything, they could have been instructed to forward a photograph of him. How convenient he had no one, was something of a loner, that his book was self-published too, with no one to contact regarding that either. The case officer would surely have passport and DVLA records by now, but they could often be a generation out of date, hence the reason police always sought as recent a photo as possible.

"I also asked one of my colleagues to find more information on the three people whose bodies were found in the woods," continued Lee.

"And?"

"Gaynor's parents are deceased, Jim Fowler's too—"

"Shit!"

"But…Samantha Lawrence's parents are still very much alive."

"Are they?" Ness almost gasped the words.

"I've just come off the phone with them."

"What? You have? Okay. And?"

"It seems Witcher got in contact with them – quite recently, in fact, a few months ago – managed to find out their phone number, although they've no idea how. He wanted to know whether Samantha was a cult member, insisted she was, actually, and that she must have known other cult members, asking them about her friends, her work colleagues, basically anyone she had contact with. It was Samantha's mother who answered, but the father took the phone from her and slammed it down, disgusted with him. And then what did Witcher do? He turned up on their doorstep, again insisting their daughter was a cult member, suggesting to them she'd riled the others somehow, perhaps even tried to break free of them and consequently been killed. He wanted the names of the people their daughter hung around with, insisting it was vital information, that it would help him on his quest to find their daughter's killer. He also wanted them to let him in, for them to tell him more about her and her activities, the type of things she got involved in, that all he wanted was justice for their daughter."

"Christ," said Ness, having put Lee on loudspeaker so that Presley could also hear, noticing that Presley was indeed listening and had Witcher's book back in his hands.

"Anyway," Lee continued, "they didn't let him in. They told him, quite rightly, to piss off and to stop sullying their daughter's name. They reported him to their local police, but for the life of me, I can't find any record of their complaint, which has annoyed the heck out of me. Heads will roll for that one. They were also able to give me a description of him. You ready?"

He began describing Witcher, and a visual duly formed in Ness's head. The man was tall, in his late forties or thereabouts, with a large nose and bulbous blue eyes.

"It is him!" she said, her voice initially a whisper. "It's the man we met outside Low Cottage the first time we came across it, the one who...who threatened us. He's not a stranger, not entirely."

"Okay, well, Ness, what the Lawrences have said is still only circumstantial, but it's cementing Witcher in place as our main person of interest. We'll be able to get Low Cottage searched, no problem now, and his flat too. They'll put more police on the job, searching for him as well as Corinna. I'll recommend a comb-through of the woods, house calls in Rayner, checking garages, the works. Her case will go straight to high risk, no delaying, not anymore. But, Ness, right now, tonight, I've got this other case to see to." He sighed, and she could imagine him running a hand through his hair, the frustration that he too was feeling. "It's gonna be a long night, that's for sure, for all of us, but tomorrow, it's all going to get stepped up. It'll be all hands on deck."

Ness nodded, tried to find relief in what he was saying but

failed. It *was* going to be a long night, not least for Corinna, wherever she was.

"Ness, get some sleep, okay? You're going to need it. We're getting closer, we really are." When she remained silent, he added, perhaps more firmly, "This is a police matter, and the police will handle it. Just…get some sleep."

Providing some half-hearted assurance that she would at least try, Ness ended the call and turned to Presley, who had graduated to holding the book out to her, as if it were an offering.

"Presley? What is it?"

"Did you underline these words?"

She shook her head; she'd done no such thing. "Me? No. Although I know certain words and sentences were underlined already."

"Not these words. Not like this."

"What do you mean? Let me see."

The page he was talking about had random words underscored, so hard in places they'd torn through the page.

"I think it's a message," Presley continued, obvious awe in his voice, beginning to recite from it again. "'He…liar. Danger…woods…evil…help…her…not…dead…not yet. Time…out.'"

Ness inhaled sharply. "A liar? Who's a liar? Witcher? It has to be! The rest…oh shit, the rest is pretty self-explanatory. Time *is* running out. We've already been warned about that."

Presley gulped. "What are we going to do, Ness? We can't just sit here. *I* can't."

Rather than answer, her eyes travelled upwards to where the spare bedroom was, where she'd heard movement over the past few days. *What do we do, Lyndsey? What the hell do we do?*

Silence sat like a lead weight between them, and then her mobile started to ring.

"Lee?" she said, grabbing it, not bothering to check the caller ID.

It wasn't Lee, however.

"Ruby! It's you! Oh, thank God! Thank God! We have to find Corinna. Now. Tonight."

PART THREE

Ruby

Chapter Twenty

RUBY couldn't just sit there, well…lie there, in a hospital bed, no matter what Cash said, what the doctors said, what anyone said. Corinna was missing, *missing*, for God's sake.

Yes, she knew the baby had to be her priority – Cash had been saying it over and over, barely leaving her side since she'd been admitted this morning, ensuring she stayed exactly where she was, imprisoned in this hospital bed, the Wi-Fi colluding with him. It barely worked in this hospital; 4G was sketchy as well. Not that many messages had come through anyway from Ness or Theo, and the ones that had only reassured her everything was being done to find Corinna and she wasn't to worry. Empty advice. As if she wasn't going to worry!

Thank goodness, at least, everyone needed the toilet at some point. That's where Cash had gone now, then he was picking up some food for himself before returning, eating it outside the ward too, as she couldn't stand the smell of anything at the moment. It'd set her off again, if not vomiting, then feeling as sick as hell, as weak.

I'm not weak!

If she told herself enough times, it might prove true. This was not a time for weakness of any sort. And no matter what Cash said and how much her friends were intent on shielding her, she couldn't not get involved. Corinna had been missing for almost forty-eight hours, no sign of her at all, with various avenues being checked and pursued. Ness was frantic – Ruby could sense that well enough from her texts, no matter how carefully worded they'd been, and Theo…something was wrong with Theo…a weakness of some sort, greater than her own, even.

I am not weak!

God, it was becoming a mantra. Good, let it. It'd help her to ignore how frail her legs felt, as if they were barely able to support her, and how much her hands were shaking as she began to agitate at the canula that had been inserted earlier. Another twenty-four hours couldn't pass without any sign of Corinna – time was running out. Ruby frowned as she remembered a case Cash had asked Corinna about in the pub early last week, the one about the house in which its occupants couldn't get a clock to work in the kitchen; time stood still in there. She hadn't given it much thought since, but right now it took on new significance. Time *was* of the essence, and the baby – little Hendrix if Cash had his way – was safe within, cocooned.

I'll let nothing happen to you, I swear. You're safe with me.

First things first. She had to get out of here and phone Ness, get a handle on the true situation, every last detail. Afterwards…well, afterwards, when Corinna was found, she'd be true to her word, honour her promise to her son and to Cash too. She'd back off again, lead a normal life, not get involved in any more cases, *not* that Corinna was a case. Corinna was an emergency.

"Ow!" The canula, as she pulled at it, made her yelp, but it was done, the connection severed.

As she stood up, she reached out a hand to steady herself, to breathe some more. She also thanked goodness she'd been given a small private room, a real privilege Cash had said, a stroke of luck. If she was on the main ward, she could never have done this. If it wasn't Cash keeping his beady eyes on her, the nurses would be, rushing over to stop her, to keep her confined. No one was going to stop her now, not even… She looked down, noticed a slick of blood on one hand as she cradled her belly, recalled the 3D scan she'd had and her baby's sweet face.

Her mobile phone was on charge on her bedside cabinet. She crossed over to it, checked it – no new messages were showing. In the bedside cabinet were her clothes and personal belongings. Slowly, she bent down to retrieve them, deep, steady breaths helping to control the nausea.

As she dug out her stuff, there was movement to the side of her. *Oh no, don't be some grounded spirit passing through! I can only deal with so much right now.*

Thank goodness paranormal activity had been zero since she'd entered here, maybe because she'd willed it to be, shutting her senses down. Would her decision to get out of bed, to help Corinna in any way she could, change that? She'd have to open herself up to the psychic world again, release the floodgates, tune in more than ever before.

She turned her head, a tentative move, not knowing what she'd see, and then her shoulders slumped in relief as the widest of grins graced her face.

"Jed!" There he was! At last. He'd been AWOL for a few days, as sometimes he tended to be, no cause for concern. "It's good to see you. Hey..." She reached out, although, as a spirit dog, that of a black Labrador who'd attached himself to her some years ago, there was nothing to embrace, no warm, furry body. "Don't skip out on me, again, eh? Not yet, at least. I need your help to find Corinna. You are gonna help me, I take it?"

Jed was wagging his tale and padding from paw to paw as if he couldn't wait to start.

"We're going soon, don't worry," she assured him.

Whilst he watched her, she started to pull on her clothes, still shaky, she had to admit, the nausea threatening to gag her on occasion. That it had returned and with such a vengeance was something that surprised her, surprised everyone. It was such a short respite she'd had from it, a cruel respite in many ways, like being given a gift and then having it snatched back.

Halfway through dressing, she stopped and took a sip of water, willing it to stay down and not make a reappearance. *I'm not weak. Just say it enough times, Ruby.*

Once fully dressed, her beloved tourmaline necklace also in place – an inheritance from her great-grandmother, Rosamund Davis – she grabbed her dressing gown and put it on over her clothes, stuffing her trainers into the pockets. God, it was hot in here, no radiators on but very little fresh air coming in either, making her private room and the ward muggy, just as it was on the outside, one of the hottest summers on record. She also unplugged her mobile, glancing at the window as she did. Nighttime. Darkness. And Corinna lost in it. *She's not weak either.*

"Come on, boy," she said, "before Cash gets back."

As Jed sprang into action, so did she, turning towards the door, watching with something akin to disbelief and panic as slowly, slowly it began to open. *Shit!*

"Ruby! What the hell are you doing?"

Damn it! Cash had returned sooner than anticipated. "What the hell, Cash, are you deliberately trying to catch me out or something?"

"What? No! I wasn't hungry after all, so I thought I'd grab something later."

"You not hungry? Are you kidding me?"

"It's not *that* unknown, for God's sake." He inclined his head to the side, those chiselled features of his forming a frown. "Actually, you know what? I reckon I'm coming out in sympathy again."

"Oh, here we go."

"I am! All this not being able to eat business."

"Cash, I know what you're up to. You don't trust me."

"I do."

"You're just trying to catch me out."

"I'm not... Hey! Have you got clothes on beneath that dressing gown?"

Ruby squared her shoulders. "I'm going out."

"What? Where?"

"To phone Ness. You know as well as I do the signal's crap in here."

"I can phone her, pass on any mess—"

"Cash, no! I need to talk to her myself."

As she made to push past him, Jed at her heels – not that Cash would know that unless she informed him – she saw his eyes travel to the pockets in her dressing gown.

"You've got your trainers with you."

Still defiant, she answered him. "That's right, I have."

"You don't need them if you're going into the corridor."

"Cash, will you stop fussing! Just let me go. Like I said, I need to speak to Ness."

"Ruby, you look awful."

"Charming," she said as she reached the door, which Cash was not daring to bar, not quite yet, anyway, "bloody charming."

"You know what I mean."

"And you know what I mean when I say I have to speak to Ness and find out the latest."

How pained he looked. "We have to think of the baby!"

She ground to a halt. "We have to think of Corinna! She's the priority here!"

"Ruby, I know, but—"

"You can't stop me, Cash. I'm going to talk to Ness, and I'm going to find out what's happening. I don't want anyone bullshitting me, not anymore. I want the facts."

"You're ill."

"I'm pregnant, not ill."

"You're weak."

"Don't say that!" Her voice was harsher than she'd intended it to be. "Don't fucking say that."

"Ruby—"

Perhaps he knew better than to argue further. He let her walk past him and then followed her out the door and along the corridor. The nurse's station was to the left, and both glanced over at it. There was no nurse in position, whoever was on duty probably busy elsewhere.

Leaving the ward and entering the main corridor, there

were a few people walking to and fro but not many considering the size of the hospital and how many there must be in it. Ignoring them, she began to tap out Ness's number.

Damn, the line was engaged. Damn again, she felt as if her legs might buckle beneath her.

"Ruby!" Cash's voice held a warning, but one she couldn't heed.

"I just need some water."

"You think you'll be able to keep it down?"

"I took a sip earlier. It was fine." Crossing over to one of the benches that lined the walls, she sat down. "Please, can you go and get my water? Ness is on the phone right now; I need to wait before calling again. Go on, Jed's here, he's with me. I'll be fine."

As uncertain as he looked, maybe even a tiny bit angry, he backed off, did as she asked. He was as worried about Corinna as she was, as his brother was too, who was distraught about her sudden disappearance. But these were unique circumstances, and so required unique action.

The baby wasn't sleeping as she'd hoped; he began kicking. Immediately her hands returned to her stomach, trying to soothe him. Jed was looking at her – at them both – with his head to the side, his deep brown eyes holding a mixture of emotions: love, that was for sure, but also anxiety.

"It's okay, Jed. I'll be all right, and the baby too."

Her watch told her they were edging towards nine o'clock – the darkness outside becoming more intense. How terrifying to be lost in it, to be at the mercy of someone or something.

Ruby shook her head, tried to displace that thought, was about to call Ness when movement other than Jed distracted her. As she'd suspected, not all those milling about were of the living variety. Amongst them was one who'd taken his last breath right here in this building.

Ordinarily, it took an extraordinary amount of energy for a spirit to manifest. It wasn't something that happened very often, but this young man, Ruby realised, was *freshly* dead, and so his energy was strong. Jed must have been aware of him too, but he was very nonchalant about it, his gaze mainly on Ruby or looking past her to see if Cash was returning with that water.

Although she tried to avoid catching the young man's attention, it was impossible.

She looked up, straight into his eyes, noting him slowly become aware that she was different too, that, unlike so many others recently, she could see him.

Inwardly Ruby groaned, tried to communicate via thought.

I'm sorry, I can't help you right now. I... There's something else I have to do.

One hand clutched at his side, a bloodstain soaking the tee shirt he presented in. He held his other hand out to her, an imploring gesture.

What happened to me?
I don't know. It looks...erm... Is it a stab wound?
Someone stabbed me?
I don't know, I think so.

The lad was younger than Ruby, perhaps in his teens, tall and skinny with longish hair. Just a kid, baffled by what had happened to him, that he was dead but still conscious.

What's your name? Ruby asked, unable to help herself.
Andy. Andy Pryce.

Andy, hi. I'm Ruby. You know…you realise you've passed, don't you?

Passed?

Dead.

I'm dead?

She nodded.

These others—he gestured around him—*are they dead too?*

No, they're doctors and nurses, a few visitors too.

You're not dead either?

No.

What's wrong with you?

Wrong? Nothing's wrong. I'm pregnant.

Oh…

That's why I'm here, pregnancy doesn't really agree with me.

Poor you.

He drew closer as he said it, Ruby glancing sideways, lifting one hand to clutch at her necklace, wondering where Cash was, what had delayed him.

I…I have to go, she explained. *Very soon. A friend of mine's in trouble, and I have to help her. But I'll come back. I can…speak to you then, help you too.*

Help me?

That's right. You're grounded. You're not supposed to be here, not anymore.

The boy lifted his hands, held them out to her again, question after question on his lips.

Who stabbed me? Why? I can't remember what I was doing before. What was I doing? I was with friends, that's it. What's happened to them? How long have I been dead for?

Still clutching her necklace, Ruby blinked; she also pushed herself upwards, standing rather than sitting. Jed began to growl a little, perhaps becoming aware of the effect the young man was having on her and how overwhelmed she was starting to feel.

"Jed, it's all right," she said before addressing the young man again.

I can help you but not yet. I really do have to go. I will come back, though, I promise.

But what about my mum? Do you know her? She'll be so upset! I've got brothers and sisters too. Oh God, what's happened to them? Are they all right? I can't remember who stabbed me. Why can't I? Surely anyone would remember who stabbed them!

"Ruby, sorry about that—"

"Cash!" Finally, he'd returned, a glass of water in hand. "Where the hell have you been?"

Hell? Is this hell? the young man asked. *Oh God, shit, am I in hell?*

"What? No. Sorry, I shouldn't have mentioned that word. This isn't hell—"

"Ruby, who are you talking to?"

"Cash, I... Look, we've got to get out of here."

"We're not taking another step until you've had some water. Come on, take a sip. Sorry I was so long – I only went and spilt the jug, didn't I, all over your bed. And then the nurse came in and asked me what was going on, where you were, said she needed to take more bloods."

"Crap, really?"

"Yeah, she noticed the canular you ripped out. I had to make up some story, that it had come loose of its own accord. She wanted to know where you were, though. I said you just wanted to stretch your legs a bit, you'd got cramp and were in the corridor. Promised you'd only be a few minutes. She's waiting for you to return, to get another canula in."

"I can't stay here—"

"Look, Ruby, stop for a moment and think about this. I'll go and see Ness, right now I'll go, find out everything there is to know, okay? Help them. I won't police you anymore—"

"No, Cash, I can't stay, I mean it. There's..." She looked at Andy and then beyond Andy, saw other people coming towards her, just one or two, but soon there'd be more, attracted by what was happening in the corridor, *realising* – not living people but, like Andy, those recently passed.

"There's bound to be so many," she whispered.

"What?" Cash responded.

"They'll come into the corridor."

"The corridor's empty."

"Oh, for God's sake, Cash, I'm talking about dead people! There's just one at the moment, but others are on their way, and they'll all want answers, they'll all want help." She held her hands up as she started to back away. "Andy, I'm going to come back, but...please, let me go for now. Let me get out of here." Turning, she grabbed Cash's arm, making him spill water again, this time from the plastic cup he held. "He's not listening. Come on, move. Now."

"Ruby, I really don't think—"

"Don't argue, okay? Trust me. Time isn't on our side."

After a brief pause, Cash put the cup on the bench. "Okay, come on. Jed, you too."

Despite herself, Ruby smiled. This was why she loved him, because he *did* trust her, because he'd help her to help Corinna.

Andy followed, as did the others, although they at least

kept their distance, still very unsure, unnerved by their new status. Poor Andy! He was sobbing, demanding that she stay.

I'll be back, she promised again, moved by his plight but having to put Corinna first.

With Jed at their heels, they fled as fast as they could along the corridor, away from Andy and the nurse that waited for them, taking a flight of steps to the ground floor rather than risk being followed into the lift, then slowing their pace dramatically so as to avoid suspicion.

"We just need to get to the entrance," Ruby told Cash, refusing to feel as tired as she was, as depleted, as sick. Never had mind over matter meant so much.

"They won't follow you?"

She shook her head. "They'll stay here, within these boundaries."

At least she bloody hoped so. If Andy and the others did go anywhere, they'd go to the light, pass fully before she returned, perhaps, shock giving way to acceptance. Some would refuse, though…

Outside, the air should have revived her, but it was so heavy it only sapped her energy more. The baby delivered another kick, short, sharp, and furious.

"Oh, Cash," she said, having to lean against him.

"I'm really not sure about this, Rubes." Again, he was agitating.

"I'll be okay in a minute. I'll get my trainers on, then phone Ness."

"Ruby, I know these are unusual circumstances, terrible circumstances, but if anything happens to you, to Hendrix—"

"It won't, Cash, not with you by my side, and Jed too."

Having put her trainers on and handed Cash her dressing gown to hold, Ruby called Ness and waited for her to answer. During that time, Ruby looked back at the hospital entrance, saw Andy pressed up against the glass and banging on it, as desperate as she was.

At last Ness picked up.

"Ness? It's me, it's Ruby. How are you? What's going on? Tell me everything."

As Ness replied, two things were obvious – her relief and her terror.

It was the latter that spurred Ruby into further action.

"Don't say another word. We're on our way, me, Cash and Jed. We're coming."

Chapter Twenty-One

"RUBY! It's so good to see you!"

Ness's complexion was often pale, even in summer, but right now she was the colour of milk, her dark eyes as large as a child's, a desperate strength in her arms as she hugged Ruby.

In turn, Cash hugged his brother, whose body was clearly shuddering with emotion.

"Come into the living room," Ness continued, "and sit down. Ruby, I'll get you some water."

As she lowered herself onto Ness's sofa, Ruby noticed the book in front of her. "What's this?" she asked Presley, shifting forward so she could pick it up.

"That's Witcher's book."

"The man renting Low Cottage?"

Presley, who'd also taken a seat, alongside Cash, nodded. Jed had followed Ness out of the room and returned with her as well.

Still holding the book, Ruby looked at her colleague. "What's its significance?"

Ness handed her the water and then sat too. "There's so much for you to catch up on."

"I don't doubt it," Ruby said, forcing herself to take a sip of water as she'd done in the hospital, grateful that the baby had stopped kicking, at least, and was still.

The next few minutes passed with Ness and Presley explaining as fully as they could all that had recently transpired, Ruby's eyes widening at various intervals.

"You think there's a body behind one of the walls at Low Cottage?"

"That's right." Ness's expression was grim as she confirmed it. "In the study."

"How long's it been there for?"

"I don't know. But it's not recent. Whoever it is, it's been a while."

"Christ!" Cash was appalled. "You'd think it might smell or something."

"Depends what state the body was in when it was interred," Ness answered. "It could just be bones."

"Charred bones..."

Ness looked at Ruby. "What?"

"It was an impression I got, of bones that had been charred."

"Okay." Ness seemed to accept this without question. "We'll keep that in mind."

"And Theo is all right, isn't she?" Ruby had worried about this when they'd first told her about Theo and found herself fretting again.

"She'll be fine. She'll be with us in spirit, just like she said."

"I know she will. I can feel her now, her and..."

When her voice drifted off, Ness frowned. "Her and what, Ruby? What were you going to say?"

"Oh, nothing, nothing. I… Is Lee taking your fears about Low Cottage seriously?"

"He is," Ness assured her, "but he's not in charge of the investigation, so he's feeding through all the information we have about Witcher. Because of my past connection with the police, they're not dismissing what I'm saying as kooky nonsense, not entirely, anyway. As for Low Cottage, it's likely there's going to be a thorough investigation, and of Witcher's studio flat in Brighton."

"And you think Witcher is the same man you first encountered outside Low Cottage?"

"I do now, yes, without a doubt." Ness was sitting there with one hand clutching the other, her grip seemingly getting tighter as she leant forward slightly. "Ruby, I'm delighted to see you, I can't tell you how much, but I'm also worried. I don't want you putting yourself or the baby at risk."

"I'm here because I have to be, Ness, because…I can't keep away. Corinna's not just a friend, she's family. So are you and Theo – all of you are. You're my *chosen* family."

Ness's eyes filled with tears. "You're my chosen family too."

There was a moment of silence, one in which everyone tried to gather their thoughts, either that or reel in emotions that threatened to choke them. Finally, Ruby continued. "What's our next step, Ness? You're pretty certain the woods are key here."

"They are," Ness replied.

"And we're going back there?" Presley checked. "As soon as possible?"

Cash looked wary. "How soon were you thinking?"

"We've had what we think is a message," Ness explained,

"in that book there. You asked what its significance is, well, I'll tell you. Not only does it say that Witcher was obsessed with the Devil's Triangle, in particular Rayners Wood, but also the cult that he believed practised there."

"The Cult of Badb?" checked Ruby.

"Yes, in that book he as good as baits them. Even after one supposed cult member made contact with him and threatened him, he continued to pursue them."

"What's his beef with them, exactly?" wondered Cash.

"You mean apart from them being murderous crazy shits?" Presley retorted.

"Look," Ness interjected, "we don't know whether his obsession is professional or personal, whether it has its roots in good intention or not. I suppose at this point it's important to note that whilst Witcher is our lead, he may not be guilty of anything. We now think he's missing too, from around the same time as Corinna. It could be that he's a victim as well."

Cash shook his head. "Don't think so, not from everything you've told us so far. He's our man." Wincing, he then turned to Presley. "Although, you know, he might not be as bad as we think."

"Really? So, he's playing at kidnapping, is he?" Presley's voice remained unforgiving, and Cash winced a second time before Ruby steered them back to the main conversation.

"You said you got a message, via Tom's book, about time running out. Can you show me?"

Ness picked up the book and thumbed through it. "There was a bang, as if someone had lifted the mug that was by the book and brought it down again. Presley and I were peering out the window at the time. It was Presley who went over to the book, discovered there'd been words underlined where there hadn't been before. The message says this, basically: he's a liar, there's danger in the woods, evil, help her, she's not dead, not yet. Time's running out."

Ruby nodded. "All of which corresponds with what Jess Biggs is trying to tell us."

"Yes," replied Ness, her voice small suddenly, worry exaggerating every line on her face.

"Right," Ruby decided, "if it's all about the woods, we have to go there. Now."

At her words Jed rose to his feet, as eager as ever.

"Ruby!" Cash protested. "It's just gone eleven."

Presley also rose to his feet. "Ness, have you got torches?"

"Yes," she said, albeit looking as wary as Cash. "The survey kit is in the cupboard under the sink. Along with the usual paraphernalia, there are various torches, all ready to go."

"I'll go and get them."

"Sure. Get whatever you think we might need."

Ruby also stood, and so did Cash.

"Ruby," he said, crossing the divide that separated them and taking her by the arms, "okay, I get it, we have to go now, but not you. You can't, not...not in your condition."

"It's no use trying to talk me out of this—"

"Look," he persisted, "Theo realises her limitations. She knows that if she returns to the wood, it'll put her health in danger. The same applies to you, and not just your health but the baby's too."

Jed barked twice before turning tail and leaving the room.

"Jed's heading for the front door," she told Cash, effectively stopping his tirade.

"What? Is he?"

"Uh-huh. He's waiting for us to follow him, and he's doing that, Cash, because we *have* to go, all of us. If we don't, if we wait until daylight…" She couldn't say it, the words that were forming in her head. "He's at the door, and he's waiting," she reiterated instead. "And Jed wouldn't do that, he wouldn't put me at risk unless he believed it was absolutely necessary, now would he?"

"I suppose not." Cash sounded resigned.

"If I stay behind, if I don't go and something happens to Corinna, then I'll never be able to live with it, and, Cash, I'm feeling okay, a bit better."

"Really?"

"Yeah, not as sick, not as…tired."

"Okay," he said, swallowing.

"Now can you let go of my arms?"

"Your arms?"

"Yeah, I need to go to the loo."

"Oh, right."

As she passed him, Presley still gathering equipment from the cupboard, she signalled for Ness to follow her upstairs. "I might need to borrow a jacket," she said by way of explanation.

At the top of the stairs, on the landing, Ruby turned to her. "Ness, you were holding something back when you told us about your trip to the woods earlier. What was it?"

Ness raised an eyebrow before smiling wryly. "Can't keep anything from Theo, and I can't keep anything from you, can I? But actually, you're right, and I *was* going to tell you, but only you, as I don't want Presley more alarmed and upset than he already is."

"Go on."

"When we were leaving the woods after Theo took a turn, trying to find our way out, I saw something in a clearing there, something not entirely unexpected but shocking nonetheless."

As she spoke, Ness's eyes filled with tears again. Theo had taken a turn, but so had Ness, something she'd only briefly mentioned, having no choice, really, as Presley might think it odd if she'd omitted it. Ruby knew how much Ness had been affected by the case of the murdered schoolgirls in yet more woodland in East Sussex, one girl remaining grounded despite Ness trying so hard to move her on. Gently, she reached out and placed a hand on her arm.

"Ness, what was it that you saw in Rayners Wood?"

"Black energy. It has a stronghold there, and, as I said earlier, it's what Theo believes is responsible for the three most recent deaths that have taken place there. Its energy is so intense, so terrifying, so pure, strangely enough, that it can stop your heart in an instant."

"If you don't know how to protect yourself."

"And if you're vulnerable in some way. We know Gaynor was vulnerable – Theo got a good insight into her, not so much the other two, Jim and Samantha – but so many people are vulnerable. They might not look it, they might not act it, but they are nonetheless."

"The world's a harsh place."

"It can be, certainly. Ruby, in amongst the black energy, I saw Corinna, just as Theo had seen her in Low Cottage. She had her arms out as if she was begging, pleading for help. I know—" she swallowed "—I know it's not ideal going back to Rayners Wood in the dark. That in itself puts us at a disadvantage. We don't know the woods, the layout. We could be rendered vulnerable too—"

"Not if we stick together."

Ness nodded. "If we stick together, we're strong."

"Stronger than the darkness, Ness. Always."

"Yes, yes."

"We *have* to believe it. Our job demands it of us."

That at least prompted a smile. "Well…if you put it like that…"

Ruby hesitated. Was now the time to mention it? "Ness…"

"Yes?"

"There's someone in your house."

"Well, yes, you, Cash, Pres—"

"You know what I mean."

Ness simply stared at her, and then she raised her hands to grip Ruby's arms, just as Cash had gripped them. "Do you think it's her?"

"Your twin?"

"Yes, Lyndsey."

"I…I don't know who it is. When I came in, I could sense a presence, but it was fleeting. Whoever it is, though, they're responsible for that message in Witcher's book."

"It *is* her," Ness insisted, dropping her hands and turning her head to glance at a door just to the right of them. "No one else could get in here. I've made sure of that. Oh, Ruby, what if it is her? There've been other things that have happened too, noises, like someone treading on a creaky floorboard, from the spare room there. Also, I was looking at a photograph of me in my bedroom, and for a moment, a split second, I was sure she was in it too, standing right by my side. Why won't she reveal herself? Properly, I mean. Why's she doing this instead?"

"You've given her so much time, Ness, perhaps give her a little bit more."

"Yes, yes, you're right. That's what I've told myself too. You can't push the tide."

"Not all tides," Ruby agreed, "but with some we have to at least try."

Ness nodded her head, her black hair swinging. "Yes, of course. Corinna. We mustn't delay. You wanted a jacket, didn't you?"

"Yes, although to be honest, I'm not sure I really need it. It's still so warm out there."

"I think it's going to change, though."

"The weather? Seriously?"

"Seriously, Ruby. I… Look, I've got a warmer jacket. Take it, please. Just in case."

"Okay," Ruby replied, still a bit bemused by what Ness had said. The air outside was close, apathetic almost, giving no sign whatsoever it was going to let up, just continue to oppress them, day in, day out, as it had done for the last two or three weeks – the surprise heatwave persisting.

"Girls"—Cash's raised voice reached them from below—"are you ready?"

"Ruby," Ness checked, "you sure you're okay?"

"I'm sure."

Her eyes flickered only briefly towards Ruby's stomach. "If it gets too much…"

"We have to find her."

Ness didn't deny it. "We do."

"Everything goes on hold until then." Her pregnancy and

Ness's twin included.

"We're ready," Ruby shouted back to Cash, Ness dashing off to grab a jacket for Ruby as well as herself, Ruby indeed using the bathroom and then hurrying downstairs.

At the bottom in the narrow hallway, the four exchanged glances, Jed still at the door, whining.

"A long night," Presley murmured.

"What's that, bro?" Cash asked.

"Something Lee said earlier," he explained, "that it's gonna be a long night."

"Best we crack on, then," said Ruby, grabbing Cash's arm and marching him to the car.

Chapter Twenty-Two

ALL of them couldn't help but note the time on the dashboard when they reached the woods – it was just before midnight, almost the witching hour, with plenty of darkness still ahead.

On the journey over in Ruby's car, Cash driving, Ness had phoned Lee, wanting to explain to him that she was going to the woods, how the evening's events had made it impossible not to with that terrible worry – that *instruction* – that if they waited until morning, it would be too late. "The energies are gathering," Ness had said whilst waiting for him to pick up. "Can you feel them?"

Ruby had nodded, Cash and Presley too, with Jed barking excitedly in the footwell. Ruby might have agreed, but it was only to be polite, guessing it was the same with the Wilkins brothers, although…opening her window a crack, she'd laid her head against it, felt the air on her skin, not as stagnant as before, as if something was beginning to stir within it. Something…exciting…

Shaking her head that she should think anything was exciting under such dire circumstances, Ruby had turned her head slightly. "Lee not answering?"

"No." Ness sighed. "He's likely busy. I'll leave it for now, try later."

"Okay." Ruby had faced the front again, listening to Presley as he gave Cash directions.

They now stopped in the same spot where Lee had apparently stopped earlier in the day when they'd come with Theo, on the edge of a small village called Rayner, which largely consisted of one street as far as Ruby could make out.

Once out of the car, she shivered, glad of the jacket Ness had made her wear after all, pulling it tight across her bump and zipping it up, token protection for the child within.

"Have another sip of water," Cash said, proffering a bottle he'd brought from Ness's.

Although not thirsty, she took the bottle and sipped from it, if only to appease him. All the while, her eyes remained on the village they'd just passed through to get here.

Ness noticed what she was doing. "Lee's already suggested they do house calls here."

"When, though?"

Ness stalled.

"Shit," Ruby said, having to bite back anger. "Sorry, I know Lee's a good man. He's doing his best; they probably all are."

"We all want Corinna to be their one and only case," Ness replied.

"She's *our* one and only case. Right now, that's what matters most."

Turning away from the village, Ruby noticed a track ahead, one that the darkness quickly swallowed. "Is it that way to the woods?" she asked, and Presley nodded, handing out torches.

"You've also got the light from your phones," he said, "you know, if these should fail."

Stuffing the torches into their various pockets, Ruby then raised a hand to her face.

"Was that a spot of rain I just felt?"

Cash tipped his head. "Don't think so. Starry sky. No mention of rain on the forecast either."

"Strange," she murmured, glancing at Ness, who had tipped her head back too as if scanning the skies, as if…waiting.

"Before we go any further," Ruby continued, "we need to take a few moments, each of us, to visualise white light like we always do, focusing on it being absolutely impenetrable, the perfect shield against…against whatever it is we're likely to encounter." She paused and touched her face again. "You know, I'm sure that's rain I'm feeling."

Cash shrugged, so did Presley. Ness, meanwhile, looked something else…hopeful? Was that it? "Ness?" Ruby quizzed.

"I told you, didn't I, at the house, that the weather might change, it might…break."

"Is there some kind of significance in that?"

"We'll have to wait and see," was her reply.

Having performed their usual ritual – Ruby visualising Cash and Presley in white light along with herself and the baby, as she knew Ness would be doing also, increasing the buffer – Ruby took comfort in knowing that Theo had their backs from afar. She hadn't had time to call her on the phone, but she didn't need to; she could feel well enough her presence. There'd be plenty of time to talk when this was all over and Corinna was home safe.

A bark from Jed was the signal for them to move, Ruby calling out, "Don't go too far."

Immediately Cash was anxious. "What if he goes missing, Rubes, like the other dogs?"

"He's a spirit dog. He's not as susceptible."

"But if he's susceptible at all…"

She had the same concerns, but she quashed them. "Jed can look after himself."

"Like you can, you mean?" There was a hint of accusation in his voice, which she ignored.

She could see his point, though. Traipsing down a dark track like this, into the thick of an unknown wood, one with a reputation, heavily pregnant with her first child, close to midnight, did seem a lot like madness. They *had* to do this, though; the spirits themselves were spurring them on, Jess Biggs and the one who'd underscored the words in Tom Witcher's book, *The Demonic Link*. Again, she shivered. Demons, is that what they were dealing with here? Energy that was as black as black could be, that had been summoned, called forth over a prolonged period. Certainly, it was the conclusion Theo and Ness had come to.

Damn it! She'd asked Corinna, she'd *begged* her to keep things ordinary – or as ordinary as could be, considering their occupation – and yet here they were again, dealing with the dregs of the spiritual world. Since Blakemort, Ruby had clung to her faith in the light. Now more than ever, it was imperative she tightened that grip, not let it loosen, refusing point-blank to allow even a fraction of doubt or fear to creep in…

"This way." Presley had taken the lead, with Cash and Ruby behind him, Cash's hand on Ruby's arm all the while, determined not to loosen his grip either. Ness brought up the rear. As for Jed, he kept appearing and disappearing, weaving his way in amongst a tangle of trees, stopping every now and then to lean his head to the side, as if listening…

Ruby tried to remember if she'd gone into woodland before at night and couldn't, early evening, perhaps, but not like this, so late. Nonetheless, she expected to hear the sounds of animals, the hoot of an owl, maybe, the birds as they called to one another, a rustling in the bracken as badgers and foxes hunted for food. There was nothing, aside from her own breathing.

"Shit, this place," Cash murmured beside her as they continued to trudge, torchlight doing its best to bring relief to the unrelenting night. Behind them, however, when Ruby glanced back, over Ness's shoulder, it was just a solid wall of black, one that kept pace with them.

"Ness," said Ruby, "any idea where we're going?"

"It's a clearing we're looking for," Ness replied. "Perhaps I'd better join Presley at the front."

Ruby and Cash stood aside to let her pass, Ruby's gaze still on the void behind them, noting how dense the wood had become and so quickly, the path they'd been following wide at first but soon narrowing, dividing into other paths that were narrower still. It was as if they'd entered a maze rather than the woods, a labyrinth.

"So, Ness, this was the clearing you saw earlier, right?" Ruby asked.

Presley stopped in his tracks. "Did you, Ness? When?"

"Erm…" As Ness faltered, Ruby cursed herself for having mentioned it – Ness hadn't told Presley she'd seen a clearing or, more to the point, *what* she'd seen in the clearing for fear of causing him further distress. Before Ruby could apologise, though, Ness had formed an answer. "Earlier in the day, I thought I saw something that looked like a clearing, out of the corner of my eye. I didn't say anything because our priority was to get Theo to safety."

"And?" he pressed.

"And it's most likely the heart of these woods, a place we need to check out, at any rate."

"Witcher's epicentre?"

"Possibly."

"If we do find it, what then?" Cash wanted to know.

"Then we tune in," Ness answered. "For any sign of Corinna."

"O–kay." Cash drew the word out, clearly torn between knowing how essential this task was and wishing fervently it wasn't. "Oh!" he continued, causing Ruby to frown.

"What is it?"

"I think I felt rain on my face as well. Either that or I'm coming out in sympathy with you again, you know, synchronising. Ruby, how are you? Are you still okay?"

"Honestly, I'm fine."

"The baby?"

"He's fine too. Come on, let's continue."

Ruby had no idea how big this wood was. Right now, it seemed endless, the sum of their entire world. Ness had already warned them of the kinds of things people had reported experiencing whilst in here: a feeling of being followed, even physically attacked; a white mist that would form, quite suddenly and seemingly intelligent; the nausea.

Regarding the latter, Ruby had raised an eyebrow. "Yeah, well, let them do their best with that one. I've already been to hell and back regarding nausea."

Did she feel sick right now, though?

With surprise she realised she didn't. That almost constant feeling that was now part of her normality had temporarily abated, almost as if being here was having the opposite effect on her, was negating it. Whatever the reason, she welcomed it, glad of some respite.

"Hey, listen up. What's that?"

It was Presley speaking, shining his torch off to the right. Ruby's head came forward as she strained to see, the light revealing nothing but more trees, old, gnarled and bunched together, low-hanging branches reminding her of a giant cobweb in which a beast lurked.

"What is it?" Ness enquired. "Did you hear something?"

"Yeah," said Presley. "Like the crunch of leaves or something."

"Animals, maybe?" Cash offered.

Presley lifted a hand to scratch his head. "I don't know… It kinda sounded heavier than that, like footfall. Do you think it's Witcher? In the woods too and tracking us?"

"We need to keep our wits about us," Ness replied, "be aware of foes of all kinds, including tree roots and potholes. Come on, it's this way to the clearing, I'm sure of it. I can feel a pull. Ruby, can you feel it too?"

"No," Ruby confessed, "not right now, but if you do, great. Let's go for it."

Again, they began to walk, Ruby opening her mind further, feeling something or someone nudging at the edges of perception. Theo? Corinna? *Is that you?* It was a good sensation, comforting, spurring her on. Theo, then. *I'm with you.* The words formed in Ruby's mind. *I'm with you all.* She was reaching out to Corinna too. *We're coming for you, Corinna. You're here in these woods, and so are we. We're coming for you, and nothing and no one will stop us.*

They were so close to each other, the four of them, staying that way deliberately, Theo and Jed with them in spirit, both of them exactly whom you'd choose to go into battle with. Perhaps it was because the nausea had abated that Ruby felt the way she did, that prickle of excitement experienced earlier in the car beginning to build. Instead of weak, she felt strong, her mantra having done its job – she felt capable, *more* than capable, invincible. Hopeful, even, when previously there'd been nothing but worry and despair. Rayners Wood had a terrible reputation, but within it she was beginning to heal. Was that the right word? As if recovering from some long illness rather than a pregnancy, able to tune in to something other than the negativity of what lingered here, to something far more ancient that endured.

Ness had said the Devil's Triangle – which included Rayners Wood, Chanctonbury Ring and Cissbury Ring – existed on powerful ley lines, and regarding that, Ruby wouldn't be surprised. So many places of note were, those that had evolved naturally or otherwise. She'd heard tell that if you looked at a map of London, significant landmarks such as cathedrals, palaces and government buildings also appeared to have been built at triangular points from each other. Was that a coincidence or deliberate? Their architects could've been commissioned by powerful elites who knew well enough where to position them, their aim to infuse such buildings with telluric energy, to harness it. The elites, the families that ruled, those that remained behind the scenes but pulled the strings of so many, were mad for power. But then so were more ordinary people. After all, once you got a taste for it…

This place – these woods – little wonder it had become a focal point for occult obsession, for Witcher's obsession too. But if she was channelling the good stuff, could it be Corinna was as well? That if she was here, she might be drawing strength from it, using it to remain alive? *Stay strong, Corinna. Bad things have happened in these woods, but there's also good, such a lot of good—*

"Shit!"

The alarm in Cash's voice not only ripped Ruby from her musings, it tore a rip in the fabric of her world too.

"Cash, what is it? Where've you gone?"

She lifted a hand, touched the spot where he'd previously held her, not letting go, not for one second…until now. There was no hand there and no Cash either, no Ness, no Presley and no Jed. It was just the woods that surrounded her, but not the woods as they had been – they were now shrouded in mist, when before there'd been none at all. It had been a clear night when they'd set off, albeit with a hint of rain in the air, rain that only she could feel. But now the mist had risen, and it was so thick in places, like a brick wall, impossible to see beyond.

"Cash!" she shouted again, having to fight hard to quell a panic that threatened to overwhelm her just as suddenly as the mist had, panic that obviously had an effect on the child within, because he was kicking, painfully hard, causing her to double over. "Shit!" She herself was swearing now, trying at once to soothe the baby with her hands, gently rubbing at her stomach, and to calm herself, to make sense of what was happening. *There's good here. There is!*

Straightening up, she dropped the torch as she dug her mobile out of her pocket. About to phone Cash, she checked the battery life and noticed it had gone from full to empty. *Fuck!* Pushing it back into her pocket, she forced herself to take a step forwards, hearing something in the distance, a bark, was that it? "Jed? Jed, where are you? Ness! Presley! Where've you all gone?"

The mist cast such an eerie light, as if it wasn't midnight at all, as if the day was caught somewhere between the dark and the light, somewhere the living weren't meant to tread.

Another kick caused her to yell. "Stop! Just stop it, will you?"

A loud crack from overhead startled her further. What was it? Thunder? Impossible! But then wasn't being torn from reality, as she'd just been, also impossible? "What's going on?"

Rain. More than a few spots, big splashes of it, and it was cold too, chasing away any memory of hot summer days. She had to take shelter, get out of it before she got soaked through. Her eyes frantically scanning this new landscape she'd found herself in, she began to head towards a group of trees whose branches were entwined and plentiful, providing something of a canopy to squat under. There was thunder again and something else, more barking, but not just one dog; there seemed to be several, a pack of them, barking, snarling, and growling, not like dogs at all, actually, like wolves, hungry, ravenous creatures, desperate to gorge themselves.

"Shit! Shit! Shit!"

A bolt of lightning accompanied the thunder at last, illuminating further this strange and misty landscape that she was now a part of, revealing shadows in the deepest part of that mist – creatures that squatted and taller creatures that were cloaked. What the fuck were they? Wolves and their masters? That's what her mind was telling her. All the dogs that had gone missing, so many over the years, were now something else, something vastly at odds with their usual sweet nature. And the taller shapes, the hooded ones, oh shit, she didn't want to be reminded of where she'd seen their kind before – at Blakemort, of course. Legions of them.

The baby kicked several more times, as if he was the one excited now. Certainly, there was no more excitement within her, no feeling of invincibility. She was vulnerable once again and exposed despite her chosen shelter, the branches reaching lower to hold her fast.

"NO!" she screamed, pushing herself away from the tree she'd been leaning against. "There's not just evil here!" No place was wholly evil, except perhaps hell itself. But hell didn't exist, not in this realm. She mustn't let the energy that she'd tuned into earlier – as pure, as organic as white light itself – become only a memory. She had to hold on to it.

Breaking into a run, both hands supporting her belly, she rushed forwards, away from what lay in wait, continuing to shout for the others.

"Cash! Ness! Where are you? Can you hear me? Can you help me?" Only those in the misty shadows responded, moving forwards too. "No! No! Not you! Stay away from me, d'ya hear? Stay away! Oh shit, shit. Someone has to help me! Please!"

Back in the open, she searched for the path she'd been on before, but it was nowhere to be seen. Still she continued forwards, one hand remaining where it was on her belly, the other shielding her eyes from the rain as she strained to see what lay ahead, refusing to look behind her – where *they* were, in pursuit – imagining the wolves set free. They'd outrun her in an instant, encircling their quarry, moving in for the kill…

Oh, but the rain was cold! The kind you got in deep winter. She was shivering, she was shaking as it drenched her, a deluge, biblical almost – ironically.

She had to find the damned path and keep moving, find the others too. "Jed, where are you?"

She was exposed now, the thunder continuing, each roll more threatening than the last, equally threatening forks of lightning like sharp daggers being thrown down.

This was surreal, a nightmare. It was unnatural. *Super*natural. Cults such as the one Witcher was obsessed with had introduced corruption to a place where only peace should exist.

"Fuck you, you bastards!" she called out, addressing those that followed at such a leisurely, such an *arrogant*, pace. "You can't touch me! You can't frighten me." But she *was* frightened, and they knew it. Their hounds could smell her fear, emboldening them further. *Dig deep, Ruby!*

Dig deep, Ruby!

Her own words were hurled back at her, shrieked at her, like an explosion in her mind.

Dig deep! Dig deep! We'll dig you deep – into the ground, never to be found, to rot there.

Where was the fucking path? She was heading into more mist, more woods, more trees that stood together, their branches extending, reaching out to grab her, ready to tear her apart, to get to the baby inside. Oh God, the baby! The kicking baby. The excited baby.

He's a thing of darkness too.

"HE ISN'T!" Ruby screamed as yet more unwanted words formed in her mind.

Only thunder answered.

"HE DOESN'T BELONG TO THE DARK. YOU CAN'T HAVE HIM! YOU WON'T!"

As tears erupted from her eyes, she wiped savagely at them, then briefly clutched at her necklace, trying to find a fraction of comfort from the stones. There was none. They were cold too. She was afraid, she couldn't deny it, but she refused to give those that taunted her the satisfaction of tears.

"I've faced your kind before," she continued, "and I've faced you *down* before as well. And if needs be, I'll do it again and again." Her voice cracked. "I will face you down. Ow!"

She screamed as she stumbled, as she fell forward, her hands held out but not protecting her enough, her stomach also colliding with the ground, causing her to quickly roll onto her side, to curl her knees up and become foetus-like herself. With her arms wrapped around her belly, she prayed no damage had been done, tears falling in earnest now as she fretted, unable to stop her mind from imagining the worst, the feel of blood between her legs, the cramps that would surely ensue, the figures in the deep mist not idling now but rushing at her, ready to cover her, to begin their feasting. The nausea returned with a vengeance, steaming hot, acidic bile that rose in her throat as if her body was trying to rid itself of poison.

"Quickly!"

What the hell?

"Take my hand. Quickly."

Ruby had shut her eyes in an attempt to close the horror out, but now she had to open them. Who was speaking to her? It was a female voice, young and breathy. Not one she recognised.

Yet there was indeed a woman crouched beside her – young, pretty, with long blond hair and the lightest of eyes. She had a dress on that was old-fashioned, a natural colour, earthy.

"Who…who are you?"

"Take my hand," the girl replied. "Take it now, before it's too late."

Chapter Twenty-Three

AS soon as their hands touched, the world changed again, the mist vanishing as if it had never been. The night, too, was gone. It was daytime, the sun as bright as the girl's eyes, a summer's day, but one that didn't choke you with heat or seek to sap your energy. There was a freshness in the air, which Ruby inhaled deep into her lungs, relishing how it enlivened rather than polluted her. As she rose to her feet, she also noted her nausea had subsided again.

Gazing about her, not in horror this time but marvelling at all she saw, Ruby's eyes eventually came to rest on the young woman. She was so young, maybe not even twenty, her beauty wholesome rather than ostentatious and as mesmerising as the woods themselves.

"Gaynor?"

The young woman shook her head.

"Samantha, then?"

Again, a shake of the head. "Come," the girl said. "Let's walk."

All around her, trees stood tall and strong, majestic even, nothing huddled or twisted about them, their sinewy branches not hanging low but soaring upwards as if in salutation of the sun. The leaves upon the trees were such vibrant shades of green, each wonderful variation complementing the next as they bathed in the light that nourished them.

Ruby looked down at the ground. In amongst the bracken were an abundance of woodland flowers. It didn't matter that she didn't know them by name; it didn't stop her from appreciating the colour they lent, the yellows – such a cheerful shade – purples and pinks too.

"Are these the same woods?"

The girl's laughter resembled the tinkling of bells. "They are."

"Then how come…?"

"This is what it's truly like."

"What it should be?"

"All land is sacred," replied the girl.

"But—"

"You can feel the energy here?"

Ruby nodded.

"Good energy?"

Ruby nodded again. It was true, she had felt it. "There's bad energy too."

To her surprise the girl didn't disagree. "There is."

Earlier, with Cash, Ness and Presley, she'd been on a path, one she could barely see. Now, though, the way ahead was clear, winding through the trees to a place not as densely packed, a clearing of some sort, the one that Ness had seen?

It might have been her imagination, but as they drew closer to it, some of the sun that filtered through the trees began to deplete, the rays not as far-reaching as they had been.

"We must continue," the girl said, sensing Ruby's reticence, her desire to stay where they were – in paradise, it seemed. "There's no choice."

"I don't understand," Ruby said, anger sparking within her. Why, oh why, was anything that was good so short-lived? Why did the darkness always have to edge its way back in?

"It's good to feel angry," the girl said. "It's right to feel that way about it."

Enigmatic, the stranger in her midst was that, all right, making Ruby angrier still. However lovely this experience was, however preferable to what had been before, Corinna was still missing. Ruby was done with riddles, with obscurities. She wanted answers.

"You'll get answers," the girl said. "I promise."

As they stepped into the clearing, the trees fell away to form a protective ring around them. Only one tree remained, positioned right at the heart of the clearing, the largest and the most impressive tree Ruby had ever seen – an oak tree, she was sure of it, its trunk so wide and so thick. Resplendent with branches, there was one in particular that caught Ruby's eye, one that protruded from the side of the main trunk, straight for a metre or two before curving upwards, as strong and as sturdy as if it were an individual tree.

Ruby was in awe. From a small acorn something mighty had indeed grown.

The girl had come to a halt, perhaps so that her companion could absorb better all she was seeing, the sheer might of it. The girl then started to pull her forwards, Ruby eager to get closer to the tree but also trepidatious, the latter feeling increasing, causing her heart to race and her to feel hot after all – her face, her entire body, engulfed in sweat, as if she were approaching a furnace.

"What's going on?" she asked the girl, aware that not only was her voice trembling but her entire body too. "Just tell me, will you? My friend is missing. I can't afford to waste time."

"You're not wasting time," the girl assured her, those light eyes of hers glittering.

Again, they stopped, a few feet from the tree. Ruby was grateful for the distance that remained, feeling as if her heart was about to explode, as if an invisible weight bore down upon it.

"That's how they felt too," the girl said, dropping her hand and turning to face her fully.

"Who?"

"The three that died here."

"Like this?"

The girl nodded. "The darkness has a way of crushing you."

"Did...did you die here?"

The girl was silent, so Ruby repeated the question.

"Yes," the girl answered at last. "I was killed here too."

"Killed? You were...murdered?"

"Many of us have been. Not just me, not just the three."

"Your body—"

"Wasn't buried here."

"Then where?"

"Elsewhere. A house."

"A house? What house?"

"In the village."

"What village? When?"

The girl shook her head. "No more questions."

"What? But—"

"We have to be quick."

The girl touched her again, and, as she did, as her grip tightened, a series of images filled Ruby's head. There was a girl, *this* girl, and a village, small in size, a road running through it, or, rather, a dirt track, dwellings on either side, a shop or two, drinking houses, and a toll booth. Smoky shapes moved amongst them, people milling about, just shades, just echoes. In amongst them the girl was more substantial than the rest, every bit as vibrant as she was now. She wore a dress with a white apron over it, and there was a basket in her hands and a cloth over the basket.

What was she doing, Ruby wondered, going from one house to the other and knocking on doors? Ah, she was delivering food. Fresh loaves and fresh eggs. Now she was going up to another house, such a grand house, far older than the others, as if…as if it had been built for a king. Strangely, though, she hesitated before knocking on the door, eventually doing so and then taking a few steps back.

The door opened, slowly, tantalisingly. A figure stepped out, indistinct, holding out his hands as the girl reached into her basket and took out a loaf of bread, having to come close again to hand it over. There was a smile on her face but not one that enhanced it; the recipient of the bread emitted a burst of laughter to see it, relishing that it was disingenuous.

The girl retreated further, turned and hurried down the path surreptitiously – in case she was being spied upon, perhaps – wiping at her hands as if to remove a stain there.

There was another house, not as grand as the other one, more of a cottage with black beams against white stucco, and the girl experienced the same trepidation as she approached the door. Not just trepidation but fear, raw-edged. Ruby had never laid eyes on Low Cottage, but she'd heard it described. Was this that same house? Oh, the poor girl! She was terrified to approach it, but customers needed serving, that's what her mam told her. Now that her father was gone – he'd died only recently – every penny counted, made the difference between them being able to eat or starve. "They're just folk," she'd say to her daughter when she complained of having to deliver to this house in particular, "ordinary folk. Don't make a fuss. Don't you dare!"

Like before, the girl rapped on the door before stepping away, as was polite. Unlike before, however, the door opened far quicker, as if…as if whoever was inside had been lying in wait. A figure emerged from the house, still obscured but clearly female, beckoning the girl forwards, something in her hand – money, perhaps. Again, the girl had no choice but to step closer, to take payment for goods, the woman staring at her. Examining her? She gave a sharp nod of her head before stepping back inside.

The girl was running now, clutching her basket to her, knocking on another door, this one belonging to a house far more modest in size. Nothing vague or shadowy about the woman who answered this time; she was as substantial as the girl. A woman in her later years, with concern on her face and anger too, although she tried hard to conceal it. She wasn't angry with the girl – that much Ruby understood. This was a girl whom she liked, whom she had regular contact with, whom she was…afraid for.

There was nothing left in the girl's basket, all goods had gone, but, even so, the woman reached out and gently stroked the girl's cheek as if trying to calm her, her mouth moving gently as she uttered a few words, although what she said remained a mystery to Ruby. *Take care,* was that it?

The scene changed. There was no more village, just woodland and a girl running through it, terrified. Someone was in pursuit of her; someone was *hunting* her. And not just one person, Ruby realised, seeing dark shapes again, this time surrounding the girl, moving towards her with that same arrogant pace they'd used when pursuing Ruby. No need to hurry – the girl was going nowhere. There was no escape. Ruby gulped, screwed her eyes shut briefly but then had to open them, no choice but to see. This girl, this beautiful, innocent girl, was being dragged through the woods, something around her neck. A rope. She was here, in the clearing, just as Ruby was in the clearing, dragged towards the oak tree now, hoisted up via the rope onto one of its branches, her feet kicking furiously, her hands trying to ease the burn of the rope at her throat.

Ruby knew full well what she was seeing: a sacrifice. Hooded figures, thirteen of them, surrounded the girl, believing such a vile act was necessary to the religion they'd devoted themselves to, all of them feeding upon each other's delusions.

There have always been sacrifices…

Ruby bristled. Whose words were they? Not hissed at her, merely imparted – a cold hard fact if ever there was one. There had indeed always been sacrifices, even those made for the purpose of good, Jesus Christ being a perfect example, to save mankind.

But this girl…this beautiful, simple girl, should never have been used in such a way. The crowd that surrounded her craved the darkness, wanted to feel it course through their veins and elevate them. Doing anything and everything to spit in the face of redemption.

The girl had stilled now, her hands dropping to her side. What had made her a target specifically? Her beauty? Her innocence? The two combined? Ruby could only surmise it was so; both had set her apart, drawing the woman at Low Cottage and her disciples to her like moths to a flame, determined to quash what they found so abhorrent, the light inside her.

The girl was cut down. Ruby didn't want to see any more, but she couldn't deny the fate the girl had suffered either. She was cut down and her body burnt, right here, in this clearing – a ritual hanging and a ritual burning on sacrificial ground, what bones remained not to be left there but transported elsewhere. To Low Cottage? Was she the body Ness suspected was entombed there? The woman who'd lived at the cottage, Hylands, regarding her as some sort of…trophy? Wanting the horror of the act she'd committed to feed the energy in her home, the girl the first of many intended victims, both animal and human. Ah, she had grand plans…

"Enough!" Ruby called, feeling her legs buckle beneath her. The girl reached out and, as delicate as she was, was able to stop her from falling. "You were sacrificed by Phyllida Hylands and her disciples, then transported to Low Cottage. It's your body in the wall there. In later years, Gaynor, Samantha and Jim weren't hanged at Rayners Wood, or knifed or anything like that, but still they were victims of what had been set in motion here so long ago, of what was unleashed, what, in effect, *lives* here. Witcher was right about that, at least. Cults still exist, offshoots. They continue to feed the legacy, no longer at Low Cottage, perhaps, but focused here in the woods."

The girl nodded before answering. "I also live here."

"You're grounded?"

"No."

"Then why do you stay? Why would you want to?"

"Remember what you saw."

Ruby did, after the nightmare a glimpse of heaven.

"Go on, look around."

She had to take a deep breath before obeying, fearful of the shadows, of seeing the girl's legs thrashing from the bough. There was no such thing. The sun was shining down upon the clearing, as fierce and as gentle as ever, no hint it had ever been overshadowed. Movement caught her attention and the sound of something, a dog barking, not growling or snarling, only joy in it.

She looked towards the trees. "Jed?"

It was him! In the trees and barking at her, his tail wagging from side to side. Overhead a chorus of birds burst into song, notes both high and low harmonising perfectly. There was more barking, not just Jed's, she realised, but a variety of dogs. She looked again into the trees. There were so many of them, all shapes, sizes and colours. All were taking their cue from Jed and were far from the ravenous beasts the darkness would have her believe they'd become.

"*This* is why I stay," the girl said. "Because this is what these woods were created to be. And what they could be again. There is strength here, there's protest against injustice, against what has contaminated it. The deluded, as you think of them, always make the same mistake. *Never* do they sacrifice one of their own, only what is good, seeking to destroy it. But it's not that easy. The good remains, and eventually it will right what has gone so wrong."

Ruby could only stare at her. "You're so strong," she whispered. "Not a victim at all."

"You are also strong. Draw on that strength, on your gift. Don't deny either." Reaching out, the girl then laid her hand on Ruby's belly. "I was pregnant too."

"What? You were?"

"Yes."

"I'm so sorry. I didn't see that, I didn't realise…"

"I was blessed."

Am I also blessed? Ruby wanted to ask the question but didn't dare.

"You're strong," the girl reiterated. "And your strength will serve you both."

"Who are you?" Ruby asked. "What's your name?"

"Tilly. Short for Matilda. Jess was always a friend."

"Jess Biggs?"

"She cared for me. I think she still does."

A breeze had struck up, toying with the girl's flaxen hair. It lifted Ruby's hair too, moving it around her shoulders. Trees were no longer static but swaying, the chorus of barking dying down, leaving just the one dog, hers, his voice echoey as if he was no longer close by but distant.

Daylight was fading, rapidly.

"What's happening?" Ruby was fearful again. "Tilly, tell me what's happening."

"The redheaded girl," Tilly replied, "she's here."

"Where, though? Where?"

"Beware of him."

"Who? Witcher?"

"A man torn between the light and the dark."

Ruby reached out and grabbed the girl by her arms, but she was no more solid than air. "If Corinna's here, tell me where!"

Instead of answering, the girl smiled, Ruby noticing that, when genuine, it made her dazzle. "Something else is here too," she said, confusing Ruby further. "Ah, there it is! Do you see? It's coming in all its fury. As I told you before, anger is good. Anger is righteous."

"What? I don't understand…"

The girl was fading as quickly as the light, the breeze now more of a howling wind, strong enough to knock Ruby off her feet, she was certain of it.

"Stay strong, Ruby, stay exactly who you are. Ah, look, look, isn't it a thing of glory? Look!"

She was gone entirely now, Ruby in the dark woods again, not in a clearing but where she was before when her friends had been torn from her, had disappeared. Thunder returned, and boughs and branches were creaking and moaning, the rain pelting down, a deluge, just as it had been in the nightmare, a bark still audible, a scream too.

RUBY! RUBY! Where are you?

Ness's voice had pierced her mind – her frantic voice.

"Ness!" Ruby shouted back, not thinking anymore, not questioning but running as fast as she was able to, not just for her life but for Corinna's and, quite possibly, Ness's.

Chapter Twenty-Four

NOT Ness's voice in her head anymore but another, whispering words from a poem, it seemed:

The woods are lovely, dark and deep,
But I have promises to keep,
And miles to go before I sleep,
And miles to go before I sleep…

A scowl twisted Ruby's face. The words were inaccurate. Rayners Wood wasn't lovely at all, not with this…this…storm raging. The rain, no longer just a few random spots but torrential, was pouring down in front of her – no nightmare, not this time, but real life, real time – the wind like a separate entity, a hysterical thing that whipped through the trees. As Cash had said, it hadn't been forecasted, the heatwave they'd been experiencing up until now set to continue. Another gust of wind swept through, this one actually knocking her sideways into the bark of a tree. Ruby gasped, clinging on to it and trying to catch her breath. Having materialised out of nothing, the storm was intense, a thing of glory, as Tilly had said, if you weren't caught in it.

Promises to keep…

The voice was in her head again. Who was it?

Theo? Is it you?

Despite shivering so hard with cold and shock, her teeth chattering, there was warmth in her chest, spreading outwards, enveloping her like a hug, one she didn't know she needed quite so much until it happened. A sob burst from her. It was Theo! Doing as she'd promised and remaining by their sides, another force for good, just as Tilly was, as all the dogs that had ever gone missing here were, and the people that had died too, the vulnerable, the innocent.

RUBY!

That wasn't Theo; that was Ness. Ruby had to find her.

Help me, Theo, lead me to her. You're right, there are promises to keep, so many, and here's another: I promise I'll find you, Ness, as well as Corinna. I'm on my way.

With no torch now to hand – she'd dropped it long ago in the mists – she used the trees to heave herself against the wind, clinging from tree trunk to tree trunk, not trusting her feet to guide her but Theo's instructions, no time to marvel at how clearly she could hear them.

Carry on… Turn right… Continue… Go left…

The wind kept slapping chunks of wet hair into her face, and each time it stung. No sooner would she swipe it away than it was back again, like Medusa's hair, a living, brutal thing.

Where were Cash and Presley? She'd seen Jed – in Tilly's reality, at any rate, but in this grim and darker version, she'd only heard him bark, and that was from afar. What was the force that had torn them from each other? Buffeted by another great gust, she had to swallow hard to catch her breath, her hands only briefly going to her stomach.

The energies are gathering. That's what Ness had said in the car coming over. She'd also insisted Ruby take a jacket in case the weather changed. She'd known this was going to happen! And if someone like her had known, then was it possible this howling wind, lashing rain, thunder and lightning was something to be embraced rather than feared, very much a thing of glory, an expression of righteous anger, a force for the greater good, determined to stamp out – finally – a force that was so low?

Turn left... Hurry...

Yes, yes, she would.

Time's running out...

What? That wasn't Theo, not just then! That was someone else, someone who spoke again.

Things happened. Dreadful! Nothing changes...

She might not know who'd entered her head this time, but Ruby replied nonetheless. *Things do change.* I'll *change it. Nature too. Not the supernatural but supernature.*

Black energy, cults, demons... They could not be allowed to have their way.

Turn left, Theo had said, and Ruby did just that, still grabbing on to trees to help her move forwards, right in the thick of them, their boughs swinging and protesting but a whisper in them too, one that echoed Theo and her instructions as if colluding with her.

Depending on who you believed, this wasn't such a bad place after all.

She continued onwards, lifting her feet to avoid stumbling, a bedraggled, pregnant mess, the baby active but not kicking as hard as before, that warm feeling she'd experienced, Theo's hug, lingering around her waist, focusing on the baby so that she didn't have to.

Miles to go…

She recalled the words of earlier, the truth of them this time – it certainly seemed like she was travelling bloody miles. Where was everyone?

Here!

No sooner had the answer formed in her mind than it was as if she was spat out of the trees, forcibly ejected into a wide-open space, a clearing, one with a mighty oak at its centre and that she'd visited before in that strange reality with Tilly. The oak, whilst still impressive in size, lacked the majesty of before, however. Rather it was menacing, this tree that Tilly had swung from.

"Ness!" The relentless gale snatched the cry from her mouth, and she spun around instead, eyes scanning the circle of trees, looking for Ness, for anyone. "Where are you all?"

Returning her gaze to the tree, her mind couldn't compute exactly how vast it was – the king of these woods hereabouts, it had to be, beautiful but abused, proud but corrupted. Its boughs twisted around each other, reminding Ruby of snakes and holding steady against the wind, resisting its onslaught, the wet bark glistening as if with freshly shed blood not rain. There were carvings upon it, although to see what they were, she'd have to get closer, erase the image of Tilly's body hanging from it, seeing it nonetheless, how she'd kicked…

"RUBY!"

Dragging her eyes from the shade of Tilly, they fixed on something more substantial.

"Ness!" Ruby shouted back. Ness and…someone else. A man. One who held her in front of him, something at her throat that glinted. "Witcher?" she said, about to rush forwards.

"Stay where you are!" the man demanded. "Don't move an inch or I'll plunge this knife deeper. That's no empty threat I'm making, don't think it is. It's a promise."

A promise? Yes, she didn't doubt it, wondering where they'd come from, how they'd suddenly appeared – but that tree, you could hide an army behind it if you wanted. She noticed also there had seemed to be a change in the weather as soon as she'd spotted them, the wind dropping a notch or two, the rain easing, as if, like her, it was holding its breath, waiting, deciding on its next move.

Ruby held her hands up in front of her, rain running in rivulets down her skin, further soaking the cuffs of her jacket. "Witcher?" she said. "Is it you?"

"What do you know about me?" he snarled. "What do any of you know about me?"

"Ruby, stay well away—"

As Ness tried to speak, the man instantly tightened his grip, causing her to briefly choke. "Shut your mouth, okay? I've told you, just shut your mouth!"

"Okay! Okay!" Ruby interjected, still with her hands up and retreating a step or two. "Keep calm, please. There's no need for this."

The man shifted from foot to foot like a boxer in a ring, gearing up for the fight. A howl in the distance – Jed, or it could have been an owl or some other creature – caused him to turn his head but only a fraction before his eyes were back on Ruby. She was scared, just as Ness was scared. Scrub that, Ness must be terrified, the danger right now most definitely human but not making it any easier to deal with, not with that knife pressed so close and that look in his eye, which was all too visible even from where Ruby stood. Such determination in it, and madness.

It is Witcher.

Theo was in her head.

A man torn between the light and the dark.

Where are the others? Ruby shot back. *Where are Cash and Presley?*

Keep him talking. Help is coming.

"Look, we don't mean you any harm," Ruby said, obeying that instruction. "We just want to find our friend Corinna. That's why we're here. We're looking for her."

"I know what you've done!" the man screamed.

"What? I don't understand—"

"Not you. God knows where you've come from, but this one." Again he tightened his grip, practically lifting Ness off the ground, her eyes bulging as her hands tried to loosen his hold, just as Tilly had tried to loosen the one around her neck, both of them failing. "I've met her before, with Corinna and another one, an older woman – her aunts, allegedly. That's the tale I was spun. I know they've been back to my house; I wrung it out of this one. They broke in."

Quickly Ruby scrabbled for an excuse. "It's because…because they were desperate, that's why. Corinna's missing, and they were trying to find her."

"So they blamed me?"

"I…"

"Thought they could harass me?"

"Look, it's—"

"People like you should leave well alone. You don't know what you're dealing with."

A low rumble of thunder overhead promised more lightning to come, but still the wind hovered rather than rushed by. "Then tell me what we're dealing with and who you are."

"Are you all psychic, is that it?"

"What?"

"Like that other one, Corinna." The way he spat her name sent shivers down Ruby's spine.

"Did she say that?"

"She said she's psychic, that she works with psychics. It's got to be you lot. She said she can sense the spirit world, get in touch with it. That she had an interest in these woods, *my* woods."

"*Your* woods? What do you mean?"

"I'm the one who knows these woods, every last detail. I've studied them all my life. I know every inch of ground, every tree that grows here. It's my domain, no one else's. Mine!"

The wind stirred as more thunder rumbled, but it soon died down. Instead of looking into Witcher's eyes, she looked into Ness's. *Go,* they said to her. *Get out of here.*

No, she returned, *help's coming. Theo's said.*

"Tom," Ruby continued, noting that he started visibly at the use of his first name but didn't deny it either, "we know these are your woods, we're not denying that. We don't want any trouble—"

"It wasn't just an interest she had. She was obsessed."

"Who?"

"CORINNA!" he screamed, making Ruby and Ness flinch once more. "That's why she came back to Low Cottage, because she knew it was linked to these woods."

"How, Tom? How is it linked?"

"Their kind, those that practised here, that have done for centuries, one of their most prolific members, one of their worst, lived there."

"You're talking about the Cult of Badb?"

In reply, he nodded his head, just a couple of times, hard and sharp, his grip on Ness not loosening, not for a second.

"And Phyllida Hylands," Ruby continued.

"That's it, that's the bitch. You know your stuff, don't you? Like Corinna. Hylands is the *only* member whose name is known, can you believe that? She just…she didn't care, one way or the other. She was…" His voice had changed subtly, and Ruby tried to think how. Had a more reverent tone crept in? "Untouchable, truly untouchable. She knew she'd never be held to account for the atrocious acts she'd carried out. She was so damned powerful."

Ruby swallowed, remembering Tilly and what had been done to her. "Why, Tom? Why'd you want to get close to someone like Hylands? Move into her house, *knowing* what she was like?"

"The evil that she was capable of?"

"Yes, Tom! Yes! Do you actually know what she did? Have you ever found proof?"

"That's what I've been looking for."

"They murdered people! I don't know about now, whether her cult still exists in some form as you say it does, whether they're responsible, directly or indirectly, for the deaths of the three found here in recent years, but a century ago they existed, all right, and they murdered innocent people."

"They did! Yes. Correct. Lots of people. More than we

will ever know!"

"So what about the three that were found here?"

"Of course they were victims! Easy pickings. Gaynor was homeless, Jim Fowler a policeman but one with a troubled past, a bad divorce and an alcohol habit, the prime suspect in a case himself, for theft. He wanted to find out what had happened to Gaynor as a way to claw back favour; he wasn't really doing it for her. They were vulnerable people, *weak* people."

People that Witcher clearly had nothing but derision for.

"What about Samantha Lawrence?" she asked.

"Samantha?" Witcher let out a burst of laughter that again had Ness reaching upwards to try to loosen his hold. Ruby could see she was tired, beginning to flag, swallowing furiously as if to gulp at what air she could. *Ness, help is coming.* From what quarters, she didn't know – Cash, Presley, maybe even Lee – but Theo had said it was due, and she had to believe her. "Samantha was an ordinary girl, it seemed," Witcher continued, seeming happy enough to tell her, maybe even trying to make sense of it too, "who just ran into bad luck, into the arms of darkness. I tried to get her parents to tell me more about her, about why she'd been drawn here, but they wouldn't, called the police on me, didn't understand I needed to see what the pattern was, that she was part of my investigation. Mind you—" he snorted, clearly pleased with himself "—dear Samantha still came in useful. She was the bait I used to get your friend to accompany me here. I played the part of her parent, you see, her *grieving* parent. Corinna's a soft touch, isn't she? A lamb to the slaughter."

Perhaps because he'd used such a horrendous term, Ness

277

attempted another rebellion, her elbows digging into Witcher's side, her feet kicking at his shins.

"Ness!" Ruby called in a bid to stop her.

"Bitch!" Witcher yelled, working hard to restrain her, that knife of his doing as he'd promised and biting deeper.

Ness screamed, her body becoming still, although she continued to gasp.

"I'm not playing," Witcher warned, as breathless as Ness, the boughs above him continuing to creak, the ring of trees that encircled them rustling too. Thunder rolled, and a ribbon of lightning appeared; even so, the weather was holding back, just as Ruby herself was holding back, as Ness had been forced into doing once more, her brief struggle subdued.

"Witcher," Ruby continued, "what do you want with Corinna, with us?"

He hurled his answer at her. "I wanted her to commune."

"Commune? Who with?"

"DON'T MESS WITH ME!"

Ruby had lowered her hands, but she raised them again. "I'm not, I'm just trying to understand. Do you mean—" she swallowed "—commune with Phyllida Hylands?"

"You know that's *exactly* what I mean."

Was that what he was obsessed with? A woman rather than Rayners Wood? A murderer?

"Perhaps…perhaps I can help? Me instead of Corinna, instead of Ness."

"Ruby—" Ness began, but Witcher quickly silenced her, glancing too, but only briefly, at Ruby's swollen stomach, the madness in his eyes increasing.

"I can see the light and the darkness," Ruby continued.

"I…I can see them both clearly. And I can help you, but you have to let Ness go and tell us where Corinna is. Let her go too."

"You'll never find her."

"Witcher…Tom, I can see more than she can. My gift…it's more developed than Corinna's. I'm being honest here; I'll be able to commune. Tell me where she is, and in return, I'll help you."

Once more, he was shifting from foot to foot, Ness dragged from side to side with him. "That's what she said." His ragged voice hinted that perhaps he was getting tired too. "She begged me to let her go, that she'd help me to see if I did. She promised, and then you know what she did?"

"What?"

"She ran, tried to escape. Oh, she's quick, all right, a young girl like her. But as I've said, and as she should have known, I've mapped every inch of these woods. She couldn't escape."

"Is she alive?"

She asked the question, then steeled herself for the answer. There was a moment of silence, perfect silence, the weather still holding its breath but growing as impatient as she was, as Witcher was too – she could feel it, the threat in the air…

Eventually Witcher answered. "Maybe," he said, shrugging. "Maybe not."

Incensed by his words, by his suddenly nonchalant attitude, Ruby couldn't help it; she took a step forward and then another, anger, *righteous* anger beginning to overspill.

"What are you doing?" He was nonchalant no more. "I said stay back!"

"I can help you," she said through gritted teeth. "You've

told me you know these woods, and I've told you I can see more clearly than Corinna. I can see those lying in wait here."

"What?" Only briefly he turned his head from side to side before glaring at her. "Liar!"

"I'm not a liar. And if you want to talk about the ability to commune, well, I already have, right here, tonight, with one of Hylands' victims, Tilly, the girl that was hanged from this tree, whose feet I can see at this very minute, dangling just above your head."

"Tilly?" His voice held both disbelief and belief. "What do you know about Tilly?"

"That she was a simple girl who lived in a small village, the one you now live in, Lindfield. A young girl, beautiful, who delivered produce to houses courtesy of a small holding run by her parents, her mother principally, as her father had died. She delivered to places such as the hunting lodge, oh, and yes, of course, Low Cottage."

"Low Cottage?" he repeated, as if in wonder. "Go on."

"She was a girl who became a target, easy pickings, as you'd say. Innocent and vulnerable, the kind Hylands and her disciples adored because…because they believed the darkness craved innocence, that it offered it a richer diet. She was brought here, and she was murdered here—"

"That's right! That's right!" He jerked his head upwards. "Like you say, she was hanged from this tree, this very one. This is…the hub of it all, Hylands' preferred spot to carry out the devil's work. But how did you know about Tilly? So few know! It was only ever documented as hearsay—"

"I told you, I've spoken with her. I also know it's her body that's interred at Low Cottage, or Owl Cottage, to give it its proper name, its secret name. I know all these things and more. I've seen, and I can help you see too. In return, all you have to do is let Ness go, tell us where Corinna is—"

Another moment of silence ensued. Was he contemplating her offer? Did it have any hope of working? If he let Ness go, her phone could be checked for a signal, they could call the police, get them over here, find Corinna, rescue her – pray God Witcher was bluffing and that she was still alive. And maybe, just maybe, Ruby would do as she'd said she would, show him the darkness, just a glimpse of it…

She came to a halt when Witcher roared at her, louder than any thunder.

"LIAR! You're mocking me! That's what they did, *supposed* cult members, ignoring me for so long, then sending a minion to talk with me, one who kept me waiting!"

Ruby was dumbstruck, had to work hard to find her voice. "I've told you I'm not lying! How would I know about Tilly if I was?"

"You don't get to mess with me! Not them and not you!"

What the hell? "Tom, why won't you believe me? I'll help you. I will. No! Don't! Stop doing that!" Ness was kicking again and thrashing, that sharp, wicked knife's edge pushing further against her skin, not enough to draw blood, but it soon would. "Tom! You have to stop! The police are on their way. You won't get away with this, with harming Ness. I can promise you that too!"

"The police…" As the wolves had snarled, so did Witcher. "They're in on it too, all this cult 'rubbish', as people call it. So many in the police force are, did you know that? Oh yeah, yeah, that's right, the bigwigs, people in high office the world over. You know how they got there? Because of evil. That's how. Because they worship at the altar of evil, and it rewards them!"

"Not everyone in high office," Ruby denied. "There are plenty of good people there too."

"You're wrong. Those who hold power, *true* power, do so because they've done precisely that – they've succumbed. They walk amongst us in plain sight, and they're untouchable, all of them."

"The cult won't protect you," Ruby warned. "Hylands won't."

"If I'm devoted to her, she will, if I prove it. I want to be taken seriously, not ignored. I deserve to be shown more bloody respect! To be untouchable, to do exactly what I want, to have people bow down to me, like Hylands had people bow down to her. Just think…"

His voice – his wistful voice – trailed off as now, managing to restrain Ness with one arm, he lifted the other, the one that held the knife, the glint from it like lightning itself. Determined to stop him, Ruby started to run, the rain pouring once again, the wind howling, carrying her forwards through the darkness.

"STOP! WITCHER, JUST STOP!"

It was coming down, down, down, that knife, Ness staring up at it, frozen now rather than flailing, caught in the horror of what was to come, anticipating it.

"STOP!" Ruby was almost upon him, her hands outstretched, no thought for herself now, or her baby, desperate to stop Ness from being harmed. "YOU CAN'T DO THIS!"

Like Ness, he froze too. Ruby was confused, wondering what was happening now and whether she could trust her eyes. Not only did he freeze, the knife dropped from his hands, seeming to hover in the air for a moment, as if cradled by the wind, before dropping to the ground.

"What…what's happening?" he said, his voice barely audible as he stared not at Ruby but beyond her, into the circle of the trees. "How…how is that possible?"

Ruby tensed. What was he looking at? Those dark figures she'd seen before, maybe, snarling beasts by their sides? Something that was even worse than Witcher.

She could hardly bear to look as he spoke again, as Ness's eyes widened.

"How can you be there as well as here? It's not possible! Who…? Who is that?"

Curiosity getting the better of her, Ruby turned her head.

There were no hooded figures, no slathering wolves. It was a woman that stepped forward. One who looked exactly like Ness.

Chapter Twenty-Five

"LYNDSEY!"

Ruby heard the name on Ness's lips, understood too who this other woman was – Ness's twin, the one who'd died at birth, who'd grown up beside her in the spirit world but whom Ness had banished from her life when she was thirteen, consequently never hearing from or seeing her again. The torment this had caused Ness! Ruby knew how much, that she was sorry for what she'd done, begging her twin to give her a sign she was safe. But Lyndsey never had, too deep in the grip of darkness, Ness feared. But if that had been the case, it wasn't any longer. She'd returned – perhaps had done so even before tonight, if what Ruby had sensed in Ness's house was anything to go by – fully manifesting, striding out of the trees, and straight towards Witcher.

Witcher. The knife might have fallen from his hand, but that didn't mean he'd relinquished his grip on Ness. As Lyndsey approached them, he dragged Ness backwards, the wind having worked itself back up to full capacity, causing the boughs above his head to swing perilously low – one bough in particular. Ruby blinked. Saw again the figure of Tilly hanging from it; she was still, what life there'd been in her extinguished, darkness having counted down the seconds.

"Who is that woman…? What…she? Can't be… Impossible! Impossible!"

Witcher was babbling, some words swallowed by the wind.

"What…dark magic…this?"

Dark magic? Ruby shook her head. This was no dark magic, but she could see how it might be misconstrued. Lyndsey was presenting as Ness, identical to her, right down to her clothing, her black hair plastered across her face as Ness's was. Only her expression was different – one of sheer determination, whereas Ness's face, despite the danger she was in, was rapturous.

Since she'd emerged from the woods, Lyndsey hadn't faltered, quickly closing the gap as the wind dipped and howled, as it got behind her like it had got behind Ruby, aiding her.

"No! No! Not happening…" Witcher still babbled. "There's…one…only one…"

"There isn't," Ruby shouted over the wind, making sure that her words reached his ears. "There are two. Ness is alive, but Lyndsey is spirit."

"What? Spirit…"

"You wanted to see. Well, that's exactly what's happening."

"Not her! Not this! Keep her away from me! Keep her away!"

Still he was retreating, more boughs from the ancient oak lowering precariously, one scraping the top of his head. Emitting a scream, he reached up. "What's that? What just touched me?"

Taking advantage of her partial release, Ness drove her elbow into his stomach again, causing him to loosen his other arm, to stagger as now both hands clutched at his scalp. Free at last, she ran forwards, towards Lyndsey, calling her name. Witcher's horror, Ness's elation – it was both terrible and wonderful to see, two emotions that sat at opposite ends of the spectrum.

"Lyndsey!" Ness continued. "Lyndsey, you're here! You saved me."

Help is coming. That's what Theo had said. Is this what she'd meant?

But what of the others? What about Corinna?

"Ness!" Ruby called, hating to interrupt them, two women who were carbon copies of each other, just a few inches apart now, their expressions ravenous. "Ness, Corinna…Witcher…"

Witcher was tearing at his neck and his waist now, and Ruby could understand why: the boughs of the ancient oak tree had wrapped themselves around him.

A beautiful tree, a natural masterpiece but used for torture. Those carvings upon it not just the names of lovers, there'd be other marks too, symbols people thought of as powerful, and perhaps they were – but, really, it was people's actions that were powerful, the good they did, the harm, and what those actions attracted. The tree – was it fighting back? Just as the whole of nature was.

There was an almighty crash, not close by but from elsewhere in the woods. A tree, it had to be, forcibly uprooted and falling to the ground. Certainly, the ring of trees that surrounded her were crashing one into the other, producing a tribal sound like the beating of drums.

Time's running out – hurry!

It was Theo's voice, a new desperation in it.

Again, Ruby addressed Ness. "We have to find Corinna!"

As entranced as she was, as long as she had waited to be reunited with her twin, Ness tore herself away, her hand reaching out to Lyndsey even as she hurried towards Ruby, begging her.

"Please don't go," she said. "Please wait."

Lyndsey simply stared at her, but already she was fading.

Ruby reached out too, to Ness, saw the tears that fell from her eyes to mingle with the rain on her cheeks. "Ness," she said, doing her best to soothe her, "this isn't the end. She'll return."

Ness was nodding, still crying, her sobs ragged. "She saved me, Ruby, for the second time. He was going to do it. Witcher was going to kill me. I could feel it. I could sense his determination to be taken seriously, as he said, by Hylands, by everyone, to be more of an authority than he already was, crazed for the power it would give him. She came back, she saved me. But—"

"No buts, Ness, not now. We have to find Corinna."

"Yes. Yes. I know."

Both turned towards Witcher, an ensnared man who'd wanted to see something other than what was material and who was now getting his wish.

"There! There!" In between trying to disentangle himself, he kept jabbing at the air. "In the trees. Who are they? *What* are they? Is Hylands there? Is she?"

If Ruby turned her head to look, she knew what she'd see – *them* – those that had swallowed the darkness whole, who'd gone past the point of no return.

Witcher wasn't a stupid man. He'd said himself he'd made a lifetime's study of these woods, of the Cult of Badb and Hylands in particular, moving into Low Cottage to feel closer to her, to prove to her his devotion, the intended slaughter of Ness proving something else: he was as bad as her. He knew what was in front of him well enough. On his lips, however, there was no welcoming cry. The man gibbered, he howled, even louder than the wind.

"Ness! Shit! What do we do?"

Ness looked from them to Witcher, alternating her gaze, another tumultuous crash elsewhere in the woods making her flinch just as Ruby did, surprise, horror, sadness and acceptance all emotions running riot on her face, running riot within Ruby too.

"Come with me," she said, grabbing hold of Ruby's arm and also heading towards Witcher. Before they reached him, she started shouting, "Witcher, we haven't got much time. This storm…those…those things that are behind us… We can help you, but you have to help yourself too."

The dark shapes, energy that had splintered from the mass, the servants of something so much bigger…Ruby couldn't look at them full on again. For herself and for the baby, she couldn't allow them to imprint themselves upon her mind and remain there, torturing her, playing upon her fears…

Ness read her mind. "You don't have to look. They're not here for us."

Words that offered only a crumb of comfort. Just as she and Ness were doing, they continued to move forwards. She could sense them well enough, and how they kept pace, the wind whipping itself into more of a fury, as appalled as she was. When Ness struggled to speak, Ruby took over.

"Tom, Tom, if you can hear me, listen! We'll help you. We'll get you out of there, but you must tell us where Corinna is. We have to get her out of here too. Tom, quickly, please."

If he did hear, he gave no indication, his hair now utterly dishevelled and his jacket and trousers ripped by the oak's branches. What was behind them was also angry, but then it always was – it was *born* of anger, nothing righteous about it at all.

"Strengthen your protection," Ness managed, having to clutch on to Ruby now in order to stay upright. They could hear another tree being torn from the soil, the devastation continuing.

"What's happening, Ness?"

"It's a culling. Like the Great Storm of '87, this will destroy everything in its path. It's indiscriminate now; it'll raze this entire area to the ground."

"Tom." Ruby pleaded with Witcher again. "Stop thrashing! Let us get you out of there."

"No time," he continued to rant. "Look…look…no time."

"There *is* time! And you can redeem yourself. Maybe you're not a bad man, maybe…maybe you wanted to expose what had happened here for all the right reasons once upon a time."

"Help…can't help…don't know…she is… Oh God, help!"

Don't know? What did he mean by that? That he actually had no clue where Corinna was, despite boasting he knew every inch of this wood?

"Shit, Ness, we've got to reach him before they do."

As they put that plan into action, Ruby continued to yell. "Tom, the fact you're calling for help shows you don't want this. You don't want anything to do with the darkness, not really. Oh, for God's sake, come on, just admit it, will you? Your intentions were good once, weren't they?"

Damn the roar of this wind! It was deafening.

"Tom, stop struggling. Stop making it worse!"

Around him the branches continued to whip back and forth.

"Tom!" Ruby tried again. "We can get you out of there if you calm down." With the black energy closer too, she begged for an answer from Ness. "What do we do?"

"We keep trying," Ness said, although Ruby could sense well enough her hopelessness.

"What about—" with her thumb Ruby indicated behind her "—them."

"I told you, it's not us they want."

"This weather, is it happening elsewhere, do you think?"

"Focus on Witcher. We still need him to tell us where Corinna is."

"But what if he doesn't know, Ness? I think before, when he said what he did, he was bluffing."

"HELP ME!" Witcher's voice cut across them as another gust of wind pushed Ruby and Ness away from him, too strong to fight against. Still he was shouting. "I don't want this, I don't want *her*," he declared. "Not anymore. How could anyone want this? Go! Go away."

What had been behind them now encircled the tree, just as they had when Tilly was caught up in it. Ruby buried her face in Ness's neck, and Ness tightened her grip on her.

"Oh no, no, no!" Ruby murmured. "What can we do? What can we do?"

"There's nothing more we can do."

"The darkness is going to devour him."

"Yes. It is."

Ruby lifted her head, began to turn towards the tree, but Ness stopped her.

"He's chosen his path, Ruby."

As wild as the weather, Ruby shook her head. "But we still don't know where Corinna is!"

"Help is coming."

"What?" Ness had just repeated the same words as Theo. Ruby noticed too that Ness was much calmer now, almost serene. "I don't understand."

"Listen."

All she could hear was Witcher screaming, the way he begged for mercy, the wind screaming too, the clash of trees, the creak of boughs, the lashing rain…

"Ness, I can't—"

"Listen!" Ness insisted.

Barking. Somehow overriding it all.

"Jed?" she whispered.

"Not just Jed."

She was right – yet again, it was a chorus of barking, in the distance, leading away. To where?

Help is here.

Not Ness but Theo.

"Help is here," Ness reiterated, hope evident on her face also.

There was another crash – this one really close – and two terrible cries, one that soared with triumph, the other so much more guttural.

The source of those cries was the oak tree. The dark figures had gone, dispersed, but Witcher was still present. Or at least his body was. A bough had been sheared off completely – a heavy bough, the one Tilly had swung from – and beneath it lay Witcher.

"He's dead," Ruby whispered, not having to draw closer to realise that.

"He is, he's gone."

Around them the storm continued to whoop, to holler, to vent its wrath.

"What happened, Ness? I mean, what *really* happened?"

"It wasn't the darkness that got him," Ness replied, again rapture in her expression.

"It was the light?"

Ness's eyes travelled to the thunderous sky. "I've seen it before, in a vision, when I was searching for Corinna. Two mighty shields colliding – the light and the dark. This time, the light won, it got to him before the darkness could. He hadn't walked so far down that path after all."

Perhaps if he'd killed Ness…but he hadn't.

Ness nodded as if Ruby had voiced that thought. "In a way, Lyndsey saved him as well."

It was a battle won, but the war continued.

"Come on, Ness…the dogs…Corinna."

Briefly Ness touched Ruby's cheek. "Are you okay to keep going?"

"Me?" Ruby glanced downwards at her belly, felt the warmth there still from Theo's hug and how the child welcomed it. She breathed in the savage air, imbibed the energy, *good* energy, able to extinguish the bad – always. "Oh,

Ness. I don't think I've ever been better."

Ness's hair slightly obscured her face. Even so, Ruby caught how wide her smile was.

"Let's get going, then," Ness said. "Reunite this family of ours."

Chapter Twenty-Six

"CASH!"

"Ruby! Christ, what happened to you? I've been looking everywhere."

"I don't know. I just…I don't know. One minute we were all together, the next we were torn apart. Not anymore, though, Cash, not anymore. Thank God. Oh, look at you, you're soaked! Presley too. And those dogs. Christ alive! There's just so many of them!"

Although there was relief on Cash's face, confusion remained, as it did with Presley, who was right beside him. Ruby and Ness had left the clearing and Witcher behind, following the barking – the sound that guided them onwards, through trees that rocked precariously, back onto the path now littered with debris, with twigs and branches – both of them praying that if any more trees came crashing down, they'd do so at a safe distance. A few minutes later, they'd stumbled across the Wilkins brothers, who'd only just found each other too. The moment Cash had clapped eyes on Ruby, he'd rushed over and clasped her to him, the warmth of his hug a match for Theo's.

"Is the baby all right?" he checked.

"The baby's fine, but Witcher's not. Witcher's dead."

"What? Dead? How?"

"A bough broke from an old oak tree, the one that's in the clearing. It fell on him."

"You saw it?"

Briefly Ruby glanced at Ness. "We did, yeah."

"Shit," both he and Presley exclaimed.

"What about Corinna?" Presley continued.

"There are dogs barking." Seeing how puzzled they both looked by these words, she quickly hurried on. "Just believe me when I say there are. Lots and lots of dogs. Jed's in amongst them too, no doubt. We have to follow them. I think they know where Corinna is."

"Shit!" Cash said again. "Go on, then, lead the way."

Without another word, all four set off, hurrying as much as the weather allowed.

In front of her Ness yelped and stumbled. Presley, however, had her on her feet in an instant.

"It's okay, I've got you. You all right?"

"There was a branch. I tripped over it. My ankle hurts. Go on ahead—"

Presley refused. "We stick together. Nothing tears us apart a second time."

A sentiment Ruby herself agreed with.

Ruby stumbled next, Cash grabbing her before she hit the ground.

"Christ, Ruby, be careful!"

"Yeah, yeah," she breathed.

"The baby—"

"The baby's fine."

"But—"

"Cash, I promise. Theo's looking after him."

He nodded, relief easing his frown.

Presley slowed, looking all around him, rain falling off his lashes. "Where could she be?" he lamented. "There's no buildings, no shelter. There's nowhere to hide!"

"There is," said Ness. "There has to be. And Corinna found it."

"We just have to follow the dogs," Ruby reiterated, encouraging them to move quicker.

"Dogs," Cash muttered even as he obeyed. "I don't see any damned dogs."

Ruby didn't correct him, didn't admonish him either for calling them damned, although she might do later, once they were out of here. There was nothing damned about them, and nothing damned about her baby either. There! She'd said it, thwarted what the boy had said to her at Blakemort, had *insisted* – that her baby was one of Legion, a disciple of darkness.

That's why she'd been so frightened, in case there was a grain of truth in what he'd said, remembering also the photograph she'd found at Blakemort in amongst others, a photo at odds with the rest and quite clearly planted. It was of a man standing outside the house, decades ago, and smiling – as if anyone could ever smile there and mean it – a photograph inscribed with the same name as her grandfather: Edward Middleton. That was *all* she knew about him, his name, and that her sweet, sweet grandmother had left him as soon as she'd realised she was pregnant with Ruby's mother, severed their connection. If it was her grandfather, what was his involvement with Blakemort? That smile of his…was there smugness in it? Some kind of satisfaction? Was it borne not from good intent but bad? How it haunted her. Was darkness in him, *truly* in him? Someone she'd derived from, that her child derived from…

It didn't matter. Hendrix also derived from Cash, and Cash was like Tilly, not vulnerable, oh no, but good through and through. And good won out, always. Against it, evil was simply no match. Hadn't she just witnessed that yet again, in the clearing? Evidence of how strong the light was.

And she was strong as well, she and Cash. Together they were also a force of nature.

To be fearful, to be *petrified*, was exactly what the boy had wanted. Enough! No more feeding it! No more weakness either or allowing her energy to be sapped day by day. She was going to actively *enjoy* what remained of this pregnancy, relish the strength of the baby within, each and every kick. He was an innocent who'd be shielded, but not by a stay-at-home mother – a working mother, one who took pride in her job and her strength, who fulfilled her vocation, not ran from it.

Right now, however, they were running *to* something. Corinna had come here willingly, not because she was drugged as Ness had suspected but because of compassion and kindness. Quickly, though, she must have realised her mistake, Witcher showing his true colours. He'd kept her here – where, they had no idea – but she'd managed to escape him, running through these woods in fear of her life, just as Tilly once had, having to find somewhere to hide…

Witcher was a man who'd allowed himself to become corrupted, a man who'd wanted to expose the darkness at first but then became seduced by it, the Morrigan especially, Phyllida Hylands. He was a weak man ultimately, a plaything. He couldn't beat them, so he'd joined them. Perhaps when your mind was occupied to such a large extent with the darkness, as his was, it was easier for evil to begin twisting how you considered things, to look attractive rather than the repellent thing it was. Corinna, however, was far from weak; she was clever, drawing power from all the right sources. She was here, she was alive, and she was close. The fact the dogs had now stopped running was testament to that.

All around them were oaks, beeches, ash trees, elm trees, so many of them, some of the world's biggest, most spectacular species. *Where are you, Corinna? Where are you?*

"Look out!"

Shouting, Cash grabbed Ruby and pulled her to him as a heavy branch broke to land just in front of them.

"Christ!" she muttered. That was too close for comfort, Presley and Ness shuddering too.

Cash was ashen. "We can't stay here in this storm, Ruby, we can't!"

"The dogs have stopped," Ruby told him. "Corinna's around here somewhere."

"Where, though?" Presley's eyes searched frantically.

"She's here!" Ruby repeated. "Ness, back me up."

Ness was also scanning the ravaged landscape. "She *is* here. Somewhere."

As if spurred by this, Presley started to race around, the beam of his torch haphazard, bouncing off every tree, illuminating dark corners, surging upwards too, desperate for some hint of where his girlfriend might be. Finally, in exasperation, he banged his fist against the bark of a thick trunk, not once but several times, prompting one of the dogs to come racing forwards out of the pack – Jed, who then proceeded to sit at Presley's feet and bark at the tree.

Ruby extricated herself from Cash and rushed over. "Stay where you are, Presley. Jed's with you."

Although clearly confused, Presley did as he was told, Cash and Ness swiftly catching up with Ruby as she, too, raised her hands and pounded the tree.

"She's in there," she said. "Corinna's in there!"

"What? Are you crazy?" Cash cried out. "That's a tree!"

"It's a hollow tree, Cash, a tree whose insides have rotted." Ruby glanced up at it, imagined well enough how majestic it had once been, not quite like the oak tree in the clearing but impressive enough in its own right. Witcher had said he knew all about these woods, but he didn't know about this – the perfect hiding place.

"Round here," Ness said, "there's a kind of opening. Presley, shine your light in, quick!"

He did, gasping a moment later. "She's in there! God, Ruby, you were right."

Ruby's head fell back as she sighed in relief. "*Jed* was right, and all the dogs that aren't missing after all but still here, in spirit."

Any relief at having found her, however, was short-lived, as Cash pulled Ruby aside again just as something else went crashing to the ground, a bough from the same tree that Corinna lay in.

Ruby swore, as did Cash. It was as Ness had said, nature was indiscriminate now, rampant, destroying everything in its wake. This tree was no exception, regardless of its precious cargo.

"Ruby," Presley continued, "she's not moving. She's...she's slumped there."

"We have to get her out now," Ruby insisted.

"Not as easy as it looks," Presley told them. "How she got in there, I don't know. She *squeezed* herself in. She's unconscious, and her shoulders are at the far end, neither of which helps."

Ruby stepped closer to examine the hollow, just as more lightning struck – so close, the next strike promising to come closer still. Corinna was petite, the opening she'd found small; her lying at an awkward angle meant dragging her out would indeed prove problematic. If Ruby weren't so heavily pregnant, she'd have had a chance to reach in, but she'd never be able to lift her anyway, nor would Ness. They had no choice, however – they needed to release her and fast, try to make the gap a bit wider. Desperate, Ruby began to tear at the bark with her bare hands.

Cash was instantly by her side. "Hey, hey, what are you doing? Stand back, we'll do that. Presley, come on."

The pair of them taking over, they continued to hack away with their bare hands, hardly anything yielding despite how rotten the wood was. Glancing at Ness and then up at the sky, Ruby urged them on. When her words died away, she started praying instead. *Please be all right. Please be all right.*

Help is coming.

It was Theo, overriding her own thoughts.

What help?

It's coming. I promise.

Another thunderous roll exploded directly over their heads, and lightning would surely follow, one billion volts' worth.

Ruby started yelling now. "Hurry! Get her out of there!"

"I can do it," Presley said. "I think I can reach her. Cash, get something, a branch, a stone, anything. We just need a bit more of a gap so I can reach in."

Cash dropped to his knees, his hands outstretched, picking up a sizeable stone and handing it over to Presley, who continued to hack like a man possessed.

Eventually, he dropped the stone and leant into the tree.

"Have you got her?" Ness asked, both her, Ruby and Cash crowding Presley as much as they dared, Ruby still glancing upwards at the furious sky, at natural forces intent on completing the job in hand, wrecking these woods and what they had become, doing so in order for them to grow again. Fresh trees, brighter flowers, birds and animals returning, all once it was cleansed.

Cleansed?

Oh shit! Fire was the great cleanser.

"There's no more time," she warned. "You have to get her out. NOW!"

Presley fell back with a thud, a weight on top of him. It was Corinna, her hair on one side not red but dark because of the blood that soaked it.

The very second the pair hit the ground, there was the blinding burst of lightning that Ruby had feared, jagged and pitchforked, she'd swear, overpowering them with a smell of chlorine – the ozone from the burnt air. It struck the rotten tree right down the middle, branches bursting into flames and igniting other trees whose branches had become entangled with it. The fire would spread, quickly, ferociously, the rain easing off at last, allowing it to do just that.

"She...she's still not conscious," Presley said, dragging Corinna away from the burning tree, Cash having recovered his faculties and drawing closer to help him.

Ness also closed the gap and took Corinna's wrist in her hand. "She's still alive," she breathed.

"Presley, can you carry her, the fire…" Ruby said, her eyes drawn back to the leaping flames.

"Of course I can." He and Cash both got to their feet, Presley then bending to lift Corinna, to take her in his arms. "It'll be all right," he told her. "I promise."

"Let's keep that promise," Ruby said, nodding fervently. "Let's get her out of here."

"Which way?" Cash had raised his hands to shield his face from the heat.

Ruby looked at Jed. Jed looked back at her and then took off, away from the burning tree.

"This way," she said. "Everyone stay close."

Added to the crackling, spitting and hissing all around them was another sound.

"What's that?" Presley asked, cradling a still unconscious Corinna close.

"That's the sound of sirens," Ruby told him, still following Jed. "Help is coming."

Chapter Twenty-Seven

IT was official. Low Cottage was now a crime scene, not just because of the fact Tom Witcher had lived there – a man guilty of abduction and attempted murder – but because of the *actual* murder of Matilda Barrow, aged eighteen, from the village of Lindfield.

Not that her name was recorded anywhere that the Psychic Surveys team or the police could find – records before the '80s and '90s were patchy enough at the best of times, and this girl had died sometime during the early 1900s. No, it was psychic information that filled in the gaps. Ruby, who'd already made a connection with Matilda that night in the woods, was able to explain how the remains of her body had been transported from there to Low Cottage by Phyllida Hylands and her acolytes as a trophy, to be walled up in her newly built home. Whether there were other bones secreted – human or otherwise – was still being investigated.

Ruby pitied the cottage's owners, the Wintertons. When informed of what was going on, they were, quite rightly, horrified, declaring they didn't want anything more to do with the property.

"Will they eventually sell it on?" Cash asked.

"According to Lee, apparently not," Ruby answered. "They're a wealthy couple with a portfolio of properties, most of which they rent out. For now, they're going to leave it empty, take advice."

"Advice from whom?"

Ruby smirked. "Us, probably. Psychic Surveys. I tend to think, though, that once the house has given up all its secrets, nature will have her way with it too." The house had suffered only minimal damage in the storm, but Ruby suspected that come another bout of bad weather, it wouldn't fare so well. As had happened with Rayners Wood, it would be destroyed.

When she told Cash this, he smiled too. "I bloody hope so," he replied before adding, "And you're sure you want to go back to work?"

"One hundred percent."

"What changed your mind? You were so determined, you know, to be there for the baby…"

"I'll *still* be there for the baby. We'll just have to share the load a bit more, that's all."

Cash inclined his head to the side. "You know, I've always said this, ever since I first met you – there's more than one danger attached to your job, something Corinna's just proved. You can't go around to people's houses, stranger's houses, on your own. They could be nutters like Witcher."

There was no way Ruby could disagree, not this time. "From now on with house calls, we'll go in twos at least, and we'll always let others know of our whereabouts."

It was something, and it had the desired effect of appeasing Cash.

Ruby was now back with the Psychic Surveys team, something Theo, Ness and Corinna were delighted about.

Not at the helm, though; they were all sharing the load there equally too, at least for the foreseeable future. First up was sorting out the cases that had been put on hold whilst Corinna had been missing, principally the Parkers' house in Barcombe Mills.

Corinna was still recovering – she'd received quite a blow to the head when fleeing through the woods. Witcher had caught up with her, and they'd fought, causing her to fall, to smash against a jagged tree stump. She was only glad he hadn't used his knife on her, because he'd told her he had one, kept threatening her with it if she didn't succeed in summoning Hylands, summoning *anything*. How she'd managed to get away from him after that particular altercation, she had no idea. He'd held her captive in her own car – which had been found at the far end of the woods, along a disused track – locking her in and, of course, destroying her phone. "When I was running," she said, "he was so close behind me, but then I don't know…it was as if my feet took on a life of their own, and I managed to lose him. It was dark, though, really dark. I had no idea where I was going. But then…then I found that tree, and I knew there was something different about it straightaway. I found the hollow, squeezed into it and then…I don't remember anything else."

The team had listened to her recount her experience, Ruby wondering if she'd been right when she'd told herself on that perilous night that Corinna would be harnessing the good energy still in existence there, even if she hadn't fully realised it at the time, drawing strength and direction from it in order to remain alive. Even so, she'd need a good two or three weeks to recover from her ordeal. No problem. The main thing was no lasting damage had been done. Willingly, she'd agreed to sit out any return to the Parker house, as had Theo.

"It's not as if I can get into the damned attic anyway," the latter had fumed.

"Perhaps if you ate less…" Ness said, duly avoiding the look Theo'd thrown at her.

With Jed for company, Ruby and Ness now travelled in Ruby's old Ford to the Parkers' house, Ness giving directions on how to reach such a small, out-of-the-way village.

"Come to think of it," Ness said en route, "are you sure *you'll* be able to get into the attic?"

"I'm not that fat, Ness!"

"Well…I mean…you know…"

Ruby laughed. "I'll be fine. You can hoist me up if necessary."

Ness raised an eyebrow at that but didn't comment further; instead, she continued to gaze out of the car window at the countryside, Ruby also admiring the trees and how they swayed in the breeze so elegantly, reminding her of dancers.

The storm a week ago might have been more intense over Rayners Wood, more *purposeful*, but it had pretty much raged over much of East Sussex despite not being forecasted, causing damage to roof tiles and greenhouses predominantly, a few branches from urban trees also having fallen into roads or on top of cars. But it was nothing, *nothing* compared to what it had done to the wood outside the village of Rayner. It had decimated it. And yet, as far as Ruby and Ness could find, there was very little reportage on the damage that had been wrought; it seemed to go unnoticed, perhaps even uncared about.

She and Ness had taken a walk there a day or so ago. Even though the ancient oak in the heart of the clearing still stood – minus its heavy bough – it had been injured by lightning, displaying several blackened wounds sorrowfully.

"You know," Ruby had said, staring at it, "Phyllida means 'green bough'. I looked it up."

Ness had raised an eyebrow. "Oh, does it? How apt. Or perhaps I should say ironic."

"Yeah, a bit of both, I reckon."

Still with her eyes on the oak, Ness sighed. "I can't help it, the woods aren't my favourite thing."

"I know they're not. Any sign of Lyndsey since that night?"

Ness had shaken her head. "No."

Ruby said nothing more about it. The sudden appearance of her twin was obviously foremost on Ness's mind – you didn't need to be psychic to realise that – but she'd need a bit of time to process it, as anyone would, Ruby supposed.

They'd walked a bit further when Ness asked Ruby, "What about Tilly? Any sign?"

"None," Ruby had said, also a little ruefully, before noticing something at her feet. A beautiful purple flower, just the one and unlike any she'd ever seen before, its green stem proud, and untarnished in any way. A thing of glory. Quickly, she'd changed her answer. "Actually, Tilly's all around us."

As they now reached the Parker house, it began to rain, just lightly, and Ruby was glad of it. If they were going to have to go into an attic, best it was in cooler weather. In fact – the storm having broken the heatwave – Ruby doubted they'd see similar, not this year, anyway.

The Parkers ushered them in, Ness introducing Ruby and putting the absence of her other two colleagues down to minor colds, extending her apologies concerning that. In turn, the Parkers assured them that all animals had been locked away, Ruby having to suppress a smile as she remembered what Theo had told her about dear little Walter and the chaos he'd caused.

Getting into the attic was a bit of a struggle, Ruby had to admit.

"You okay?" said Ness, extending a hand and indeed hauling her upwards.

"Yeah, fine. Tell me, though, this house, it's not built on a triangle, is it?"

Ness smiled. "No, Ruby, it isn't."

"And you know that for sure?"

"I've taken to studying houses we're called to on a map."

"Good idea. Oh, and David and Christopher, they're not twins?"

"No." There was a sigh in Ness's voice, one of nostalgia, perhaps? "I've been assured of that."

That's right, she had, by records at The Keep and by another twin...

"Do you want to start the address, Ness, or shall I?"

"Go ahead," Ness replied.

Facing the corner where Ness, Corinna and the family dog had sensed something, Ruby was about to open her mouth. No sound came out, however, as the something they'd sensed came rushing out of the shadows and straight to her.

"Oh wow!" said Ruby, staring down at the top of the spirit's head. It was a child, aged about eight or nine. The top of his scalp was bald and shiny, hair evident but only in tufts. She couldn't see his face; he'd pressed it up against her stomach, as he'd also done with one hand, a hand that had suffered damage too, that was burnt.

Quickly Ruby checked if Ness could see the spirit that was cleaving to her.

Ness shook her head. "No, not a thing. What's happening?"

"He's here, the boy, with me. He's…he's hugging me, my bump."

Such a tender action, it brought tears to her eyes. Inside her, the baby kicked, but only the once and then lay still, as soothed by the boy's hug as he'd been by Theo's.

In the gloom cast from the yellow light above them, Ruby reached down, wishing the child were more substantial, that she could wrap her arms around him too, burns or no burns. "Who are you, little man? What's your name? Your true name?"

Christopher, he whispered, keeping his cheek firmly pressed against her.

"You're on record as being David."

Christopher! Adopted.

"Adopted?"

Replaced.

"Replaced? What do you mean?"

Their child.

Ruby looked briefly at Ness before readdressing Christopher. "You replaced their child, David, but your name is Christopher?"

Dead.

Ruby frowned. Was he referring to himself?

Parents.

"Your parents died?"

War.

"War," she murmured. "Your parents died during the war. Oh, Christopher, I'm so sorry."

Not theirs.

"Your adopted parents?"

Not adopted.

"But...you said you were."

Not really.

"Not really adopted." Again, Ruby looked at Ness, who was nodding.

"A war child," she suggested. "Sent away, perhaps. Evacuated."

Evacuated!

The child lifted his head at that word – although not enough that Ruby could get a good glimpse of him – repeating it excitedly before continuing to hug Ruby with his tortured hands.

Not David.

"No, no, you're Christopher," Ruby said. "We know that now."

Not him, not good enough.

"Oh, I'm sure you were."

Burnt his clothes.

Ruby nodded, remembering also that a bundle of partially burnt clothes had been found in this corner of the attic. They'd been removed and were now in the shed.

Hid them.

"In here? In the attic?"

The boy nodded before answering again.

I…I like fire.

Ruby inhaled. There it was. A confession, one full of shame.

But fire…burns.

"Oh, Christopher, what did you do, sweetheart? Did you hurt yourself?

There was silence.

"Did you hurt others?"

NO!

"Okay, okay," Ruby quickly backtracked, "you didn't hurt others, that's good, Christopher, really good. But you hurt yourself, didn't you?"

Don't play with matches.

"That's right, I was told that as a child. 'Ruby,' my gran would say, 'never play with matches.'"

They said that too.

"Okay…" Ruby said, gently prompting him, waiting for more of the confession.

Didn't like being told.

"You didn't like it? Why?"

Not my parents!

"No, no, they weren't."

Not David!

"Had David died?"

Before me.

"Before you arrived?"

A furious nod of the head told her she was right.

I'm not bad.

At that, he seemed to hug her stomach tighter.

"I know that, darling. You're a child, innocent."

I burnt his clothes.

311

"I know that too."

Sorry.

"It's okay, Christopher, I can...well, I can understand it. You were confused, you were hurting. You wanted your own parents, your own identity."

I caught fire.

It was as Ruby had guessed: the little boy had burnt David's clothes in a fit of anger, most likely, but anger that was understandable, that was righteous, at least in his mind. Unfortunately, somehow he had also managed to set fire to himself.

"Where's your body, Christopher? Do you know?"

Out there.

"Where?"

He shrugged.

"What about your surname, what is it?"

Hayle.

"And where did you live before here?"

Birmingham.

"You're Christopher Hayle from Birmingham." A little boy torn from his family through no fault of his own, a boy who'd then gone missing, who'd disappeared – no one looking for him, not during wartime, when so many disappeared, never to be seen again. What had David's parents done with his body? Had they buried it locally in a plot of earth? Unmarked, of course. Had they done that because they'd panicked? Were they bad people or victims too, a couple who'd already lost a child and had seen Christopher as a gift, perhaps, someone to replace him? What a tall order for Christopher to live up to; what a shame they couldn't have loved him for who he was. Not a bad boy, a lost boy, as so many were lost in the darkness for so long, hiding, confused and ashamed.

Ness had clearly got the gist of what was happening. There were tears in her eyes, just as there were tears in Ruby's own eyes. From below, sitting at the foot of the ladder on the landing, a dog barked, Jed, and in it was something victorious.

"Christopher Hayle," Ruby said again. "We'll find out all about you and what happened to your parents, where they're buried. We'll try to get your name added to their headstone too. We'll do that for you, and something else…the baby, my baby, his middle name, do you know what? I think it's going to be Christopher. It's a strong name, a name I really like. Yes, it is, it's definitely going to be Christopher, after you, a good little boy. Meanwhile, Christopher, don't linger here anymore, you don't belong in this house, you never did. It's time to see your mum and dad, to go into the light because that's your true home. You've nothing to be ashamed of, okay? They can't wait to see you. They're not angry with you, not at all."

Promise?

Ruby smiled, the words of the poem Theo had recited in her mind coming back, Robert Frost's 'Stopping by Woods on a Snowy Evening', as she now knew. *And I have promises to keep.* She did, both now and in the future. Good promises. Those *meant* to be kept.

"I promise," she said, noting Ness's head hanging low, tears likely coming in earnest now.

The pressure she'd felt around her stomach eased as Christopher began to fade, his hands no longer burnt and his hair not patchy but abundant and full of curls.

313

This, exactly this, was what made her job so worthwhile and why she couldn't turn her back on it, because to do so was to turn her back on those like Christopher. He was just a kid, a kid who'd grieved, who was troubled, but still just a kid.

Before he faded completely, he grew in strength again for a fraction of a moment, no more than that, and leant forward, not hugging Ruby's stomach now but planting a kiss upon it.

Just a kid, he said, fading completely, causing Ruby to smile through her tears.

"Is that the end of it?" Ness asked.

"The end, the beginning, call it what you will," Ruby replied. "It's the end of Christopher Hayle, that's for sure. He's gone, but actually there's another kid at the hospital, Andy Pryce. I promised I'd go and speak to him, try and explain his new circumstances. Don't fancy popping in there, do you, before we call it a day?"

"Certainly. Yes, of course. Talking of hospitals, you're looking so much better now, Ruby."

"That's because I am." Again, she was smiling. "All the tests came back fine. I got a clean bill of health." Gently she patted her stomach. "Ness, everything's gonna be just peachy."

314

Epilogue

Ness

There is a time for everything,
  And a season for every activity under the heavens:
  A time to be born and a time to die,
  A time to plant and a time to uproot,
  A time to kill and a time to heal,
  A time to tear down and a time to build,
  A time to weep and a time to laugh,
  A time to mourn and a time to dance,
  A time to scatter stones and a time to gather them,
  A time to embrace and a time to refrain from embracing,
  A time to search and a time to give up,
  A time to keep and a time to throw away,
  A time to tear and a time to mend,
  A time to be silent and a time to speak,
  A time to love and a time to hate,
  A time for war and a time for peace.

As Ness read these words, those quoted in the Bible, in

the Book of Ecclesiastes, there was both sadness and acceptance in her at the truth of them, how poignant they were personally.

In the living room of her home, her hand reached out to grab a tissue so she could wipe at her eyes and blow her nose. Scrunching the tissue in her hand afterwards, she stared at it.

Soon after visiting the Parker house with Ruby, Ness had returned alone to see the Bows. The clocks had started to work in their house again, including in the kitchen.

"I know everything's all right with the clocks now," Karen Bow had said, "but is she still here? Jess Biggs."

"I don't know," Ness answered, "but if she is, I have a message of my own to impart, as well as my thanks."

Although Karen looked confused, she agreed to Ness filling her in later on the full story. At that moment, there was still work to do.

"Jess," Ness said, once more in the Bows' light and airy kitchen. "*Are* you still here?"

She got no reply, but what she did get was a sense of something…a hint of the woman's presence, as if she was standing in a doorway, one foot here, one foot somewhere else entirely.

"Jess," Ness continued, "we realise you knew Tilly as well as the kind of thing that was happening in your village, that you'd become aware of it. You liked Tilly; she was a sweet girl, a girl who didn't just visit your house but other houses in the village, including the hunting lodge and—" here she paused for a second "—Low Cottage. When she went missing, only you made the connection, perhaps because, forming a triangle with those other houses, you felt just that – a connection – and in your own way you were as powerful

316

as them, *more* powerful because your compassion, concern and love won out in the end.

"Jess, thanks to you and your persistence, we found Tilly. She was hanged in Rayners Wood by Hylands and her followers. In short, she was sacrificed, and her remains brought to Low Cottage as some sort of terrible memento, walled up in a small living room there. She's now been removed from there, and will get the burial she deserves, her life and death recorded. But I want you to know, and my colleagues Ruby, Theo and Corinna want you to know too, that she's free, Jess, entirely free of any harm, any fear, any anger and any hatred. Her spirit is pure. It's untouchable, very much a part of the light. She chooses to stay in Rayners Wood because, regardless of what happened there, it's beautiful – heavenly, you could say."

From outside the kitchen door, a clock chimed, just the once, but it echoed. If she'd had any sensation of Jess before that, it was gone now, leaving her able to tell the Bows something of the full story of what had caused Jess to linger, skipping over the more colourful parts.

Since the successful resolution of both those cases another week or so had passed, fairly dull and drizzly days, quiet days, spent mainly in the company of Lee, who was mortified at not having answered his phone the evening they'd gone to Rayners Wood. The kids he'd been called out to see in Saltdean truly had caused a rumpus, with several arrests made plus one boy having to be coaxed away from the cliffs after taking drugs. Despite how busy Lee had been, though, someone had managed to get through to him. He'd had a sudden urge to step away from the mayhem, temporarily leaving his colleagues to it, whilst he'd dialled in a request for a unit to be sent to Rayners Wood on suspicion of activity there.

"I just had this sudden conviction all was not well," he'd explained to Ness. "As if there was a little voice in my head telling me to send help, not to delay any longer. I tried calling you too, of course, but I couldn't get through, Witcher must have grabbed you by then. Oh, Ness, I'm so sorry, but…do you reckon I've got some kind of sixth sense after all?"

It'd been Theo's voice in his head, of course, but Ness let him believe in his sixth sense, not because she was worried about his reaction, but because to think it was his idea to help them in their hour of need went some way to assuaging his guilt at not being there.

And now it was time to do something about the guilt she felt, not sit indoors any longer, especially as the sun had made something of a reappearance, chasing the drizzle away. There was a place she needed to visit. The woods. But not Rayners Wood. Elsewhere in Sussex.

She glanced again at the extract she'd just read. It was time…

In the car as she drove to her destination, there was complete silence. Normally, Ness would have the radio on, Smooth Radio, perhaps, where they played the golden oldies that she loved, but today she didn't want any distractions, none at all. All that occupied her mind was Claire…and Lyndsey. Lyndsey, who hadn't shown up again since that night in the woods, no sign of her at all despite Ness continuing to plead with her, picking up that photograph in her bedroom and staring at it, praying she'd materialise in that, at least, listening out for creaky floorboards…

Give her time.

She was prepared to do that, as much as was needed. Just to know she wasn't trapped in the darkness was enough for now.

But Claire *was* trapped, and it simply couldn't go on.

Parking her car at the woods, she got out, locked it, and then, with her hands shoved deep into her pockets, walked determinedly to the clearing where the girls' bodies had been found, passing not one person on the way. Like Rayners, this was also a place people tended to avoid, what had happened here well publicised, making it an even lonelier place to be.

It took just over twenty minutes to reach the clearing, her eyes scanning the circular enclosure as they always did. Actually, there *was* evidence of someone having been here, and she moved nearer to examine further. A small fire had been lit, although now only black ash remained and, in it, a few cigarette butts, indicating that perhaps there had been more than one person, two or three. She knelt closer, not wanting to reach out and actually touch the butts, recoiling from doing so, but noticing a couple of them had lipstick stains, so, yes, definitely more than one person. A man and a woman, a ghoulish pair, drawn to this site for reasons she didn't want to entertain.

She returned to her feet and straightened her back before speaking.

"Claire, I know you're here. I wish to God you weren't, but, sadly, that's not the case."

The silence in these woods was as intense as it had been in Rayners Wood before the storm, no birdsong to punctuate it, to lend any sweetness.

"Claire," she continued, "I also know how scared you were, how scared you still are, how memories of those last

319

terrible moments endure. And they were terrible moments, moments I can't even imagine, your agony and your bewilderment. But enough now, Claire. Enough!"

Kicking at the ash, dispersing it, she walked more towards the centre of the clearing, peering into the shadows of the trees ahead, her resolve growing.

"I want you to come out of the shadows, and I want you to do it now!"

Ness had never spoken to Claire like this before; it had always been softly, sympathetically, cajoling her and pleading.

"You can hear me, Claire, so do as I say. Come out of the shadows. I've run out of patience, and you've run out of time. I promised you I'd send you to the light, and, that's exactly what I'm going to do."

God, she sounded like a schoolteacher, one you daren't disobey. Fingers crossed Claire thought the same.

"Claire, I'm waiting…"

There was a rustle in the trees, just to the side of her. Rather than turn fully to investigate, she allowed only her eyes to travel to that spot. Movement. Definitely movement, albeit slight.

"Good. Good," Ness continued. "That's what I want to see. Hurry now. We haven't got all day."

More rustling, a slight breeze responsible, perhaps, but Ness didn't think so.

"Will you please hurry! I do have others to tend to."

Ness hated the words leaving her mouth, but if they had the desired effect, then hate would turn to love – two extremes working together for the sake of a common cause.

"I seriously do *not* want to wait anymore. Step forward,

Claire! Now!"

Not just a rustling, there was a figure. Ness's legs almost buckled to realise it. It took every ounce of strength she possessed to remain upstanding, to maintain her no-nonsense veneer.

"Come on! Come on! Walk towards me."

As the girl continued to materialise, further words failed her. Instead, Ness had to clamp her lips together and squeeze her hands tight, contain the emotions within her. She was such a forlorn figure! So small, so vulnerable, long dark hair falling about her shoulders, clothes in disarray and soiled, a scuff on her cheek too, a bruise from where she'd been struck.

With all her heart Ness wanted to rush over to her, apologise for talking so harshly, just hold her, pour love back into such a bleak and shattered heart.

All of which was impossible.

All she could do was send her to the light.

All, Ness?

A voice beside her startled her. Although not wanting to take her eyes off Claire, she had to see who'd uttered those words. The cry that left her mouth could not be stifled. "Lyndsey!"

It *was* Lyndsey who'd spoken, who was there too, not as she'd been in Rayners Wood, a carbon copy of Ness, but as the child Ness remembered, barely older than Claire.

"Oh my God, Lyndsey! I... It's wonderful, to see you. I was so hoping..."

Her voice trailed away as Lyndsey looked pointedly from Ness to where Claire was standing.

"Oh yes, yes, it's Claire that's priority here, yes, of course."

A little girl who was staring back at them with so much

hurt in her eyes.

Without another word, Lyndsey walked forwards, her hands outstretched. Claire's hands remained by her side, but just before Lyndsey reached her, one began to lift.

Go on, Lyndsey! Silently Ness cheered her on.

Finally, the girl placed her hand in Lyndsey's, some of her fear dissolving, a look of trust developing instead, the kind that one child would place in another because it could never be placed in an adult again, not whilst she presented as Claire, anyway.

The two of them started to walk, into the clearing but not towards Ness, keeping their distance from her, still hand in hand. A fragile child and a fragile moment. There were so many questions Ness wanted to ask: *Lyndsey, are you going all the way into the light with her, or are you coming back? Where were you all this time? Do you forgive me?*

Claire kept her gaze straight ahead as they drew parallel with Ness, fear gone entirely now as she stared into the distance, at the light, realising at last it was nothing to hide from.

Lyndsey, however, turned her head.

We would have made a good team, wouldn't we, Ness?

Another cry escaped Ness, a sob, one filled with so much regret and yet so much hope.

Yes, she answered. *We would have.*

They were fading. Damn it, they were fading! Which was a good thing, but a bad thing too. She didn't want Lyndsey to fade, purely for selfish reasons.

Will I see you again?

The girls were beyond her now, their forms so faint, shimmering as the light wrapped itself around them. Claire was going home, where she belonged, after so long. It was a cause for celebration, but to take Lyndsey with her…

Lyndsey! Will you wait for me?

They'd gone, were no longer visible.

Ness fell to her knees, right there in that clearing, the scene of so much tragedy, so much evil and so much innocence, loud, gasping sobs haemorrhaging from her mouth.

"Lyndsey! Lyndsey! Lyndsey!"

She was making so much noise, she barely caught the words that started to form in her mind, had to work hard to quiet herself, to let them form more fully.

Three simple words, but so full of promise.

I'll wait. Always.

Afterword

If you're a Sussex reader with an interest in the paranormal, you'll most likely know about the Devil's Triangle. If so, however, you'll be asking yourself, "Where the hell is Rayners Wood?" Rayners Wood is inspired by Clapham Wood, a renowned psychic hotspot. I've given it a different name because, although I like to weave lots of facts into my books, they are ultimately works of fiction, and so I also make liberal use of artistic licence. Clapham Wood, Chanctonbury Ring and Cissbury Ring are all beautiful, but the legends of these places are rooted in fact. Go ahead and visit them, but make sure you leave before sundown…

As much as I love writing, building a relationship with readers is even more exciting! I occasionally send newsletters with details on new releases, special offers and other bits of news relating to the Psychic Surveys series as well as all my other books. If you'd like to subscribe, sign up here!

www.shanistruthers.com

Printed in Great Britain
by Amazon